Hanif Kureishi grew up in Kent and studied philosophy at King's College, London. His novels include *The Buddha of Suburbia*, which won the Whitbread Prize for Best First Novel, *The Black Album*, *Intimacy* and *Something to Tell You*. His screenplays include *My Beautiful Laundrette*, which received an Oscar nomination for Best Screenplay, *Sammy and Rosie Get Laid*, *The Mother*, *Venus*, which was directed by Roger Michell in 2006, and *Le Week-End* in 2013. He has also published several collections of short stories. He has been awarded the Chevalier de l'Ordre des Arts et des Lettres, the PEN/Pinter Prize, and is a Commander of the Order of the British Empire. His work has been translated into thirty-six languages. He is professor of Creative Writing at Kingston University.

Further praise for *The Last Word*:

'[A] provocative, powerful new novel from Hanif Kureishi . . . grippingly explores the point at which a real human being becomes a character . . . A novel about how "it's frustration that makes creativity possible" is at times itself a frustrating, but ultimately rewarding, read about the terror and wonder of writing.' Anita Sethi, *Metro*

'In the story's resolution, kindness, humanity and affection prevail and the last few pages touch a depth of feeling previously not seen. They are impossible to read without a lump in your throat.' John Harding, *Daily Mail*

'It describes the business of an artist approaching death with a brio which makes this Kureishi's best novel since *The Buddha of Suburbia*.' Amanda Craig, *Independent on Sunday*

'*The Last Word* is a highly spiced, tongue-in-cheek addition to the respectable subgenre pioneered by A. S. Byatt's *The Biographer's Tale* and Penelope Lively's *According to Mark* - a novel about how a biography comes to be written, the pressures brought to bear on both biographee and anatomist, and the procedural difficulties that lie in wait along the way . . . There are some splendid bite-the-hand-that-feeds-you jokes and Mamoon's titanic ego is deployed to considerable effect.' D. J. Taylor, *Literary Review*

'Writing for both Mamoon and Harry – and presumably Kureishi, too – is a visceral business and the patter between all the characters has a sharp edge. It is not so visceral, however, that Kureishi forgets to be thoroughly entertaining or steer his conversations with great variety and skill. Biography, as he notes, "is a process of disillusionment"; fiction though, as he shows here, can be every bit as perceptive but also much funnier.' Michael Prodger, *New Statesman*

'Writing is the devil, Kureishi says here. *The Last Word* has devilry in abundance. Swiftian and Hogarthian, this would be gloomy reading, a tale of shattered communities and the imagination monetised, were it not for the delicious wickedness of the lampooning.' Chris Dolan, *Herald*

'A page-turner that reads like a broad Gothic farce with a coiled Pinteresque power-struggle at its centre.' Pico Iyer, *Prospect* magazine

'Contains deeper reflections on the businesses of writing, reading and biography, and their fate in what may be a post-literary culture. Although the magnificent comic monster of Mamoon provides much of the book's pleasure, it is finally as significant for what it is about as for whom it might concern.' Mark Lawson, *Guardian*

'This is a gripping, somewhat shocking and darkly funny tale . . . set to be another of Kureishi's most memorable works.' Harriet Shepherd, *Irish Examiner*

THE LAST WORD

HANIF KUREISHI

FABER & FABER

First published in 2014
by Faber and Faber Limited
Bloomsbury House
74–77 Great Russell Street
London WC1B 3DA
This open market edition published in 2014

Typeset by Faber and Faber Limited
Printed and bound by CPI Group (UK) Ltd, Croydon, CR0 4YY

*This is a work of fiction. Names, characters, places and incidents
are the products of the author's imagination or are used fictitiously.
Any resemblance to actual events, locales or persons, living or dead,
is entirely coincidental*

A CIP record for this book
is available from the British Library

ISBN 978–0–571–27754–4

6 8 10 9 7 5

For Carlo

ONE

Harry Johnson gazed out of the window of the train at the English countryside and thought that not a moment passed when someone wasn't telling a story. And, if his luck held for the rest of the day, Harry was about to be employed to tell the story of the man he was going to visit. Indeed, he had been chosen to tell the *whole* story of this important man, this significant artist. How, he wondered, with a shudder, did you begin to do that? Where would you start, and how would the story, which was still being lived, end? More importantly, was he, Harry, capable of such a task?

Peaceful England, untouched by war, revolution, famine, ethnic or religious disturbance. Yet if the newspapers were correct, Britain was an overcrowded little island, teeming with busy immigrants, many clinging to the edges of the country, as on a small boat about to capsize. Not only that, thousands of asylum seekers and refugees, desperate to escape disturbance in the rest of the chaotic world, were attempting to cross the border. Some were packed in lorries, or hung from the under-carriages of trains; many were tiptoeing across the English Channel on tightropes slung across the sea, while others were fired from cannons based in Boulogne. Ghosts had it easy. Meanwhile apparently, since the financial crash, everyone onboard the country was so close together and claustrophobic they were beginning to turn on one another like trapped animals. With the coming scarcity – few jobs, reduced pensions, and meagre social security – people's lives would deteriorate. The post-war safety Harry and his family had grown up in was gone. Yet, to Harry now, it seemed as if the government was deliberately injecting a strong shot of anxiety into the body politic, because all he could see was a green and pleasant England: healthy cattle, neat fields, trimmed trees, bubbling streams, and the shining, early-spring sky above. It didn't even look as though you could get a curry for miles.

There was a whoosh, and beer spattered his face. He turned his head. Rob Deveraux, sitting opposite Harry and cracking open another tin, was a respected and innovative publisher. He had approached Harry with the idea of commissioning him to write a biography of the distinguished writer, Indian-born Mamoon Azam, a novelist, essayist and playwright Harry had admired since he was a teenage book fiend, a nerdy connoisseur of sentences, a kid for whom writers were gods, heroes, rock stars. Harry was immediately responsive and excited. After years of study and obedience, things were turning good for him, as his teachers had predicted if he concentrated his thoughts and zipped his fly and lip. This was his break; he could have wept with relief and excitement.

He deserved it, he reckoned. A couple of years before, in his late twenties, Harry had published a well-received biography of Nehru containing much new material, and although the familiar story had now, in the modern manner, to be lightly spiced with interracial copulation, buggery, alcoholism and anorexia, the work was considered, on the whole, to be illuminating. Even the Indians liked it. For Harry it had been 'homework'. He was reviewing books and teaching now, while looking for a new project to invest his creative passion, energy and commitment in; something, he hoped, that would make his name, launching him into the public world and a rosy future.

Today, on a bright Sunday morning, Harry and Rob were on the train to Taunton to visit Mamoon at the house where the legendary writer had lived for most of his adult life, sharing it now with his second wife, Liana Luccioni, a spirited Italian woman in her early fifties. The world from the window – his England – would have kept Harry calm and easy, except that Rob, like a boxing coach, insisted on coaxing and goading his boy in preparation for the fight ahead.

Rob was explaining that it was both an advantage and a nuisance writing about someone who was alive.

3

The subject himself could help you, he said, as Harry dabbed beer from his face with his handkerchief. The past might take on new tones as the subject looked back – and it was Harry's job to inspire Mamoon to look back. Rob had no doubt that Mamoon would help Harry, since Mamoon had finally recognised that the book was becoming essential. Liana was proving to be extravagant, if not more expensive and, indeed, explosive than any woman Mamoon had experienced before. Rob had said it was as if Gandhi had married Shirley Bassey and they'd gone to live in Ambridge.

Mamoon had been much respected by the literary world, as well as by the right-wing newspapers. He was, at last, a writer from the Indian subcontinent they could like, someone who thought domination, particularly by the educated, informed and intelligent – people, oddly, who resembled himself – was preferable to universal stupidity, or even democracy.

But being too cerebral, unyielding and harrowing to be widely read, Mamoon was becoming financially undone; despite the praise and the prizes, he was in fiscal turnaround. Currently he was in the process of selling his archive to an American university. Before it also became necessary for him to remortgage his house, his wife and his agent had agreed that the best way to perk up his quiet career – Mamoon had become the sort of writer of whom people asked 'Is he still alive, do you know?' – was for a 'controversial' new biography to be published with, on the cover, the subject as an irresistibly handsome and dangerous young man. The sharp, memorable image would be as important as the words: think Kafka, Greene, Beckett, writers whose taciturnity never stood in the way of a hot, moody photo. This, then, was the book Harry would write. The biography would be an 'event', a 'big bang', accompanied, of course, by a television documentary, interviews, a reading tour, and the reissuing of Mamoon's books in forty languages.

On the other hand, continued Rob, the fact the author was alive could inhibit a biographer. Rob had met the man about a dozen times; and he said that Mamoon, to his credit, was more Norman Mailer than E. M. Forster. Inhibition, Rob reckoned, was something Harry needed none of here. It wouldn't suit the subject.

On his side, Harry considered Rob to be more of a Norman Mailer than Mamoon, who had seemed restrained and dignified on the one occasion Harry had met him. Rob was a dishevelled unshaven brilliant maverick, who usually smelled of alcohol. Today he had turned up actually drunk and began drinking beer the moment they got on the train – while eating crisps continuously, bits of which adhered to his face and clothes like flakes of dandruff. Rob considered writing a form of extreme combat, and humanity's 'saving grace'. For him, the writer should be the very devil, a disturber of dreams and wrecker of fatuous utopias, the bringer-in of reality, and rival of God in his wish to make worlds.

Now Harry nodded gravely across the table at Rob, as he always did; he didn't want to betray any alarm.

If Harry thought of himself as a cautious if not conservative person, Rob appeared to encourage his authors towards pugnacity, dissipation and 'authenticity' for fear, some thought, that the act and art of writing, or even editing, might appear 'artistic', feminine, nancy, or, possibly, 'gay'. Never mind Mamoon, Harry had heard numerous tales of Rob's 'sociopathic' tendencies. He didn't go into the office until five in the afternoon, though he would stay there all night, editing, phoning and working, perhaps popping into Soho. He had married, not long ago, but appeared to have forgotten that wedlock was a continuous state rather than a one-off event. He slept in different places, often in some discomfort and with a book over his face, while appearing to inhabit a time zone that collapsed and expanded according to need rather than the clock, which he considered to be fascist. If he became bored by someone, he would turn away, or even slap them. He would cut his writers' work arbitrarily, or change the title, without informing them.

Not that Harry had minded about the tales of madness, being aware that it is only the insane who achieve anything significant. Besides, Rob's publishing outfit had won numerous big prizes, and Rob was powerful, persuasive and potent. Having lunched and chatted with him at parties for five years, Harry couldn't say, until today, that he'd witnessed much debauchery himself. Rob had the hippest list in London, and was as much an artist as an innovative movie or record producer. He made things happen and took risks; he was said to be 'lateral'. Harry had never dreamt that Rob would invite him to work with him. Not only that, Rob would pay Harry a substantial advance for this book. If Harry borrowed money from his father, he should be able to afford the deposit on a small house he wanted to buy with Alice, his fiancée, whom he'd been seeing for three years, and who had moved into his bachelor flat. They had talked about having children, though Harry thought they should be more settled before committing to this.

It had occurred to Harry, in the last year, at least, as he matured, that he needed to be well off. It wasn't his first priority, which was to be serious, but he was beginning to see that his list of life achievements might have to include a hefty amount of money in the bank, a token of his status, ability and privilege. Rob had volunteered to help with this, aiding Harry on his journey. It was about time. 'I am your Mephistopheles, and I pronounce you now officially rock 'n' roll,' Rob had said.

'The day will come, of course, when you will have to thank me for this. And thank me hard. Perhaps you might gratefully kiss me on the lips, or give me your tongue.'

As the train drew them closer to the meeting, Rob's instruction was that Harry should write 'as mad and wild' a book as he could. This would be Harry's break-through. He should practise his autograph; he would be feted at literary festivals in South America, India and Italy, appear on television, and give well-paid talks and lectures on the nature of truth and the biographer's ser-vitude to it. It would be his ticket to ride. If you wrote one successful book, you could live in its light for ten years.

'Let's not get carried away. It'll be a fire-walk.' Rob gulped at his beer. 'The old man will exasperate you with his stubbornness and taunting. As for his wife, you know she can be sweet and amusing. But you might have to sleep with her, otherwise she could smoke you down like a cigarette.'

'What? Why?'

'In Rome, where she lived, and where she grabbed Mamoon, she was known as a man-eater who never passed on a meal. And you are a hog with a keen snout, when it comes to sniffing out the truffle of a woman.'

'Rob, please—'

The editor went on, 'Listen up: that clever old sly

fox Mamoon might seem dull and dead to you, and indeed to everyone, including his own family.' He leaned forward and whispered, 'He comes on like someone who has never knowingly given pleasure to a woman, someone who has never loved anyone more than himself. He has stolen a lot of enjoyment. He has been a dirty bastard, an adulterer, liar, thug, and, possibly, a murderer.'

'How common is this knowledge?'

'You will make it known. Extreme biography: that is your job.'

'I see.'

'Marion, his ex-mistress, a Baconian torso on a plank, is bitter as cancer and spitting gobbets of hate to this day. She lives in America and not only will she see you, she'll fly at you like a radioactive bat. I've organised your visit – some people accuse me of being a perfectionist. There is also the fact he drove his first wife Peggy over the edge. I'm sure he wrapped oranges in a towel and beat her blacker and bluer than a decayed Stilton.'

'He did?'

'Investigate. I've insisted you have access to her diaries.'

'He agreed?'

'Harry, the Great Literary Satan is weak and woozy now like a lion hit with a monster tranquilliser. It's his time to be taken. And it's in his interest to co-oper-ate. When he reads the book and learns what a bastard he's been, it'll be too late. You will have found out stuff that Mamoon doesn't even know about himself. He'll be dead meat on the skewer of your insight. That's where the public like their artists – exposed, trousers down, arse up, doing a long stretch among serial killers, and shitting in front of strangers. That'll teach 'em to think their talent makes them better than mediocre no-brain tax-paying wage slaves like us.'

According to Rob, the publishers would sell the 'juicy' parts of the book to the Sunday newspapers; it would be reviewed internationally, and there could be excellent sales in numerous languages. And again, when Mamoon died – 'I hope', said Rob, not someone to miss an opportunity, 'in about five years' time' – the book would sell once more, with a new chapter ripping through the author's final flirtations, last illness, death, obituaries, and the unacknowledged children and, of course, mistresses who would flock to the funeral, and then to the newspapers, thrashing at their breasts, pulling out their hair, and preparing their memoirs as they fought amongst themselves.

The train rolled through graveyard towns, and Harry found his body rioting at the thought of meeting Mamoon today; indeed, he felt afraid of the whole pro-ject, particularly since, as Rob drank more, he kept repeating that this would be Harry's 'break'. Rob 'believed' in Harry but had gone on to insist Harry was far from fulfilling his potential, a potential which he, Rob, had recognised against considerable opposition. With Rob a kiss was usually followed by a clout.

'I have been priming Mamoon for you, man,' Rob added, as the train approached the station.

'Priming him how?'

'He's been told you know your stuff, and stay up for nights reading the densest material, Hegel, Derrida, Musil, Milton . . . er . . .'

'You've said I understand Hegel?'

'You're not an easy sell. I was starting from zero with you.'

'Suppose he asks me about Hegel's dialectic?'

'You'll have to give him an overview.'

'What about my first book? You must have sent it to him.'

'I had to, finally. But it had its *longueurs*, even your mother would agree. The old man struggled to get through the introduction and had to lie down for a week with Suetonius to clean his palate. So reach the new level, man, or you'll be so fucked you'll have to get work as an academic. Or even worse—'

'Worse? What could be worse than a former polytechnic?'

Rob paused and glanced out of the window before

delivering the news. 'You'll have to teach creative writing.'

'Please, no. I'm not qualified.'

'Even better. Imagine being lost for ever in a dark forest of uncompleted first novels that require your total attention.' He gathered his rags and got up. 'I see we've arrived at the wasteland! Look outside – look at this bog, peopled by tattooed dolts, gargoyles and turnip heads sniffing glue. The horror, the horror! Are you ready for the rest of your life to begin?'

TWO

Mamoon's pretty house, much altered in the last seven years of this marriage, was at the end of a winding potholed track surrounded by flat countryside, a good tranche of which Mamoon had bought up and now rented to local farmers who used the land to make hay. His land was surrounded by an electric fence, to keep deer off. The original house had been purchased in the seventies for Mamoon and his young wife Peggy, by her parents. Peggy had died, a furiously aggrieved alcoholic, twelve years ago, and a couple of years later, Liana, whom Mamoon had been seeing only for a few months, strode through the door bearing her suitcases.

Since then one small outhouse had been restored as Mamoon's work room. Another run-down barn apparently housed his unused books, copies of his own works in numerous languages, and a disorganised archive, but nobody had been in there for some time. A 'studio', where she would write, paint or design, was semi-built for Liana, but remained unfinished, and she used it to dance in. Liana had also been planning, with an architect, a further extension for guests. It was partly this development, along with all the work she'd had done to the house itself, which had busted Mamoon, forcing him to say that if things didn't improve, he'd have to work for a living.

Mamoon himself, now in his early seventies, stood waiting for them in the yard with Liana and Yin and Yang, their two young, barking springer spaniels. A handsome and seemingly strong man still, with a wide chest, goatee beard and black eyes, Mamoon was diminutive and dressed in tweedy English country clothing, greens and browns. Liana appeared to be dressed almost entirely in fur, the tails of dead animals dripping down her chest.

The couple greeted their guests warmly, but it was clear, as Rob fell out of the taxi and gazed deferentially at Mamoon, that Mamoon wasn't interested in him: Mamoon, to Harry's satisfaction, gave Rob one of the scathing grimaces he was famous for.

Rob lurched away to shout at people on the phone. Then, while Liana went off to cook, Rob hurried towards the sofa in the living room, dragging a rug from the floor and plunging under it. 'The fresh country air always relaxes me. Don't let it happen to you,' he said, passing out. 'And – make sure you impress him.'

While waiting for Mamoon, who had gone to get changed, Harry contemplated Rob, horizontal rather than lateral, and thought how enviably free and individual the editor was, beyond the disappointing pull of reality.

'Come, please, Harry. Will you?'

Harry did a double take, for Mamoon had appeared at the door in head-to-toe blue Adidas and trainers. Waving at the young man, he said he would show him his land, two ponds, and the river at the bottom of the field.

'Let's walk together and talk, since we are both interested in the same thing.'

'What is that, sir?'

'Me.'

Harry had heard that with his sarcasm, superiority, scrupulosity and argumentative persistence, Mamoon had made hard men, and, in particular – his forte – numerous good-hearted, well-read women weep. However, as they went out of the house and across the garden, Mamoon said nothing about the biography, and made no jokes or cutting remarks. Harry had been taken to meet Mamoon and Liana three weeks before, at a lunch organised by Rob. The talk then had been gossipy and light; Mamoon had been gentle and charming, and had kissed his wife's hand. Harry imagined that this meeting in the country would be the serious audition. But he seemed already to have been given the job. Or had he? How could he find out?

They looked at the flowers, vegetables, ponds, and the closed, grubby-looking swimming pool. Then Mamoon looked at Harry and explained that he needed exercise. It turned out that, among other things, Rob had told Mamoon that Harry was an intellectual with a fine singing voice, and also that he'd been a schoolboy tennis champion. Unfortunately, the reprobate now snoring and groaning on the sofa had failed to inform Harry that playing tennis with Mamoon was part of the deal, and that he would be introduced to a pair of Mamoon's old shorts, while hitting balls for him in the court adjacent to his garden.

That afternoon, as Mamoon puffed and thrashed, and Harry helped him with his backhand grip and even sculpted Mamoon's body into his as they worked on his serve, Harry was terrified that Mamoon would drop dead on the court, murdered prematurely by the man sent to embalm him in words.

The tennis session cheered Mamoon. Clearly seeing that Harry's presence wouldn't be all bad, he punched his fist into the palm of his other hand, and said, 'You have the look of an English gentleman cricketer. Did you play for Cambridge?'

'Yes.'

'And you're not terrible at tennis. You even tested me. I like that. I need it. While you write me, we can be competitors. It will lift our games. We will improve together, side by side. Okay?'

Mamoon went to shower; Liana took Harry into the garden, sat him down on a bench and patted his knee.

Simultaneously, a dark-eyed country girl with tied-back black hair and a tight white blouse began to pad across the infinite lawn with a tray of tea and biscuits. When the girl finally arrived, after what seemed like forty minutes, and began to pour the tea – things in the country appeared to take place in slow motion; the stream petrified between pot and cup – Liana looked Harry over with a mixture of severity and pity, and indicated the surroundings.

'What is your impression?'

Harry sighed. 'The peace, the silence, the distance. This place is paradise. Perhaps I'll get to live like this, when I'm older.'

'Only if you work very hard. I can reveal the truth now, young one. My husband approves of you. He whispered to me while changing that you seem to be among the few decent and bright Englishmen left on this island. "How did they turn out one so decent?" he said. But, Harry, it is *my* job to ask you what you intend to do with this man I love, admire and worship.'

Harry said, 'He is one of the greatest writers of our time. Of any time, I mean. His fictions are stand-out, but he got to know, and has written up, some of the most violent and powerful men in the world. I want to give a true account of his fascinating life.'

'How can you tell it all?'

Rob had warned Harry that you couldn't go wrong if

you mentioned 'the facts'. No one could have a beef with 'the facts' – they were unarguable, like a punch in the face.

'The facts—'

But Liana interrupted him. 'I must tell you that it will not be easy, but Mamoon is compassionate and wise. You will write a gentle book, remembering that all he has, apart from me, is his reputation. Anyone who besmirches that will suffer from nightmares and boils for ever. By the way, do you take drugs?' Harry shook his head. 'Are you promiscuous?'

Harry shook his head again. 'I am almost engaged,' he said.

'To a woman?'

'Very much so. She is a PA to a clothes designer.'

'And you don't have a criminal record?'

'No.'

'Dear God, with you we are getting everything at once!'

He was becoming dizzy; Liana stared at him in admiration until he felt uncomfortable and sipped his tea.

'How is it, your tea, sir?' said the girl, who was still standing there. 'You like Earl Grey? Rrrr . . . if it's your favourite and you're coming to stay, I'll get you a hundred tea bags.'

'Thank you, I do like it.'

'Digestive?'

'No thanks.'

'Jaffa cake?'

'No thanks.'

'Shall we go in and eat properly?' said Liana.

Rob missed lunch, and woke up when the taxi arrived.

'I can see', said Liana, as she and Mamoon stood together in the yard with their arms around one another, waving goodbye to Rob and Harry, 'that it is going to be a lot of fun to have you here, and we will all get along well as Team Mamoon. You will be so welcome here at Prospects House! I can feel already that you will become like a beloved son to us.'

'They're so happy together,' said Rob, as the taxi drew away. 'Makes me spit. Harry, don't go straight home. I'm not quite as married as I used to be. Let's go out and rip some rectum, yeah?'

'No, please—'

'I am adamant, friend.'

That night, since he thought it would be Harry's last glimpse of civilisation for some months, Rob insisted on taking him and Alice to a smart place in Mayfair frequented by bankers, gangsters and Russian prostitutes. They began with vodka, oysters and tiger prawns, but as with all of Rob's sprawling meals, it was some time before they even reached the base camp of the first course. Hours later, staggering out into the quiet, grand city, and feeling as if he'd swallowed someone's head, Harry said, 'Who would have any idea that the financial system has collapsed?'

Rob embraced Harry and said, 'My man, never mind that – I see difficulties ahead for you. This project could be a nightmare, but never forget how fortunate you are to have such a great subject to explore. Now your real work begins.' Dashing at lithe Alice, almost knocking her off her high heels and then holding her unnecessarily tight, Rob said, 'Do not worry, you divine thing. The love of your life will triumph. By the end you will admire him even more.'

'You're a clever man, Rob,' she said. 'But you haven't convinced me.' She had already emphasised that Harry, though he had passed thirty, was still a little naïve; Mamoon could eat his soul alive, leaving him humiliated and empty. 'Surely it might cause him permanent damage, psychologically. Didn't you say that Mamoon's wife even called Harry her son? What sort of woman would say that to a stranger?'

Rob was giggling and said he'd be sure to oversee everything. He had dedicated his life to problematical writers – they were always the most talented – and Harry only had to phone him. Anyhow, Mamoon was lonely, but couldn't admit it. He would more than welcome Harry's company; he loved to discuss literature and ideas. It would be an education for Harry. He would emerge with a new sophistication.

In the taxi Alice put her arm around Harry and kissed him on the side of the head. 'I know you so well, and you'll feel guilty, simplifying everything, putting the emphasis here or there according to your interest. Or the interest of Rob, more like, whom you're bullied by.'

'Am I?'

'See how you listen to his every spitting insane word, and even do that doggy nod when he stops talking? Surely you'll have to write stuff about Mamoon that he won't like?'

'I hope so. I've said to Rob it'll be *my* book. He agreed. He called me an artist.'

'When?'

'Just before he put his face down on the table.'

'What if Mamoon and his wife take revenge on you? Rob was telling me at dinner that the old bird's capable of mad furies. I read that she tossed a computer at a journalist's head for asking Mamoon if he'd sold out to become a pseudo-gentleman.'

'The British Empire wasn't won with that attitude. Alice, why aren't you backing me? What would you like me to do?'

'Truly? I wish you would be a teacher in an ordinary school.'

'With us living in a comfortable semi in suburbia?'

'Why not?'

'You wouldn't last five minutes on that money.'

'We'd be different people, with fewer shoes.'

He said, 'My love, you know very well that I've got to get my life off the ground. Even my dad said I still resemble a student. In my family, it's always a good idea to be a man.'

'What does that really mean, Harry?'

'To be amusing and articulate company. To play sport, to be successful in the world – top of the heap. This book is my debt to Dad. Besides, Rob will take care of me. He's recommended cunning and silence, and has some other advice up his sleeve.'

She turned away. 'You don't care what I say.'

'Listen. Something important happened on the train. Rob slammed the contract down in front of me and insisted I sign it.'

'And you did?'

'It was my moment of decision. Now I'm excited. Please, will you visit me there in the country? I'm sure they won't object. They'll adore you as I do, I'm sure.'

'I don't think so.'

'Why not?'

'Too intimidating. I won't have any idea what to say if he asks me about the long-term effect of the Iranian revolution. I'll just have to occupy myself in London. I want to learn to draw.'

'Oh, Alice,' he said. 'Please.'

'Don't pressure me. Give me space,' she said, kissing him again. 'Let's see how it goes. I have a feeling you'll come home to me quite soon.'

THREE

A week later, Harry moved into a little upstairs room at the front of Mamoon and Liana's house.

The night of Harry's last supper in Mayfair, a gurgling Rob in his cups had quoted a sentence from Plum Wodehouse's *Uncle Dynamite*, 'The stoutest man will quail at the prospect of having the veil torn from his past, unless that past is one of exceptional purity.'

Not that Harry could be put off. He had prepared for the veil-tearing task ahead by rereading Mamoon, going to the gym to work out with an orange-toned trainer, and keenly seeking the advice of his father, a psychiatrist, about the mind contest ahead. At the top of his list of imperatives was the one from Rob which informed Harry that he was to approach silkily from the side, charming and working Liana, the gatekeeper, until she knelt before him with the key to Mamoon on a velvet pillow.

'Turn it on, dude, as previously stated. The full beam, innit – as you did so fruitfully with my weepy assistant Lotte, now in three-times-a-week therapy, poor thing.' Rob went on, 'She'll seem deranged to you, the wife, but she worked hard to find the right person to frame the husband, hassling every agent and publisher in London. I guided her to you.'

'What clinched it?'

'What do you think?'

'I guess my potential and writing style. Possibly, my intellect.'

Rob said, 'Her first two choices dropped out after meeting Mamoon. One of them he called an "amateur".'

'And the other?'

'"Excrement". You were the cheapest of the decent, available ones, and, from her point of view, probably the most naïve. She thinks she can intimidate you into a hagiography.'

'Ah.'

'We'll let her believe that, pal, before taking them down – all the way to Chinatown. It'll be a long game of intrigue and deception. Remember, his vanity will be quite a force. Let it be your lever and use it against him.'

For the first few days, after breakfast, and when Mamoon had walked with his eyes down to his work room across the yard, Harry sat at the kitchen table with Liana and made sure, while adopting his therapist's face, to enquire about her hatred of her sister, her spiritual beliefs, why men had always adored her, why she preferred tea to coffee in the afternoon, the temperaments of her numerous dogs and cats as well as that of her parapsychologist, and wondering, with her, whether she should ditch yoga and take up Pilates. But their main concern was whether it would be possible for her to lose five pounds from her ass. In London, she said, all the women were anorexic and in the country they were all obese.

He learned that Liana's mother had been an English teacher, and an expert on Ariosto and Tasso; her grandmother had written for De Sica and Visconti. But when she brought over a box and began to offer him photographs of herself as a child – 'that little child is still in me, Harry, wanting to be loved' – he saw his empathic face had worked too well. Somehow he had convinced Liana that as well as researching a book about her husband, which would include a lot of material about her, he was also an odd-job man. 'Please, darling, such a tall strong blond boy, with – oh, wow – thick legs and fine arms, would you accompany me to the supermarket, if you don't mind, just five minutes, otherwise we won't eat or drink a thing tonight.'

He was to carry the stuff to the car, and then into the house. His work had also come to involve hauling boxes of books around the place, fetching firewood from the barn, putting down poison for rats, making the fire in the library, and removing half-eaten mice from the front step, as well as numerous other domestic chores that the two women from the village, who came in five mornings a week – sometimes accompanied by the slow-moving daughter of one of them – didn't have the time or strength to do. As he wasn't staying in a hotel, Harry knew, encouraged by Alice, that he just had to muck in and 'embed' himself.

His therapeutic charm offensive, and the fact she had little company, had made Liana indecently adhesive. The wisest thing for him to do, he figured after a few days – while he surveyed the material he might begin to look at – was to have breakfast at six thirty. After, he'd scoot off to do 'research' before experiencing the couple in their dressing gowns and hearing Mamoon complain about his eggs, the temperature of the toast, the fatal burden of being a writer with nothing left to say, and only blindness, incontinence, impotence, bad reviews, death and obscurity ahead of him.

After breakfast Liana would be busy instructing and harrying the staff, including two people who came to work in the garden, which gave Harry the opportunity to escape to the barn to which she had handed him the key, saying, 'There, *tesoro*, now go – find him.'

He found, as he barged open the creaky door, that the place hadn't been opened for some time, and was semi-derelict. Scattered around were unwanted books, discarded coats, busted furniture, mouse and bird mess, a pool table, boxes full of drafts of novels, and, most valuably, Mamoon's first wife Peggy's diaries in a wooden crate. Carefully, he lifted them out and wiped them with a cloth. Then he scrubbed down a table, found an un-broken chair, fixed up a light, and plunged in.

Mamoon had lived a long time, and written a lot: plays and adaptations of classics set in the Third World, essays, novels, some poetry. Harry's work would be immense, and his most significant resource was Mamoon himself. Harry was intending to conduct detailed and serious interviews with him. He would hear it from the horse's mouth; Mamoon's view would be the coup. However, when Harry approached his subject and opened his mouth to ask him if he might spare a moment to answer a few questions, far from being co-operative, Mamoon hurried on, as if past a tabloid reporter. The fourth morning, after breakfast, when Harry had worked out that Mamoon would be crossing the yard to his study fifty metres away, he made sure to be lurking behind a tree, smoking. Spotting his prey, Harry suddenly dashed out. 'Sir, sir—' he began.

Mamoon put his head down and thrust his arms out, and beetled on.

Liana shot out of the kitchen. 'What do you think you are doing? Never approach Mamoon when he is in the zone!'

'When will he speak to me?'

'He is deeply committed to you.'

'Are you sure?'

'I have to work on him. He has to be softened.'

'Will you do that?'

'Believe in me, darling boy. I will take you there. We will reach his marrow.'

While he waited to approach Mamoon's marrow, Harry was at least pleased to see that the most accurate source of information about Mamoon's early years as a writer were the journals which Peggy had kept from the beginning of their relationship. There were eleven volumes piled before him, in such tiny writing that Harry had to squint over them with a magnifying glass and ruler. They were also beautiful: Peggy had used numerous different coloured inks, writing at various angles across the page. Between the pages there were flowers, notes from Mamoon, an outline of his hand, cuttings from newspapers, Polaroids of her cats, lists, and postcards from friends. Since he had agreed not to remove or copy the diaries, which would soon be sent to America, Harry had to hurry through them, making notes as he went.

He had already begun to think of the young couple's relationship in terms of chapters: the callow scholarship-winning Indian, down from Cambridge and living in London; the budding author also working as a journalist; the writer begins to make his name with an amusing and well-observed novel about his father and the old man's scoundrel poker-playing friends; he and Peggy marry and travel; he and Peggy settle down in the house, where Mamoon begins to write the long family novels set in colonial India that he would be remembered for, as well as sharp essays about power and empire, along with extensive profiles and interviews with dictators and the Third-World crazies created at the collapse of colonialism.

In the late morning Liana would bring Harry his coffee, along with half a baguette and some sardines. A woman of Rome, who had spent time in India with Mamoon, Liana wore bright shawls, vibrating bangles and heavy rings, along with wellington boots in various colours for tramping through the mud and rain, which was, Harry was learning, what people who lived in the country appeared to do a good deal of the time. Her overcoats – often in fur, and fashionably spattered with mud, creating a Jackson Pollock effect – looked expensive.

'How's darling misery-guts Peggy?' Liana asked Harry, patting the pile of diaries and sitting right next to him. 'Is she drunk again?'

Harry, from an academic family, had always been capable of hard work, of bearing a large load of necessary boredom. However, he was finding the diaries both alarming and monotonous, particularly the later pages where Peggy enjoyed describing her numerous symptoms: brain-splitting migraines, stomach aches, her fear of cancer, and her regret. There had been an abortion;

she had allowed Mamoon to mistreat her. She had turned away; she hadn't insisted sufficiently; she had been weak with a strong man. She had been masochistic, even. Her OCD, her desire to slit her wrists and so on, would be interleaved with: 'I love my solitude, but fear I'll go mad. I love to read but it's not enough. Here, in the country in the winter, when it is dark at three, things can get very dark with me. I drink, and fall over and wake up on the floor in my own vomit. If Mamoon saw me, he would be appalled. But he disappeared on a book tour, where he meets only sycophants and pussy, as he puts it. Now he is sleeping with one of the women – Marion – on another continent. Kindly, he informed me she is the first woman who truly knows how to satisfy his renewed appetite. I never quite achieved that, apparently. He loves her soft body, her mouth on his cock, and the way, since the word "no" doesn't agree with him, she is ready for him whenever he wants her.'

'Didn't you read them?' Harry asked as Liana looked at a photograph of Mamoon he had found.

'I wish I could have known him then,' she said. 'I could have saved him. But *grazie a Dio*, why would I read them?'

Liana sounded like Mamoon, but he didn't sound like her. With her Indian-inflected English in an Italian accent, Liana had a loud abrupt voice, like the wind tearing at your hair, particularly when offended, and there was usually something offending her. Even her emails were loud.

'Curiosity?' he said.

'I am living the damn dream here.'

Before Mamoon she'd had two miscarriages, a fierce marriage and a divorce. Alone in a small flat in Rome, near the Tiber, ten minutes from the Piazza del Popolo, she went to discos, loved to drink, made love when she could—

'With whom?' he said, making a note.

She held his arm and whisperingly told him that she worshipped all forms of sexual expression. But dressing up and dancing could make her light up the city with erotic love. At that time she liked younger men.

'Of which age?'

'Late twenties, *tesoro*. They are still playful then, and their bodies are lovely, and still firm. Their minds are almost grown up.'

At night she sat at her window reading Turgenev and thought she was done with serious passion. Then, by chance, one day the maestro was generous enough to stroll into the little English bookshop she managed. She recognised him right away and was ecstatic. His books were her truth, and he was her *kismet*. Though she was shy, and had hair like a witch's web, she could do nothing but beg for his signature, for him to touch her book with his actual hands – the ones that held the pen of genius. He wrote down his number.

She informed him, the second time she saw him, as they strolled in the sunshine in his favourite place, the Villa Borghese, that she had fallen in love with his primal creative power. He was relieved. He was parched. He took her to dinner. She wore her blue lace skirt. She had never had a dark man. They made love with their eyes. He played the man part well, and invited her to his bed. Though he was a little older than she was used to, what could she do but open herself to him? She was pleased that he was not just a talker like some clever men. In her experience intellectuals were not sufficiently devoted to sex, with weak erections and watery, even frothy semen. But Mamoon undressed her slowly, he knew how to look at her body and let her show herself to him; he knew what to say about a woman. He kissed and caressed her feet, and had her at least three times.

In the morning he kissed her coffee mouth. He said he loved that taste on her, of bitter black coffee. She had happily stayed in his arms ever since.

'God didn't grant me children, Harry, but He granted me Mamoon when I thought it might be too late! For a time, I could come just by thinking of him. Can't we throw Peggy and her diaries away and live the life of the living? I am Tolstoy's wife: it is like running an estate, this place!'

33

'Did Mamoon read the diaries?'

'Why, are they so shocking?' She said, 'He wasted his life attending to that poor woman who killed herself just to spite him. Why would he want to fritter away another moment on such a spoilt and sullen creature?'

'He acknowledges in interviews that the two of them worked together on his manuscripts. She was the only person who wasn't afraid to edit him.'

'See how kind he is, praising her when we know the truth – that it was obviously all his work!'

Harry said, 'Perhaps she was like the Beatles with George Martin – impossible to subtract from the work.'

'Please, stop these stupid distractions. You know we are in need of a career boost up. I can tell you, to help the finances even more, I am going to write my own book. If I let you see some of it, you can offer advice.'

'I'd love to. But Liana, I must speak to Mamoon if I'm to make a picture of him alive, here and now. Otherwise I think I will pack right up and go home at the weekend.'

'*Acha*, tonight then,' she said.

They would have a proper supper and Harry would join them.

At seven thirty a bell was rung downstairs. Harry left his work. He learned that Liana liked the round supper table by the window to be properly laid with crisp napkins, shining cutlery, candles, and the best champagne and wine. She was in jeans and a V-neck jumper, and Mamoon wore a fresh shirt. When Harry entered, Liana glared disapprovingly at his raggedy T-shirt, which he would be sure never to wear again, or would perhaps incinerate. Their housekeeper, Ruth, who had veined arms and a grey, bitter mouth, and was wearing black with a white apron, served them silently. Her sister was cooking.

Harry had heard from Rob that being merely a literature lover, Liana had had inflated ideas about Mamoon's standing and wealth, with little notion of what the life of a professional writer was like. She'd been shocked by how modest an income his books actually generated. A small but lofty reputation didn't translate into cash. Her accountants had told her that unless things improved, the couple would, in the near future, have to sell the house and land and move somewhere smaller. 'Perhaps to the lowest of the low, Harry – even a bungalow!'

It became clear that Liana had convinced herself that the solution to this was for Mamoon to become, as she put it, 'a brand'. Harry was amused to learn that Mamoon, who said little at supper, appearing to park his mind somewhere more congenial and with a better outlook, wasn't sure what being a brand entailed.

'Brand, did you say, darling *habibi*? Would I have to become like Heinz ketchup or a Mont Blanc pen?'

'Not ketchup, no, but more like brand Picasso,' she said. 'Or Roald Dahl. Crowds of people are in and out of that dismal little shed every five minutes, paying through the nostrils.' When Mamoon pointed out that Dahl was long dead, Liana said, 'Never mind that – he is alive in people's minds. We must sell you better so you are similarly alive.' She nodded at Harry. 'This biography will be a good start. Don't we quite like nice Harry?'

'The boy has a powerful forehand.'

'Mamoon, I have to remind you over and over that you haven't been fairly remunerated for your genius. I go to meetings with our accountants and I can tell you, they may not have read your books, but they have looked at your figures and sighed.' She took his hand, kissed it, and rubbed it against her neck. 'Darling, an essay on Tagore won't repair the jacuzzi.'

Mamoon winced and leaned forward. 'We have a jacuzzi?'

At least Liana was trying – to sell the film rights to his books; to use Mamoon's contacts to set up a cookery programme for herself; and to persuade him to give a lucrative lecture tour in the US. She was also intending to 'pen', as she put it, a novel about a beautiful, Italian woman who falls in love with a genius. Harry would, he'd been informed, help her with this task. Who these days, apart from old-fashioned Mamoon, bothered to write their own novels, any more than they designed their own houses? Would Harry read what she'd done so far and make suggestions?

Harry got up and went out into the yard for a smoke. Liana followed him, saying, 'Why did you make that distasteful face in my house? Mamoon lives in a dream world! If I didn't protect him, he'd be broke. Don't forget you're here to show the world what an artist is.'

'That's what I'm trying to do.'

'You know, Harry, I get a little tired of you sniffing around listening, suddenly coming up with a sly question about what happened whenever and why. Let me ask *you* a question. How many bedrooms were there in the house you grew up in?' When he hesitated she went on, 'There you are. You can't remember. Five? Six?'

'It was a Norman Shaw house, in Bedford Park, in Chiswick, West London. They were a bit run down. Dad sold it when I went up to Cambridge. Silly really, as those houses are worth millions now and film stars live there.'

'But your father was a surgeon.'

'He was a doctor, and became a psychiatrist, working first in an asylum and then in a hospital.'

'*Salaud* – never mind that! Mamoon and I have had to work like dogs to achieve all that we have, while you were brought up in the top one per cent of the world's population. In another time, Harry, you'd have become a politician, a diplomat, an economist or a banker. What went wrong?'

'It's all gone right. We were brought up to feel at ease with mad people. Dad would invite his former patients over to the house. Some stayed with us. Dad encouraged us to follow them into their delusion, which he called their story, the narrative which held them together. What was called their madness was really their writing.'

'What has this got to do with my husband?' she said.

At one time, he explained, while the Left was railing against imperialism and American influence, and often supporting Third-World fascists, Mamoon interviewed and wrote about powerful politicians, dictators and bearded mass murderers who had, on occasion, personally beheaded their enemies that morning – men who wrote their 'novels' in the blood of the people. Mamoon understood this to be a form of story-telling, the making of history by writing. His voice was cool, never judgemental but morally firm. He understood the need for dictators, prophets and kings, and our love for them. 'And anyway, Liana,' Harry went on, 'while we're talking about my family, my long-dead mother ran a bookshop for a time.'

'Oh you poor thing. Do you miss her?'

'Every day.'

'Do you speak to her?'

'Yes. How do you know that?'

She shrugged. 'The hills are a radio. There are voices everywhere. This house is an ear. Did you hear Mamoon speaking at night?'

'Not yet, no.'

'I think you will.'

'That would be better than nothing,' he said.

FOUR

Harry was waiting for a way in. It would happen, he knew. He had to be patient.

Meanwhile, during the following week, he found the routine he needed: reading diaries, letters and papers in the barn until one o'clock, when Liana would announce lunch.

Then, one day, he saw Mamoon in a green velour tracksuit heading for the garden carrying weights. Harry figured that he would be mistaken if he believed for a moment that Mamoon's vanity, or his competitiveness, had declined with age. In the mid-afternoon, after it had occurred to Harry to invite Mamoon to stretch, run a little, work out a bit, and warm down with him, he learned this would be an opportunity for him to enter the old man's confidence. Mamoon loved dressing in a variety of sports gear and was keen to kickbox and learn some capoeira moves. 'If, or rather when, all else fails,' puffed Mamoon, 'you could become my personal trainer.'

In the early evening Harry would talk to Liana and help her make supper, before writing up his notes. Later, when he could no longer concentrate, he would become restless. Sometimes he ate alone in a local restaurant, with a book in front of him. If he was lucky, Mamoon would shout out his name, inviting him into the television room. Mamoon was proud of his television, which he called 'Pakistani', since it was vastly out of proportion to its surroundings and characteristic, he liked to believe, of deprived immigrants crouching in front of it like primitives contemplating the transit of Venus. Rob had prepared Harry for these whisky sessions, saying that it was in confrontation with the TV that Mamoon came into his own. For most of his adult life, Mamoon had been his own kind of radical, going to some trouble to mock and invert political correctness, rebelling against the fashionable contrarians of his day, hippies, feminists, anti-racists, revolutionaries, anyone decent, kind or on the side of equality or diversity. This was, for a short time, an unusual and even witty idea. Now Mamoon was as bored by this pose as he was by everything else. Occasionally he would try a provocation. 'Look at that ugly lazy black bastard,' he'd say, as, instructed by Liana, they drove into town to pick up some local cheese, and having noticed what looked like a shy but enthusiastic African student visiting local churches. 'Off to rob, rape and mutilate a white woman's cunt, no doubt.' But Harry felt Mamoon's heart wasn't in it, and that he preferred to ask simple questions about things which genuinely puzzled him. 'Tell me, Harry,

41

what exactly is Happy Hour? What is lap dancing and *The X Factor*? What is wiffy?'

'Wiffy? Oh, wi-fi.'

Mamoon adored Indian and, even, Pakistani cricket. He had loved, on first coming to Britain, to watch English county cricket on provincial grounds. Monday morning in chilly weather and a light rain, a train ride from London, he would sit down on a bench with a Thermos and a cheese sandwich to watch an obscure game. One wall of his library was covered with pictures of post-war players. In pride of place, though, Mamoon kept a framed photograph of the 1963 West Indian cricket team. Rob had told Harry to be sure to tell Mamoon that his uncle had captained Surrey, and had instructed him to prepare Mamoon by never turning up without either gossip or DVDs of his heroes, Rohan Kanhai, Gary Sobers, Wes Hall, and, from a later period, Malcolm Marshall, Gordon Greenidge, Alvin Kallicharran, and Vivian Richards. It didn't bore Harry to repeatedly watch them with Mamoon, or even to hear him say 'Oh good shot, sir,' like any other English buffer. Sport, which was unpredictable and existential, and where men were truly tested in the moment, was more important than art, which was 'soft'. Bowling at Lord's, taking a penalty at Wembley, playing at Wimbledon, that was 'the definitive', as Mamoon called it. 'If one had played a shot like that at Lord's, one would die happy, don't you think? I am a poor entertainer compared to it.'

Mamoon was chatty and alert when he watched football, and liked it if Harry sat with him, drinking whisky and discussing the players and managers. 'Watching the World Cup with Nietzsche,' Harry called it, having realised he learned more about Mamoon listening to him discuss the future of Manchester City than by interviewing him about his books, or his ideas on colonialism. Harry's questions were, at the beginning, gentle and general, and Mamoon made no attempt to conceal his boredom. 'When did you know you were a writer?' 'But I don't, even now.' 'Did you love your father?' 'Too much. I was a son rather than a man.' 'When did you become a man?' If a question seemed impertinent or irritated him, Mamoon said nothing but stared into the distance, waiting for the fatuity of the enquiry to occur to Harry.

While Harry sat with the great man, he ruminated on the writers he had grown up loving. Forster, tearing colonialism apart, absurdity by absurdity; a serious Orwell; Graham Greene, prowling around, looking for trouble and death; Evelyn Waugh, who saw almost everything, and hated it. Mamoon was one of the last of that sort, and of equal merit, in Harry's view. And Harry was in his house; he was walking and discussing seriously with him; he would write his life. Their names would be linked for ever; he would have a small share in the old man's power. But biography had learned a lot from the scandal sheets; it had been sucked towards the dirty stuff, a process of disillusionment. Unmasking was the thing, leaving just bleached bones. You think you like this writer? See how badly he treated his wife, children and mistresses. He even loved men! Hate him, hate his work – whichever way you looked at it, the game was up. The question had become: what can we forgive in others? How far do they have to go before we lose faith in them?

Harry had loved most of the arts long enough to know that artists had to be excused failings which would condemn the general population. The artist was the proxy, the brave one, the one who spoke, was thanked, and who paid the price. Artists were allowed, indeed encouraged, to lead more libidinous lives on behalf of others who had, of necessity, to leave their *jouissance* at the door while they worked. And as Harry began to read through the material in the barn, he became aware that he was thinking about the matter Rob had specified. What would he do with Mamoon? Who can think of Larkin now without considering his fondness for the buttocks of schoolgirls and paranoid hatred of blacks – 'I can hear fat Caribbean germs pattering after me in the underground . . .' Or Eric Gill's copulations with more or less every member of his family, including the dog? Proust had rats tortured, and donated his family furniture to brothels; Dickens walled up his wife and kept her from her children; Lillian Hellman lied. While Sartre lived with his mother, Simone de Beauvoir pimped babes for him; he envied Camus, before trashing him. John Cheever loitered in toilets, nostrils aflare, before returning to his wife. P. G. Wodehouse made broadcasts for the Nazis; Mailer stabbed his second wife. Two of Ted Hughes's lovers had killed themselves. And as for Styron, Salinger, Saroyan . . . Literature was a killing field; no decent person had ever picked up a pen. Jack Nicholson in *The Shining* had the right approximation of a writer. If Harry showed merely a decent man rather than a mercenary, he wouldn't be believed. No one wanted that: it didn't get anywhere near the hate, heat and passion of a real artist.

Harry wanted Mamoon to know that he would 're-spect and honour' him because he loved his work. Mamoon might have been mean, drunken and dirty at times, as all men and women were, but it was important that prurience didn't distract him, or his readers, from the increasingly important lesson that great art, the best words and good sentences, mattered – and mattered increasingly in a degraded, censorious world, a world where the passion for ignorance had increased through religion. Words were the bridge to reality; without them there was only chaos. Bad words could poison you and ruin your life, Mamoon had once said; and the right words could refocus reality. The madness of writing was the antidote to true madness. People admired Britain only because of its literature; the pretty little sinking island was a storehouse of genius, where the best words were kept, made and remade.

If Harry felt guilty that he was attempting to look into the intimate life of a considerable man who had invited him to stay in his house, it wasn't because Mamoon, with his high-mindedness, fastidiousness and dignity – a man formed and active before the Murdoch empire altered for good our ideas of a 'private life' – was beyond such trivialities.

But trivialities make a man, and, when he could find them, Harry brought and read to Mamoon bad reviews of books written by Mamoon's contemporaries, friends or acquaintances, knowing that he would be unable to refrain from chuckling and purring with pleasure. Then Harry learned, during their runs through the lanes with the dogs, that Mamoon loved gossip, particularly if it was demeaning. Harry cursed himself for not noticing, in his reading, that humiliation was the touchstone of Mamoon's character; it was where he had come from, and where he continued to find his enjoyment. His father had humiliated him continuously, driving him towards excellence and a lifetime of semi-repressed fury, and Mamoon never forsook its awful pleasures. Mamoon didn't appear to respond to his wife's kisses or caresses, or even her attempts to take his hand, but he was fascinated when there was prohibited contact between other people. Before he drove down to the country, Harry had to ring around the gossipocracy of agents, publishers and writers, to stock up with as many stories of infidelity, plagiarism, literary feuding and deceit, cross-dressing, backstabbing, homosexuality, and, in particular, lesbianism, as he could. At present Mamoon was fascinated by stories of formerly 'normal' women dragged to the 'other side' by '*les Sapphics*', whom, he seemed to believe, had 'mesmeric' powers.

'Anything lesbic to cheer me up?' he'd say when Harry arrived from London. 'Have their moustaches been twitching this week? Do they have fresh batteries in their vibrators? Let's hike across the fields and discuss it fully.'

Harry had begun to feel like a Bloomsbury Scheherazade. But he had learned that Mamoon's definition of lesbianism was almost non-discriminatory: he referred to all women writers as lesbian, including Jane Austen, Charlotte Brontë and Sylvia Plath. 'I'm going to bed with a lesbian,' he'd say, tucking an Austen under his arm and going upstairs.

'At least *you're* going to be having a good time,' mumbled Harry.

'I'm sorry to be trivial,' said Mamoon. 'I told Rob I'm just a hollow man. The novelist is the same – a trickster, deceiver, conman: whatever. But mostly he is a seducer.'

'Aren't you fascinated by seduction?'

'Isn't that all art is?' said Mamoon. 'Turn over, show us what you have, that is what you readers want.'

Even if Harry did have gossip, Mamoon rarely stayed up beyond nine in the evening, and it was soon after that hour when the revenge predicted by Alice – you could call it truth's price – began to occur.

Harry was having peculiar experiences when alone in his bedroom.

The staff hadn't been allocated time to clean his room. Perhaps Mamoon hadn't encouraged them; he didn't like guests, and few came. In Harry's room there were dead flies and dust; the television didn't work – all Harry could do was play *FIFA* and *Grand Theft Auto* on it, before watching movies on his computer until he fell asleep. He'd been driving back to London to see Alice and their friends whenever he could. Perhaps the close proximity to his subject, and to the countryside, was getting him down.

Harry had been brought up with his twin sporty, clever brothers in West London, one of them now a philosophy lecturer and the other a restaurateur. Unlike many of his friends, his parents hadn't owned a country place, preferring to spend the weekends at galleries, exhibitions and the theatre, having picnics at Chiswick House, or throwing parties in the garden for those whom the boys sneeringly referred to as 'intellectuals', who talked about feminism, politics, and Lacan. These people's idea of a good night out was to catch a double bill of Jean-Luc Godard at the ICA. Harry's father, who never wanted to stop thinking about and, unfortunately, discussing the psyche – being much exercised by the philosophical problems of psychiatry and 'notions of normality' – believed there was no one to talk to in the countryside, and that the people living there were as bovine as the animals they reared.

But it wasn't only this inherited aversion to the countryside which was making Harry discontented. After ten days, at about three in the morning, he was woken up by a terrifying male howling and yelling, as though something were being slaughtered. At breakfast Liana said, 'Are you exhausted?'

'But yes.'

She took Harry some eggs, and then began to dig her fingers into his shoulders as if she'd mislaid some loose change in his muscles. 'Were you awake? The murderous yelling has begun again. It happened the last three nights but you didn't hear. Your questions are condemning him to a terrible wakefulness.'

'I've hardly started with the enquiries. If I ask him if he wants milk in his tea, he runs for the hills.'

'Mamoon is a worldly man, with childish fears. He won't tell me what these dreams are, but when he wakes up, soon after he sleeps, he cries like a baby. Sometimes he barks like a dog. Even the animals have insomnia then, and become suicidal. Please, swear to me, you won't mention it in the book and embarrass us in London, Bombay and Rome.'

Harry said he couldn't cram in every wink, burp and gesticulation. He took her hand as he turned to face her. 'But Liana, surely you know indiscretion is the essence of biography? Who would read a portrait of a saintly saint?'

'I don't believe you are a filthy merchant only, Harry. What people want is upliftment, to learn the path to greatness so they can follow down it. Thank God I am here to educate you. And when the book is finished, you will bring it to me and I will strike out anything remiss with my sharpened pencil.'

He laughed. 'You won't be doing that, Liana.'

'Rob has agreed. Mamoon would cut his balls otherwise. Who do you think you are – Joan Crawford's daughter?'

'I had no idea that Rob had made some sort of deal with you.'

'What does it have to do with you?'

'Sorry?'

'When you hire a decorator to make the walls green, you don't invite him to say he doesn't like green. You invite him to put the green up and shut up.'

'I'm only the decorator here?'

'You do the paperwork. We do the rest. Coffee?'

He was compromised already. What else might she swear him to omit? Would he have to defy her? And if he knew he would have to do that, why couldn't he say so now and make everything clear to her?

That was the least of it. Harry rang Rob to tell him how it was going, and how inhibited he felt already, as well as to complain about the other noises which prevented him from sleeping – the wildlife.

Rob yelled, 'Get a gun and fire off a few rounds from the window. When the goats get the idea you mean business they'll retreat to their stables.'

'They're not goats.'

'Horses?'

'They're birds, I think. It's cold in the room, the light doesn't work very well, the window doesn't shut and at about four o'clock in the morning these animals – what are they, bats, geese, ducks, fish, pigs; anyway most of Noah's ark – start up this atrocious animal disco. I'm trapped in a rectum here!'

'You fucking wuss, complain to your agent, not to me. Thank God I didn't put you forward for the Freya

Stark gig, redoing her African walks or wherever it was the old girl traipsed around.'

Harry said, 'Is it true you've given Liana creative control of my book?'

Rob put the phone down.

Before retreating to his room, Harry began to go out into the yard and smoke a joint to help him sleep. Then he'd lie in bed thinking about Peggy, with a notebook and pen beside him. This was how he often had ideas. But sentences from the 'miseries', as he called the diaries, began to circulate in his head. One night, after he'd been there for ten days, these whispers appeared to have their own agency, or to be coming from another source, a hubbub he couldn't turn off.

Harry got up, stumbled across the room, and put on the dim light. There she suddenly was: Peggy, perched on the foot of the bed, perilously thin, exhausted but fiercely energetic, and glowing.

'What will you say about me, Harry?' she said. 'Will I be defined by my bitter end? Isn't there more to me than that? And who are you to judge?'

Peggy had been a quiet, articulate, academic girl with well-off alcoholic parents who had taught French at private schools. After university she'd worked for a small literary magazine and been introduced to Mamoon by the editor in one of the Bloomsbury pubs he frequented. In Harry's view Mamoon, whose school-

teacher father had trained him hard to win scholar-
ships, was traumatised by being sent to an English public school and then to Oxford. There wasn't a moment
when he didn't feel awkward and out of place amongst
the English toffs his father was so keen for him to join,
though the father also claimed, at the same time, to hate
the British. On his first date with Peggy he had embarrassed himself by getting into the front of a black taxi
next to the driver, and shuffling about trying to find the
seat, until the outraged driver threw him out.

In cold, sooty London, a city full of people who believed Indians to be backward and inferior, while the
sexy white kids were dressing like Syd Barrett, Peggy
helped Mamoon negotiate the master race of Belgravia
for whom he was a failed white man barely acquainted
with cutlery, and persuaded him to meet her friends in
the literary world. Half the people he charmed: he was
sympathetic, and was considered to have class and quiet
wit. The other half he offended with his arrogance. But
his father wanted him back, and wrote all the time begging him to return. He would have gone; he couldn't
see a way forward. It was Peggy who persuaded him to
stay in London and make a career as a writer, one of the
most difficult choices a man like him could have made.
It was she, when he wasn't getting enough work done in
London, who pleaded with her parents to loan them the
money to buy the cottage in Somerset.

As couples are at the start, they were together all the time, exploring their new neighbourhood, and driving around the rest of the country, visiting second-hand bookshops. Mamoon then took her to India for a few months. Meanwhile, intellectually, she never let him off the hook; she even accused him of having a lazy, 'play-boy' mind, which stung him into arguing and debating back. He started to really think.

It was here, in the early seventies, in the library she began to create in the house – the one which he was still developing – that he began to read ferociously, to 'catch up'. She was a European, an internationalist, who loved Miles Davis and Ionesco; they learned about wine and listened to Boulez while smoking Gauloises. Like a lot of English intellectuals, she was exhausted and frus-trated by English isolationism. She worshipped D. H. Lawrence, but otherwise the established view of writ-ing was dry and scholastic: pointless talk of 'lit crit', 'the canon' and Leavis, and then, later, of Marxism. Harry was learning that Peggy formed Mamoon as much as his parents had, and his scorn for totalitarian – mostly Marxist – political and religious systems, inherited from her sixties libertarianism, had remained un-changed. Eventually he drained her, it was thought, and wanted to be gone; she wanted to settle. After, for years, they just stayed 'suspended'.

And so, addressing the ghost, Harry said, 'I will be

fair and compassionate. No blame or excuses. Just the facts and a warm voice. You spoke for yourself, in the diaries. You were clear. You can go now, Peggy, please. You don't have to worry, I'm not from the newspapers.'

'But Harry, I've been waiting to see you for a long time,' she said. 'Don't you know me?'

'Aren't you Peggy?'

'Look at me closely, if you can bear to.'

It was when he recognised his mother and heard her say, 'Oh Harry, it's so good to see you. I want to hear every detail of your life after I left. Was it awful? Have you been okay? Can we talk now?' that he jumped out of bed, fled soundlessly along the corridor past the rooms where Liana and Mamoon retired, and out of the house and into the cooling night air.

In the yard he sat helplessly in the family 4×4, pulling his eldest brother's scarf from the glove compartment, putting it around his neck and hugging it to himself. His brothers, at his father's insistent urging, had made him sell his motorbikes, which he had only done when they promised to replace his wheels with the loan of this vehicle.

It was turning out to be useful. It was twenty minutes' drive to the village pub, where he'd never before been. He had no idea how he'd be received. But he needed to see people who weren't yet ghosts.

FIVE

Every morning, once upon a time, Harry's mother got up early to make him a cooked breakfast, before taking him to school. Whenever they were in the kitchen together, she'd talk over her shoulder about films, politics, men, poltergeists, neighbours, feminism, dreams – a surreal stream of hard-to-follow continuous conversation for which, it was understood, he would be the link man.

She kissed him a lot, or would suddenly sob. She had a mad laugh which could be alarming, or would suddenly say, 'You have no idea how I hate this middle-class shit!' Sometimes, to illustrate a point, she'd enact a scene, doing the voices. Or she'd sing: pop, folk, opera, with, a good deal of the time, a joint burning in the ashtray. She'd quote Lautréamont so often he remembered the words even now 'Silent, foul spiders/spin their webs in the base of our brain.'

Most evenings she went to see friends, or to parties or the theatre or dance. Apparently she hated boredom, as well as the tyranny of possessiveness and control. Harry's father had once said, with some irony, that she considered sexual opportunity to be the vanguard of political liberation. She also condemned her husband for not believing in the sixties' idea that madness brought wisdom. For her, it was not the purpose of living to be as sane as possible, and she believed her husband to be 'a policeman of the soul', since he considered it his work to make people sane, as others might want to free people from the tyranny of alcohol. But it could only make them duller, she believed. How many people was she? How many people could we be?

Harry didn't know what he thought about any of this. He did remember, though, that most nights, at the end of her life, she crept into his bedroom, and he slept in her arms, almost like a young lover, until morning. Was that love, or madness? Later, a friend of his mother's said: Harry, you are very much like her; of high intelligence, you can understand anything. Both of you are bright but brittle – and you'll go down under the slightest knock, worrying and fearing failure.

When he was twelve, she died. It seemed that after she was gone he was alone for ten years. He had to get up in the dark, feed himself and cycle to school without his mother offering him a pear, cutting the crusts from his sandwiches, or running after him with books and football boots. His identical brothers, four years older, were at Latymer, while he was at St Paul's. Where the other boys had much more of their mother, he was forced, too early, into independence. And the twins had always had one another: they bickered, disputed and had bloody fist fights around the house, but there was barely a moment when they were not in resentful or eager contact with each other, almost but not quite a closed circle.

Harry cared for himself by reading in his room, while playing his siblings' records and tapes, and speaking constantly to his mother in his mind. The family had disposed of her other clothes, but when Harry took over her wardrobe for himself, many of her shoes remained at the back of the cupboard. It occurred to him to lie with his ear on the carpet and speak to them. Harry would make films in his mind of her choosing them and putting them on; he would wonder where she had gone in each pair, who she had been with, and what they had talked about.

He saw now that the idea of isolation he had had about himself was only partly true, a myth he'd made. He was motherless, and his father might have been at work, or attending to the house, or dating. But his brothers had never been awkward or shy. At school they were rugby and soccer stars who earned money modelling and later formed a band, the Ha-Ha Fish, playing at the opening of hip shops in Carnaby Street and the sticky back rooms of Camden pubs in front of school friends. They said if he learned bass, he could perform with them, and so he did.

A teenage girl with a mass of dark hair, in a short skirt, T-shirt and black tights, opened a bedroom door to see a little boy, younger than her, sitting on his bed blinking over a book, scratching and twisting with anxiety, a plate of food untouched. Harry's brothers' pals, and their numerous girl friends, were in the house constantly, and from the beginning the boy was the object of much pity and attention from young women. There's nothing like a blond motherless child to bring the girls running with kisses, sweets and more. Who would want to give that up? The twins began to refer to the pretty little pasha's 'harem', the girls who were keen to assist him with his homework, cook for him, select his clothes and cut his hair, and accompany him to the cinema, the shops and other treats at the weekend and during holidays.

A girl beginning to move away from her parents and wanting to grow up can be persuaded into appalling acts of love. Once Harry hit thirteen and began to sweat and shower, a relay of fragrant teenagers were kissing, petting and spending the night with him on sleepovers. The motherless boy hated to sleep alone; sometimes he crashed on the floor in one of his brothers' rooms. Soon he learned that numerous girls were susceptible to his pleas for them to care for him. He needed to replace one woman with a horde of other women. From the age of fourteen he was seducing more of them than those amateurs his brothers. It would cheer his father up, when he came home, to find the house garlanded with girls in flower. 'St Trinian's', he called it, or 'the Kingdom of Pubescent Girls'. He made sure to warn Harry that he'd be envied – hated, he meant – for his gifts, charm and ease, as he got older, and that he should conceal but not suppress his virtues. Harry didn't then understand what his father meant.

His father had a superb library: philosophy, psychology, fiction, art. That was that, for Harry; he developed himself there. Not that he didn't miss his mother; he was still angry with her, to say the least, which was how she remained alive and active in his mind. What he didn't want was her sitting at the end of his bed when he was alone in the country.

Now he sped through the dark winding lanes, and then ran from the car. Soon he was at the warm bar of a busy pub, and others were turning to him, the stranger, the curiosity that everyone seemed to know about. People gathered round. Apparently the locals – farmers and ageing rock stars who lived in the big houses, and their fans who lived in smaller places – were keen to hear about 'the writer'.

Was it true Mamoon had no friends? Was he cruel to his wife, violent even? Was he a devil-worshipper? More importantly, was he really broke? And wasn't it true that he had certainly made the most of the country which had welcomed him, and where his talent had been allowed to flourish? Hadn't he complained too much? Had he ever been sufficiently grateful?

Nothing can be still while it lives in the minds of others, including, of course, a character and reputation. It didn't take long, Harry saw, for a personality to enlarge and inflate, as the subject became what others preferred him to be. Like Harry's mother, Mamoon had travelled beyond and above himself, a process Harry himself was now correcting but also abetting, in his own way. What was a person then, but a self which travelled between private fantasy and public creation?

Hadn't Mamoon been in that place for Harry when he read and reread Mamoon's interviews, profiles and essays in *Playboy*, *Rolling Stone* and *Esquire* as a young man? That Mamoon had willingly journeyed into the darkness of the contemporary world itself, and returned with testimony, witness and thought, revealed an intrepid man who was a conquistador, determined to expose and explain the harshest truths. Wasn't he the first to track, in the dark cities of northern Britain, the change in the Muslim community from socialist antiracism to a radicalism built around a new worldwide form, a reactionary idea of Islam? His essay 'The Axe of Ideology' had been crucial. Didn't his analysis then go further, as he followed the trajectory of Islam from a form of liberation theology to a death cult demanding sacrifice, built around obedience to the law of the Absolute Father?

Where was Harry in this now? Like Mamoon, Harry couldn't just hold up the mirror; he had to explain why he was there, and what this man meant. His words had to keep the writer alive in the history of literature, however much he might want to kill him personally.

Glad to be out of the house, and to have alcohol in him, Harry felt more buoyant. The less he said to the locals the more he'd enjoy his evening. He did make the mistake of suggesting, to the irritation of those around him, and at the risk of appearing superior, that a good way to make contact with a writer might be to pass one's eyes over his sentences. After this faux pas he thought it best to settle himself in a secluded corner of the bar where he could keep a look out for the local interest: the ardent young wife of a farmer bored by dipping sheep in antiseptic, or dragging on the udders of recalcitrant animals; or perhaps the partner of a long-distance lorry driver eternally delayed by a French strike.

Then he looked up; it was dim in the pub, but he saw what he wanted. His instinct had been correct. The skin game was on. He finished his drink. Before fetching another one, he went into the toilet, popped some money into the condom machine and pushed the button for plain rubbers. The girl who had been smiling and flicking her long hair at him appeared to be younger than he'd wanted. He didn't need a scandal. But she had sent her friends away. Sensibly, she was standing up. She would lead him.

He was keen to follow this siren, even into a crepuscular corridor which led to the pub's back room, an undecorated and unheated grave fragrant with urine and worse, as if the toilet were parked under a table. The drinkers were here. A hairy man with the face of a pit bull, wearing only boxer shorts and tattoos, played pool under a flickering striplight. A couple of Medusas, pulling on chained dogs, waited, squinted and cursed. Harry was afraid. He went to the girl.

They sat close together. When, quite soon, the words ran out, she licked her fingers and extinguished the candles on the table, rubbing hot wax into his hands, and onto his arms. She was plain and lovely, and not too young at all, a dramatically dark-haired busty girl in her mid-twenties or perhaps older, with black eyes, her thick legs packed into a tight, if not straining miniskirt. She introduced herself as Julia. He followed her out, and indicated his car.

They drove for half an hour, until she told him to stop in a wide street of old council houses. It was otherwise quiet in the misty rain, but dogs barked.

'Follow me,' she said.

But Harry wondered if he might be getting too old

for the dispiriting adventure that seemed to inevitably accompany the need for human contact. Did he want to creep half drunk into a damp-walled council house at midnight in the countryside, particularly since, as the girl hauled him along the dim downstairs corridor, he glimpsed, through an open door, a scene of Hogarthian dissipation.

A late middle-aged woman with her shirt open and arms in the air and three older rough men in clothes they must have slept in for weeks were dancing. They punched their arms in the air, and shouted with drunken violence.

Julia would not let him linger. She jerked him away. Soon he was two floors up in an attic room, perhaps deluded, but certainly crammed into a single bed clinging to a thin pillow and what appeared, now, to be a fat-faced proletarian girl in her early twenties. Still, once she'd finished her cigarette, and – if he hurried – before she lit another one, he'd have her again, this time on her knees on the floor, clearing a space amongst the cups and clothes, while regarding the underwear hanging from the mirror.

Not that anything important could be achieved without inconvenience, if not suffering; and he was happy to see she was more than he'd imagined. As was often the case, he feared he might become afraid and lost in his own mind, and might begin to dwell, once more, on the fact that he and his brothers could have made their mother crazy. His father had said, not long ago, 'There's no ambivalence: children make their parents die. The three of you were much too much for her.' Thinking of this, Harry required a night's comfort and companionship. A girl is an umbilical cord, a lifeline to reality. His mother wouldn't have wanted him to be alone.

Despite the thud of music and the occasional shock of abrupt yells from elsewhere in the house, he relaxed. As she stroked him and he kissed her hair, he could consider how things were going with the book. There had at last been progress; Harry believed he'd been asking the right questions. He'd pressed on.

That afternoon, passing the library on his way back from the barn, he'd spotted his foe through the window. The old man was halfway up a ladder searching for a book, and appeared particularly vulnerable. Harry, with a burst of spontaneous confidence, and, by now, a certain amount of desperation, had hurried into the house. 'There you are, sir,' he said, and peppered Mamoon with queries until even he became curious about himself.

The writer had, at last, come gingerly down the ladder, made himself comfortable in a chair and said almost mournfully, 'I must give you more, dear man. You seem upset, and even angry, now.'

Mamoon talked about his father with respect and affection; his mother he hardly mentioned, but when pushed was kind. As for his siblings, again Mamoon talked of how much he liked them, having supported one through college in America. The sister he hadn't spoken to for thirty years he said nothing about. 'It's not an interesting dispute.' About Peggy he didn't add much, claiming he'd repressed the details but that it was 'all in the diaries'.

'What's your view of it now?' Harry asked. 'Of her. Your lover.'

'You know, Harry, I loved her for a long time,' Mamoon said. 'But, once intelligent and attractive, the poor woman became increasingly distressed. She made herself so very ill with the drinking. She was even unwashed at times. Born for disappointment, she only wanted what I couldn't give. The drink made her aggressive – mostly with herself.'

Harry said, 'Would a more ruthless man have removed her?'

'How could even a more ruthless man have removed her from her own house? I could have moved somewhere else. But there is a lot I love here – the quiet to write. The long story, the novel, is an old-fashioned and, people say, defunct form. Perhaps it resembles oil painting, in that its creation is labour-intensive and enjoins an iron discipline, patience and forbearance. It is all I can do. As for Peggy, you can't just let people down, dammit. That's the hell of compassion. But I did think, next time I must marry a real woman.'

'As opposed to?'

'A case history.'

'You are compassionate, sir. That is well known,' said Harry. 'But did you go with other women?'

'Much less than you might like to imagine.'

'Didn't you say that no one has been truly married until they've committed adultery?'

'I hope so.' Mamoon went on, 'She and I always worked together on my manuscripts. That was our intimacy and the purpose of our conversations.'

'It was your love for one another?'

'Many artists have had a muse. The idea confuses idiotic people as to art's origins. They want to believe it springs from a single pure source. It has been said that my work hasn't been up to much since Peggy died.'

'Do you agree with that?'

Mamoon shrugged and began to head for the door. 'I work on, when I can. What the hell else could I do all day – talk to you? An artist, you must remember, is at his best in his art.'

This was duller than the much-gossiped idea of a diabolic intransigent Indian driving devoted women mad. Rob's late-night calls – he hollered into the phone, saying everything at least twice and with exclamation marks: 'What have you got on him? What have you got? You got *it* yet? Make sure you tell me!' – were making Harry so anguished he was beginning to wonder whether he could write a first book at all about a man about whom there would be many books, eventually. And if he didn't have the book, he explained to Julia now, he wouldn't have a career. His brothers were doing nicely, but could be very damning, while he, Harry, would be nothing.

Harry awoke when the light came up and peered about the dark blue-walled room he had landed in.

Stroking and smelling the lovely, plain woman beside him, he then recalled a lashing rant he'd received from Liana the previous afternoon, just after he'd spoken to Mamoon. She had dashed from the kitchen and into a field where he believed he was safe, reclining for a breather with a notebook in the shade of an old apple tree.

'Why did you insult Mamoon so?'

'Oh God, I'm sorry.' He sat up. 'What was it?'

'Wasn't it something about your father being a real man – and an example to you – because he had had three sons and brought them up alone?'

'Dad educated us. He called it his only duty. It's commendable. I want to do the same, Liana.'

Liana stared at him. 'How almost impossible it must be for you to imagine what it was like for a shy, preco-

68

cious Indian boy to come here and not only make a life, but a triumphant one, among such strangers, enemies even – certainly amongst people who didn't encourage him. He showed people his stories and they literally said to him, "Why would you think anyone could be interested in these bloody Indians!"'

'How could I not understand that?'

'Do I need to remind you repeatedly that you have flown through life on a magic carpet of privilege? The world has always been the private garden of tall, blond, good-looking men who can stroll anywhere and ask for anything.' She went on, 'And never forget that whatever Mamoon and I are like, and however snobbish you think we are, if we'd failed, we'd have been left with nothing. How many so-called coloured writers were there before my husband? People didn't even believe the blacks could spell Tchaikovsky!'

He was considering what sort of lesson this might be when he said goodbye to Julia early the next morning.

She put her arms around his neck and said, 'It's like being struck by lightning. I've fallen in love. I will love you now, Harry, and never let you go. Do you remember my name?'

'Julia. Is that right?'

'I won't forget yours. I could have kissed you when I poured the Earl Grey.'

'What Earl Grey?'

'Don't you remember? The first time in the garden at Mamoon's. You sat there looking so beautiful and worried. I wanted you then. I've seen you in the yard. I know you've been concentrating. Your mind always seems to be somewhere else. But something eternal passed between us. Didn't you feel it?'

'A bit,' he said. 'It was *you*.'

'Yes. I'm confused. Didn't you know that?'

'Sort of.'

'You don't remember? I offered you a digestive biscuit and a Jaffa.'

'I would never forget a Jaffa. But I must have been wondering if I'd ever be able to write the book.'

She whispered, 'Your penis is my dog. I love the taste of you in my mouth.'

'Bon appétit.'

He was surprised but gratified by her love. He guessed he was a novelty in the town, where the gene pool was limited; the ecstasy would soon wear off. He would enjoy it while it lasted.

SIX

A few nights later, having removed his boots upstairs, Harry snuck out of Mamoon's house like an errant teenager, quietly closing the door behind him.

He breathed in: the evening air was a whisky shot; the music in his car was soon rocking, and he sang as he ripped through the lanes. It was true: his genitals were deaf to reason. But wasn't it rather that his reason had become deaf to the cry of his genitals? Hadn't his mother said, 'Take love where you find it, little boy, and consider yourself lucky'? But it wasn't just a cry of lust: he was quivering and insomniac. He was finding it impossible to spend the whole night in the house of cries.

He had read through most of Mamoon's early relationship with Peggy, and had begun on the part where Mamoon, whilst travelling, first saw his 'luscious' Colombian lover Marion. What vertigo she had given him: Mamoon had found a woman who had challenged, desired and infuriated him.

Meanwhile, Peggy, who in her diaries was suffering more than even she liked – perhaps bringing forward her own death – had continued to come to Harry, usually in the guise of his mother. Something about the past hadn't been settled or organised; the story wasn't complete. This ghost of a mother had begun to ask him questions about who he was and who he truly loved. Was he capable of love? Could he truly be with anyone? 'Why are you talking to me?' he shouted. She was frightening him. 'Please, I beg you, leave me alone.'

And so, when Mamoon and Liana had retired, Harry once more went for a drink with the locals. He waited for Julia to hurry through the door and slide in beside him, a block of warmth and scent. Though she had eagerly invited him to see her again, and he saw her in the house, emptying the dishwasher and ironing, he had sworn to himself that he would eschew her. But now they would spend the night together. Delighted to be of service, he would smack her with a hairbrush as she requested, sleep in her arms, and leave early in the morning before anyone was awake.

But in the morning he was still tired; he had been up late talking to her, and this time he overslept. He could hear people moving around the house. He looked for his clothes and phone, and noticed, on a desk, along with copies of *Closer* magazine, several atlases, anthologies of poetry and books on myth. He was creeping down the stairs and trying to reach the front door without being heard when Julia's arm shot out from behind the living-room door.

'Five more minutes with me,' she begged. 'Just five. Look—'

She must have risen early to tidy up. The curtains billowed: the beer cans had vanished, the ashtrays were emptied, and the furniture returned to its place. In the front room, filled with a monumental TV, a sofa, some low chairs and a table, Harry quickly ate the bacon and eggs Julia had insisted on cooking for him. She sat opposite, drinking her favourite strong country cider – cloudy, with bits in it – eating a profiterole, and smoking a cigarette.

'What is that doing there?' Harry indicated the flag of St George above the mantelpiece. He noticed, on the mantelpiece itself, three bottles of the champagne Mamoon and Liana drank, and a big chunk of fine cheese next to it. There was also an old, passport-sized photograph of Mamoon leaning against a Toby jug.

'My brother Scott the Skin is with the National Party. We're British stock. Aren't you?'

'Julia, haven't you noticed – I apologise for talking about it too much – but I am writing a book about an Indian.'

'Shut up. The old man's no trouble,' she said. 'By the way, were his parents and brother coloured too?'

'Oh yes. The whole family. Black as night.'

'But he isn't Somalian and he's always giving the Muslims a criticism, they say.'

'Yes, I guess.'

'Do you really like Muslims?'

He said, 'The world's full of people with unusual beliefs, Julia. Scientologists, Rastafarians, Catholics, Moonies, Mormons, Baptists, Tories, dentists, captains of industry – every madness has its cheerleader. The asylums and parliament are crammed full of delusionists, and only a madman would want to eliminate them. My father had the right idea. Begin from an assumption of insanity and then laugh, where possible.'

'Scott says they think we're unclean filth who'll burn in hell. He says, where's our country gone? Who took it away?'

'But the country's much nicer now. Everyone's broke, but it's stable, unlike everywhere else in Europe. And there's less hate around than there used to be.' He said, 'Talking of unusual beliefs, when I finished my last book and was waiting for a good idea, I went down to South London and researched a long story on the new skinheads. They're all huff and puff. A bunch of Widow Twankeys pissing in the wind.'

She put her finger to her lips. 'Shhh . . . Jesus, zip it up and put it away. The local town, where I bet you've never been, is full of Poles and Muslims. White workers like us no one cares about. There's a mosque in a house they watch, the lads. The boys set fires to scare the towel heads and black crows. They follow them and hit them.

74

That'll teach 'em to try and blow us up.'

He got up. 'Thanks, but I'd better go write a book.'

'Please, Harry, I like you so much. I'm not like them. I don't go round hating. Are you trying to cliché me?'

'Don't give me reason to.'

'Good, you lover boy. Now, five more minutes.' She asked, 'If you like the writer's work so much, give me one of his stories.'

'Now?'

'While I finish my roll.'

While she held it up and took a tiny nibble, Harry said, 'Mamoon's last big work, a novella, *Afternoons with the Dictator*, was a top piece of comic satire about a raggedy bunch of five overthrown Third World dictators meeting in a cafe on the Edgware Road for tea. It was adapted as an opera at the Barbican and one weekend at the beginning of this job, Mamoon sent me, as a test, I suppose, to see it. It was all stilts, inflated uniforms and industrial music. I liked it, but it would have killed him to see it. According to him, the world needs no exaggeration.'

'What's in the story?'

'These dictators – men who would roast your dachshund or drink your eyeballs in soup – walk about with their shopping in plastic bags; they play cards; they drink. At first their talk is mostly banal, about how the lifts in their buildings don't work, or what a nuisance it is to get your army uniform adjusted for a good price, particularly when you're getting fat sitting on the sofa watching *Big Brother*. Not only that, they cannot watch *Newsnight* without anxiety, and they complain about how the money they stole from the populace doesn't go as far as people think in these straitened, inflationary times.

'Although they're still pursued and admired, like ageing popstars, by crazies and eccentrics, what they dream of is returning to active dictating and torturing. What good is an unemployed dictator with time on his hands? Once they've talked about traitors and spies, and how badly they were let down by their own side, they start to argue with each other. The problem is, if they fall out, they won't have much company. But they lack self-knowledge, and, one day, it all comes down . . .'

'How?'

'One of them finds he is beginning to fall in love with a young waitress in the cafe they go to.'

Julia said, 'Is she beautiful?'

'And kind and young. Like you.'

'Shut up.'

'Listen: he never comes in without bringing her poetry books and little wooden figures, and she is flattered.'

'Any girl would be if a man did that.'

'He seems kind and sensitive, our dictator, though he has three unmentioned wives already.'

'Did he eat them?'

'They would be tasty,' Harry said. 'And usually, such a gorgeous girl – the waitress we're talking about is Spanish, dark; there are no English people for miles—'

'Really?'

'You'll see, Julia. I'll show you London.'

'Would you?'

'Well, parts of it.'

'Please, Harry, don't make a promise if you don't mean it. I take your meanings for truth.'

'Never a good idea,' he said. 'Now, usually, in the dictator's world such a juicy girl would be raped and her family burned alive, just for starters, to keep them on their toes. But with this particular beauty, one day, while paying the bill, he was unable to resist – he whispers to her, asking her out to the cinema.

'But one of the other dictators notices what's going on. He is jealous because he likes the lovely waitress more than a bit too. And he knows the waitress will never go out with the first dictator if she finds out who he is. Who would want to go on a date with a mass murderer – a man who has personally tortured some of his victims?'

'Yuck. Not even me.'

'But, in fact, he has been pretending to be a journalist, an artist even . . .'

'She believes him?'

77

'Yes.'

'What happens? Does she go with him?'

'They do go out together.'

'Don't tell me she sleeps with him on the first date?'

'Would you?'

She shrugged. 'If I wanted him. You've got to find some fun around here.'

He went on, 'They have a good night out. He is mature, polite and gentlemanly. He gives her a sweet kiss on the lips. Something stirs. She begins to feel fondly towards him. Meanwhile, the other dictator is plotting to show her a newspaper article about the first dictator—'

'And? Do the two dictators fall out?'

'But another dictator enters the picture . . .'

At that moment the door opened and a tragic-looking woman with a swollen eye, which was turning blue, hobbled into the room and stared about distractedly, as if she'd never seen it before. Harry looked up and realised he had seen *her* before – last night, of course. But somewhere else too. What was this house called, Déjà Vu?

'You're late, Mum,' said Julia.

'Morning, sir,' said the woman to Harry, almost curt-seying, but also appearing to shiver. 'Roof.'

'Sorry?' said Harry, looking upwards. 'Damp?'

'Ruth,' said Julia. 'My mum.'

Ruth said, 'Would it be all right, sir, if you gave us a lift to the house? We all overslept due to illness. Mrs

78

Azam can be very harsh and vile.'

'She can?' said Harry.

'She slapped my Julia.'

'Where?'

'Kitchen. I had to physically stop my Scott going down there. After all we've done, years upon years of all sorts of things, long before she was here, treating us like servants, she reduced our wages and said, "I know you don't know what's going on out there beyond the haystack, but these are hard times." You should see their champagne bill. She an' Sir get through three bottles a night. What can you do, if you want to work?'

Harry continued to blink at the woman until he could assemble all the information he had and place her. Julia's mother Ruth worked in the house for Liana and Mamoon; she had served him supper not long ago.

'No problem,' he said uneasily.

The mother left and he was finishing his food as quickly as he could when Julia said, 'They like you, Sir and Her. I hear them talking. They don't even notice me.'

'What do they say about me?'

'He caught your description.'

'What description?'

'On the phone. When you called him Saddam Hussein and said he had a face like a soiled arse.'

'Ah. Did he comment on it?'

'He repeated it slowly, like he was taking it in. Then he said something like, you'd never be a novelist, and the biographer is the vulture – no, sorry, what was it? – the undertaker, of the literature world.'

'Thanks, Julia.'

'Who was that you spoke to? Was it your girlfriend?'

'Yes. Alice Jane Jackson.'

Julia said, 'She's lovely, isn't she? Liana has heard she is. Is it true she's coming to see us?'

'Yes. No. Perhaps. She looks at magazines and chews her hair. She's not keen on literary people and their talky talk, their going on about reviews and prizes and stuff. She doesn't think I should have taken on the book. Negative, eh, but at least she's protective.'

'Harry, trust me, *I* can help you more than you know. I can keep you informed.'

'You can?'

'I catch onto a lot of things, going about.' Here she hesitated. 'I think I might have something, and could find it. Some writing of Mamoon's I got hold of. Notebooks. They would be useful.'

'How did you get them?'

'It was a couple of years ago. I found them in the barn when Mamoon asked me to tidy up.'

'There's a lot of damp stuff in there, packed away, rotting. Apart from me, no one's looked at it. Why did you take and read private material?'

80

She tapped her nose and grinned. 'I wanted to learn something.'

'Like what?'

'Flicking through, I saw my name in one of them. And my mum and Scott.'

'I see. Why?' She said nothing. He said, 'Can I look at them?'

'I think so. Sure.'

'You're so cute.' He kissed her head and said, 'Please keep me up to date when necessary.'

She kissed him on the lips. 'Keep me satisfied.'

'Will do. I'm your man.'

'Are you, Harry? I'm so pleased. I can't believe it.'

'It's just a saying, Julia, not a contract.'

Julia's mother climbed up into the front of Harry's 4×4 with her bag on her lap. Julia got in the back and put her headphones on. Ruth said, 'Is it all right, please sir, if we pick up Whynne, me sister? She's helping us out today.'

'Of course, Ruth,' he said. 'The more the merrier on this fine warm day in the country with the sun coming out and it not raining yet.'

'Thank you ever so much for coming to our house. You like Julia, my daughter, sir?'

'She's kind and affectionate. You've done a good job there.'

'Thank you, sir. I take that as a high compliment,

coming from you. A man so high, a doctor even. You do prescriptions?'

'Only philosophical ones.'

'I have a son too.'

'You are twice blessed. What does he do?'

'He frightens people.'

'Professionally?'

She gurgled. 'Scares the frigging daylights out of them.'

'In what capacity?'

'Security. Don't they have that in London?'

'Yes, we have so much of it we're frightened all the time.'

'Good job you're down here. He's lucky, my son.'

'In what way?'

She said, 'To have work which suits him.'

'You can't say fairer than that, Ruth. Clearly a fulfilled life lies ahead of him despite these hard times.'

'Have you met him?'

'I don't think I've had that privilege.'

'You will.' She went on, 'Do you think he could work up in London one day?'

'Why not?'

'Would you help him, if you could? You must know people who need security.'

'Indeed.'

'I'd be ever so grateful. These children had no proper father. The men down here are no good.'

82

'Apparently men everywhere are no good, Ruth. But ambition in a young man is a wonderful thing.'

Far from living, as Harry had imagined, in flower-strewn Aga-heated cottages in the verdant enchanted English countryside, the part of the town Julia's mother directed him to was composed of run-down ugly council houses – many of them boarded up, seemingly abandoned – and shabby graffitied streets. The people looked pasty-faced, slow-moving, ill-kempt, both dozy and violent. Clearly the fathers had scarpered, or been driven out by unemployment, or by the women. Harry seemed to have discovered an island run by teenagers: a semi-violent English poverty and hopelessness unrelieved by years of government investment. You wouldn't leave your car here, let alone your family.

When the sister emerged, she also sat in silence, her lunch in a plastic box on her knee. To avoid any unnecessary enquiries, Harry dropped off the women halfway up the track. Looking up, as he handed Ruth the £20 loan she had solicited for 'expenses', he had the impression, though he couldn't be sure from such a distance, that Mamoon was standing at his bedroom window, adjusting his collar, his hooded eyes seeming to lift and sparkle with mischievous interest.

Harry hurried into the kitchen to make coffee. Liana looked at him, but said nothing. Soon after, Ruth, her sister, and Julia arrived and began pulling up the carpets and plunging their arms into the toilets. Harry would go to the barn and continue work, for another day, on Peggy's letters and diaries.

But he went to his room first, to change. While he was doing so, he heard a knock on the door.

SEVEN

'Harry?' Mamoon's gentle tap alarmed Harry, and he dropped the papers he was holding. 'I need to see you.'

'You do, sir?'

'Oh yes. Can we talk later this morning? Will you be available?'

'Talk? That's why I'm here, sir, getting under your feet like vermin, as you put it the other day.'

'See you in the library, my friend, *insh'allah*. I'm looking forward to it.'

'You are?'

'Why not? There's much to say.'

This was a surprise; Mamoon had never before solicited Harry's company. He either wanted to put the record straight about something, which was unlikely, or Harry was going to be kicked out.

Distracted, tired and guilty after his exertions with Julia, Harry was also concerned he hadn't got far with his most recent questions to Mamoon, which were about Mrs Thatcher. Why, Harry had asked, would Mamoon like someone with no discernible culture, and who had driven Britain towards vulgarity and consumerism? Besides, anyone would have thought that a scribbling Indian would be the last thing Thatcher would have liked. Apparently, she'd enjoyed Mamoon's company, and he had been asked to visit her late at night, in Downing Street. A few days ago Harry had got Mamoon to say that Thatcher 'stood up to the mob' and to 'pointless demagogues like Scargill', and that 'Margaret liked men'. While a scoop about Mamoon's private conversations with Thatcher would have helped the book, Mamoon wouldn't say more.

Now, in an attempt to think about how to approach Mamoon more profitably, Harry took off to the woods with Yin and Yang, who could run all day. He said to Alice on the phone, 'This is turning bad. Mamoon has given me only titbits. I've got a thousand facts and dates, but who wants that? What am I to do, my love? How can I really open him up?'

Harry had known he would have to ask Mamoon questions he wouldn't have put to his friends or, indeed, to any other man. There were many aspects of his friends, and indeed of his girlfriends, that Harry, with English restraint, didn't want any knowledge of. Forgetting, along with hypocrisy, were, to him, the necessary arts central to living, just as they clearly were to Mamoon. Why then, he wondered, of all things, had he decided to become a literary biographer – someone who sought the truth of another and wished to remake them in his own words? Was this what he should be doing, or would he have been better off as a coastguard, as one of his brothers had recently suggested?

In London last weekend, strolling with his father in Richmond Park, he had consulted him about making progress with Mamoon. The old man said, 'Persistence is the key, surely you must have learned that from me? If you want to treat a schizophrenic, for instance, particularly one who is more or less catatonic, the only prescription is time and close attention. And you have to enter the fantasy rather than attempt to refute it. It could take months or years before you get anywhere. Sometimes you get nowhere. Not only that, the patients try to make you crazy. They want to deposit their illness in you. At the same time, the doctors get very annoyed with the patients for not getting better, and often punish them, just as teachers become impatient with their pupils. The truth is, Harry, in these relationships there's a lot going on even when nothing seems to be going on. The sane have always envied the mad for their freedom and ecstasy. Look at your mother,' he said, 'she could be adorable, and was adored. But all our love and attention couldn't keep *her* alive.'

'Can I ask you now – I've never said it. Did you love her?'

'I did, Harry. She loved other men. I don't happen exactly to believe in the bourgeois marriage settlement, a form designed to limit sexuality, and which obviously

87

demands too high a price. But she made it difficult for me. She was curious about the world, she was a believer: it was her weakness. If she wanted to know someone, she just followed them, any faker or fakir, and damn the consequences. She disappeared; we were mad with worry; but she came back after a week saying she'd hung out with some DJs in Brighton. You know some of this? Did the boys tell you?'

'Pretty much.'

He didn't want to tell his father that he still dreamed about a family holiday in Italy, when he went to his mother's room to find the door ajar. Looking through, he saw her in bed with a man. They were lying still; he was in her arms. Her clothes were on the floor, but her shoes, oddly enough, were together on a chair – either, he wondered, as a sort of exhibit, or for their own safety. Harry pushed the door a little and went into the room. His mother jumped up, pulling a sheet over herself; the man was exposed. She screamed at Harry to get out.

He ran away, and when he saw her a few hours later she was unaffected, and didn't mention it. He knew then there was another mother within the mother he believed he knew, and after that he wondered often when he would see his real mother again. But which one would it be? Had she deliberately given him erections by lazily rubbing eczema cream into his skin?

He learned from his brothers that he had escaped awareness of the worst of her extremity, though he assisted when their mother searched the house for bugs and closed the curtains against spies. When that didn't keep them away, she stowed her three boys in the car and drove them singing, a bottle of vodka in one hand – water was poisoned – to Scotland to escape an abuser. When she went to the police station to report him, her children saw her held in handcuffs, taken away to a locked ward where she was drugged, only to be returned to the family months later, in a worse state.

His father said, 'You should know, she would be proud of you being a literary man. She was fond – often over-fond – of any prick who could wield a pen nicely. The writers always put their art first, as they should. But they are usually available in the afternoon, at which point their minds give way to their genitals. Women are attracted to artists, of course, as they are to doctors, and prisoners on death row. The powerful and the vulnerable. If you want to continue to get laid, particularly as you get older, that's where to head, boy.'

'Did her infidelities hurt you?'

He shrugged and said, 'I can't quite count the ways in which we hurt one another. It was the means by which we tried to help one another – me, turning her into a patient, her, turning me into a dull authority – which were as bad as, if not worse, than our actual abuses.'

His father then said the harshest thing that Harry thought he had ever heard.

'The truth is, she was your whole life and she'll be in your dreams until your dying day; she was your mother, Harry. But to me she was just another woman. You boys are a very happy memento. You know, when you end a relationship and say you fell out of love, you actually mean you were never really in love. The past is a river, not a statue.'

Although Alice had been against the biography, before he had set off to Mamoon's at the very beginning, she had insisted Harry practise his interview technique. She was worried that with Mamoon's short-temperedness and indifference alongside Harry's blithe politeness, Mamoon would run rings around the boy, and the two would exchange only small talk. Alice had therefore insisted that she and Harry draw up a list of demanding and incisive questions for Mamoon, which she had videoed him asking in as mild and neutral a voice as possible. But Mamoon had conducted numerous interviews with some of the world's most unpleasant characters, asking them about the children they had murdered and the women they had raped – 'Did strangling the woman to death complete your pleasure or did you consider it a supplement, like brandy at the end of the meal?' – and he used silence like a knife. The 'master' would always be the one who could wait without anxiety; Mamoon could also, as Rob had predicted, become bored and prickly. 'The sight of you, Harry,' said Rob, early on, 'will no doubt remind him of how little time he has left to live truly and authentically.'

Harry had inadvertently discovered that there were some literary subjects which would rile and arouse Mamoon. These provided usefully unguarded moments, which Harry had to utilise sparingly, for fear of alerting his opponent to the baiting. It was more like road rage than literary criticism, and Mamoon would sit up in his chair. 'The enervated nancy boy of English writing, the slack-arsed lily-livered mother-loving faggot?'

Harry had referred, in passing, and in a low voice, to E. M. Forster. 'Why, what is your view, sir?'

'View? I have no views on a man who claimed he wanted to write about homosexual sex, a subject we certainly needed to know about. Since he lacked the balls to do it, he spent thirty years staring out of the window, when he wasn't mooning over bus conductors and other Pakis. An almost-man who claimed to hate colonialism using the Third World as his brothel because he wouldn't get arrested there, as he would showing off his penis in a Chiswick toilet. Apparently he preferred his friends to his country! How brave and original! Of course,' he went on, his eyes flashing, 'Orwell was even worse. He's the worst of the Blairs. Do they still take him seriously in this country?'

'Mostly as an essayist.'

'He wrote books for children, or, rather, for children who have the misfortune to be studying him. All that ABC writing, the plain style, the bare, empty mind with a strong undertow of sadism, the sentimental socialism and Big Brother and the pigs, and nothing about love – intolerable. No adult apart from a teacher would bother with one of his novels. If I think of hell, it is being alone for ever in room 101 with nothing to read but one of his books.'

'Didn't you once say that the mystery of human cruelty is the only subject there is?'

'That sounds like me, though I repudiate that view. There is love. Neither of these writers, the poof and the puritan, has described a beautiful woman. What sort of writer cannot do that?'

He shuddered; then, having appeared to climax after this jihadic uprush of hatred, he would sink back in his chair, his mouth open, murmuring, 'I much prefer little Willie Maugham or randy H. G. Wells. Yet the only one I still love to read is the Goddess.'

'Which one?'

'She who reminds me of my lonely mongrel alcoholic wandering in London and in Paris, when I first arrived – Jean Rhys. She's the only female writer in English you'd want to sleep with. Otherwise it's just Brontës, Eliot, Woolf, Murdoch! Can you imagine cunnilingus with any of them? As Jean said, the world is simple: it's just a matter of cafes where they like you, and cafes where they don't.'

Harry knocked softly.

EIGHT

He was standing at the door of the library. Since he couldn't remember the mantra Alice had insisted would calm him, he repeated to himself, 'Doom, doom, doom . . .'

'Come.'

The book-lined room was quiet and cool, the heavy curtains keeping out the light. The desks, piled with the world's most obscure and difficult books, were antique. Busts, sculpture, paintings and tapestries, some exquisite, some vulgar, had been shipped from Liana's parents' house near Bologna. Harry took off his shoes, stepping onto a long Venetian carpet selected by Mamoon when shopping with Liana. It was like walking across a Mantegna towards a hanging judge.

Mamoon had changed out of his usual roomy tracksuit, and was dressed in grey flannel trousers, Italian loafers with grey woollen socks, and a white shirt with the sleeves unbuttoned. The ginger tom on his lap closed his eyes as Mamoon stroked his head.

Harry sat down opposite and placed his notebook and pen, as well as his tape recorder, on the low table.

Mamoon said, 'Harry, please, dear boy, before you

ignite that dreadful recording box, can't it be my turn to bore you with a question?'

Harry nodded. If he didn't fall asleep, Mamoon would, occasionally, ask Harry a question which would be direct and difficult to answer, a question which, nonetheless, Harry believed he should answer in order to illustrate that silence was no use.

'Harry, do you believe in monogamy and fidelity?' Harry started. 'Do you?'

'Yes. Yes I do, yes, in theory.'

'In theory?'

'Ah-ha.'

'You are a theoretician, you say?'

'In a way.'

'In what way are you in fact a theoretician?'

Harry said, 'People say fidelity is the best solution, that everything is simpler inside the prison of love. Fewer people go crazy. The various alternatives make for more unhappiness, don't they?'

'How would I know?' said Mamoon. 'I have lived this long and still cannot answer the unanswerable questions. People come and ask me for universal truths, but this is the wrong address. You'll only get universal questions here, the ones that make literature.'

'How can you expect *me* to answer them?'

'I've seen the way you look at women. We researched you, and heard rumours which shocked us. Luckily Rob vouched for you, otherwise we wouldn't have considered taking you on. Perhaps, though, you're not ready to withdraw from the game yet.'

Harry said, 'My mother died. I needed female attention. There were aunts, Dad's female friends, and my brothers' girlfriends. It was a sumptuous pleasure, running into the arms of the women at that age, with many of them being more than nice to me. Perhaps it became something of an obsession, to try and satisfy a woman after being in her debt.'

'To pay her back for her kindness?'

'You should know, sir, that at the moment I am very seriously detoxing as far as that side of things goes. I learned I could have a very powerful effect on women. When they wanted to be desired, their passions could be huge. But I'm trying to stop, or at least quieten down, after certain somewhat hazardous escapades and scrapes.'

'Recently?'

'Oh God, I should have learned my lesson by now.'

'What are you saying? I must have an example.'

'I'm not sure we should get distracted, Mamoon, sir.'

Mamoon leaned forward. He was becoming impatient. 'The point is, Harry, if I'm not to find you abhorrent, there will have to be more reciprocity all round. Particularly from your side.' Mamoon tickled the stirring cat under its chin. 'Do you follow me?'

Harry said, 'Sir, I'd been on a bit of a binge with the women. I'd asked for too much. My debts were being called in. I picked up a woman on the tube.'

'Which line?'

'Central.'

'Ah yes. Marble Arch. Bond Street.'

'She was a woman I adored and then pitied – but perhaps led on – an isolated person, an overseas mature student, who eventually wouldn't leave me alone, and then deliberately became pregnant by me. Or so she said. Apparently it was her last chance, at her age. She wanted nothing else from me – but a child! I was worrying. I remembered that she wrote everything down.'

'Ah-ha. Everything is recorded. Go on.'

'At some peril, I climbed up the side of her building and broke into her place, to read her diary and find out the facts about her pregnancy. The door opened while I was consulting the evidence. I thought I would die of a heart attack. It was her flatmate, who had a knife. She was so terrified I thought she might accidentally kill me.

'I said I would explain everything. We put away some whisky. I slept with her. Then I refused to do it again. So this woman confessed everything to her friend, who got in her car and hunted me down. It turned out that for three days she waited for me in various places, before trying to run me over while I was cycling. My back wheel was crushed. When I looked up and saw her eyes, I threw the bike down and ran for my life. Meanwhile, I had to keep all this from my girlfriend, with whom I'd begun living.'

'Alice – is that her name?'

'Yes, she's gentle and hopeless, and sort of flounders about. But she's good to look at, and I'm mad about her. Before, if I could, I liked to have three girls a day.'

'Three? You could manage that?'

'Four is my record. No, five. What is yours, sir?' When Mamoon said nothing, Harry said, 'Now I am determined to put the devil behind me and go straight. But at that time there were others I hadn't quite finished with – left over from an earlier period, you might say. One had an abortion. Another attempted suicide – in front of me. One of my brothers said I should never have to resort to touching my own penis, though it would have saved me some trouble.'

'You seem to specialise, if that is the word, in making others crazy. Can it be deliberate?'

'It's been a bad run, Mamoon, sir. But at times it seemed worth it.'

'In what way?'

'The women were spectacular.'

'How?'

'One of them had big eyes,' he said. 'Every time she opened them wide, it was as though all the clothes were peeling from her body. She was a violinist who'd play Bach, and sing to me.'

'Ah.'

'So you see, they required the sacrifice. I knew I'd be a fool to follow them, but more of a fool not to.'

'Good. A man who hasn't left behind him a string of broken women has hardly been alive. And if anyone manages to get their sexuality and their love lined up together, they are indeed lucky. It is as rare as a fine spring day in the country.'

Harry said, 'I am glad, I have to say, to be here in the countryside, where it's quieter. I can be more monstrous than I would like to believe – in my passions, and in the way they suddenly end, as if the relationships never happened. I'm one of those people who needs to know where their next meal is coming from – just in case it doesn't come at all. Not that women like to be so used, of course.'

'Why behave in such a way?'

'I have thought about this, Mamoon, sir, you'll be surprised to hear.'

'And?'

'I love the razor's edge. I want to be cut open. My terror is of a bourgeois, ordinary life. I can't bear the everyday constraint. I believe that ordinariness would put out my spark, such as it is.'

Mamoon said, 'I have said this: we must bow down

99

in gratitude to the fundamentalist, who reminds us how dangerous books and sex are. All sex, and indeed all pleasure, must include a poisonous drop of perversion, of devilish transgression – of evil, even – for it to be worth getting into bed for. It's become banal, now that it is ubiquitous. As a keen student of the scandal sheets, I have learned that adultery – pleasure plus betrayal – is the only fun left to us. Marriage domesticates sex but frees love. It is unsuitable as a solution to human need, but as with capitalism, the alternatives are much worse.

'But all this,' Mamoon continued, waving at the room, 'that which you refer to as the everyday, the bourgeois and the dull? I want it. I need it. I love it.'

'You do?' Harry leaned forward to turn on the recorder.

'Do not touch that,' said Mamoon. 'I've come home, Harry. I did, the other day, have to lower a knife into the toaster and it was more danger than I can bear. I'm sure it will happen to you – the desire for comfort and contentment. The desire not to be special. But I had heard from someone, perhaps Rob – aren't you intending to get married?'

'I hope so. Yes, that's what I want to do. Definitely. I see marriage as a kind of defence, a levee against the turbulence of desire. Do you think it might work like that?'

'Why would you think that?'

Harry picked up the tape recorder and showed it to Mamoon. 'I'm supposed to ask you the questions.'

'Your life is more interesting than mine.'

'You won't write about me, will you?'

'I'd like you more as a fictional character, and you should be flattered to appear in one of my works, even without your trousers. However, Harry, my clock has stopped. The embalmer is rolling up his sleeves. Even as we speak, seventy-two virgins are slipping into school-girl uniforms for me. You must live, and I confirm: always put your penis first. Harry, you know I consider you to be an ass and a twerp, but it doesn't follow you haven't taught me a lot.'

'Thank you for that. It cheers me. But what did I teach you, sir?'

'My backhand was all over the place, you know that. I'd been making that wrong swing for years. It was too high.' Mamoon went on, 'You're far more sophisticated, thoughtful and well read than I was at your age. But in other ways you're very crude and self-deceiving.'

'I am?'

'I'm sorry if I just laughed at you.'

'Did you laugh at me?'

'Didn't you hear my noise?'

'I did, sir, and became alarmed that you were unwell. Why did you make your noise?'

'The juxtapositions you described are laughable.'

Mamoon said, 'On the one hand there is the banal bourgeois existence, and on the other a fantasy of what could be called limitless enjoyment – as though those were the only alternatives.'

'Yes,' said Harry. 'It seems royally stupid now you put it like that.'

'I'm sorry if I was abrupt. But the way you picture it is misleading. The frame, one might say, is in the wrong place. You haven't applied your considerable intelligence to this matter and I want to know why. It's almost a fundamentalist separation you have going.' He stared at the ceiling. 'The novel is contamination. The novel sees the complication.' He went on, 'You'd be advised to attend to something Joseph Conrad once said, not that he's a writer I can care much for now – very little gives me pleasure, as you know, since I am almost dead.'

'What did Conrad say?'

'"The discovery of new values is a chaotic experience. This is a momentary feeling of darkness. I let my spirit float supine on that chaos."'

'Floating supine on that chaos,' repeated Harry. 'That's what I need.'

'It's the values bit I would attend to, if I were you.'

Harry noticed that Mamoon was looking at him with some amusement. Harry said, 'Am I a weak young man, do you think? Or someone who has more pleasure than they deserve?'

'Pleasure?' Mamoon laughed. 'Most people don't know how to maximise their pleasure, Harry, they sexualise their pain. Surely you've noticed that most people live without love, spending their lives trying to find people they're not turned on by.'

'Why?'

'Think about it.'

'Could that possibly be a picture of you, sir?'

Mamoon leaned forward in his chair and said, 'I hate to express a view, but you insist on forcing me. I never want to be too clear. Nothing confuses like clarity. The best stories are the open ones, those you don't quite understand. But my idea of these matters is very simple: the loves you describe are very reduced encounters, of course. Not relationships, no. They couldn't be described as such. They're addictions, or anti-relationships. Perhaps you only like to be with people you hate?'

'How so, sir?'

'Relationships which don't develop become sadistic. There has to be an exchange which develops both participants: there must be some sort of transformation, or new thing, otherwise there is violence. The violence of those who wish to explode out of a situation.'

'Do you know that well, sir?'

Mamoon shrugged. 'Mutual transformation is rare, as good things are. In my view, a person should live as they wish until they find someone they want to be faithful to. After all, as you say, one can't suck oneself off.'

'Exactly.'

Mamoon went on, 'I think we've said enough for today. I feel the need to lie down for some time and think about what you've made me say.' He smiled at Harry. 'Why don't you invite your girlfriend to stay here? I would like to see her.'

'You would?'

'I have the feeling that a young woman's presence would make me more voluble.'

'How come?'

Mamoon closed his eyes and said, 'Perhaps it is again time for me to be reminded of the finer and baser things. When Victor Hugo was buried, you couldn't find a whore in all of Paris. They were too busy paying their respects. That was a man – and he still has a show on in the West End.'

'Right.' Harry collected his things and began to pad backwards down the carpet towards the door.

But before he got out, Mamoon opened his eyes and said, 'You might find that you can't buy your sexuality off the peg in some sort of one-size-fits-all fantasy – that crass bourgeois idea, the morality of slaves. If you thought about it seriously, you would see that people have to shape and form their sexuality out of what they're given. But it's more like writing a book than reading from a script.'

'Thanks.'

'My pleasure. How is our little psychonarrative – my monument, your hauntology – coming along?'

'It's getting there, sir. But there's some considerable distance to go.'

'Good. There always will be, I suspect. I hope you are turning me into a story I can enjoy. Am I interesting? I'm so looking forward to being surprised by how I come out.'

Harry said, 'You will be very surprised.'

'Why?'

'The truth is a tattoo on your forehead. You can't see it yourself. I am your mirror.'

'You. Fucking hell.'

'Bad luck.' Harry stopped for a moment. 'I must ask, have you thought about whether I could visit and interview Marion?'

'Why bother with her? There are always women. They come and go, apparently. So what? Don't pursue them. Let them flock to you.'

'Why do you refuse, sir?'

'I've said it's not a good idea. You'll only irritate her. As if the poor woman hasn't been through enough already.'

'What exactly has she been through?'

'Get out.'

'There is one more thing, sir. Your backhand still needs work.'

'Yes, I thought so. We must do that. I want to get back in physical shape again. I need you to encourage me through some stomach crunches and press-ups on the push-up bar. I need my body to work again. It might come in useful some day.'

Harry hurried away, but Liana was waiting outside for him, as he anticipated she would be, since she had no other company apart from Julia. She walked beside him through the fields, wanting to talk with him. When she said talk she meant she wanted him to listen. It was some relief to listen because he was exhausted after what he'd said to Mamoon, as if he'd attended, without wanting to, a down-to-the-bone therapy session.

She said, 'You know me well enough, Harry, to see that I am a woman of longing.' She wanted to talk about how much she wanted to get out of 'the mud', which was how she had begun to refer to the country. 'The country smells of shit,' she said. 'Mamoon likes it, since it reminds him of back home. But now I need to get to London, and we must raise money to buy a flat. I hate to be so far from my hairdresser. My clothes are falling apart. We will give parties and dinners. You know I am keen to meet Sean Connery and the *Gandhi* actor.

But in the meantime, I am giving a dinner for Mamoon nearby. Will your girlfriend attend, and then join us for a few days? I am so weary, Harry. Perhaps she will cheer us all up? Is she funny? I would so like someone out of the ordinary to come here.'

'The invitation from both of you is very kind, but I am uneasy about inviting her,' Harry said. 'Alice is from a council estate, with a schizophrenic father. She didn't go to university, and her brother's in prison.'

'For what?'

'Drug dealing and burglary. She got into art school, but otherwise she's uneducated. She read fashion magazines in her council house as if she were studying samizdat material, and, somehow, found a job in fashion. She's not well paid, but she loves clothes and takes wonderful photographs of them. But as for literary talk – I can only say Valentino is her Dante and Alexander McQueen is her Baudelaire.'

'The Roman maestro is her Dante? Once I took his hand in my city, as I did that of Fellini. Please, do invite her. Mamoon works but won't complain too much if people come to the house and don't irritate him. If he takes against them, of course, they can abandon all hope.'

Harry said, 'The other morning, when I drove Mamoon into town to see his chiropodist he said he wished he had a shotgun.' He did Mamoon's ludicrously posh voice, '"Would anyone notice if we eliminated some of these young people? Would anyone care when there are so many of them just hanging about?"'

Liana said, 'He says the same about cyclists. But if someone doesn't come, I'll scream like a banshee. Will you bring her to Mamoon's birthday dinner – anyone young is welcome.'

'I will ask her. I know what she'll say.'

'What?'

'"What will I wear?"'

'A woman after my own heart. Oh Harry, as Dante the famous writer says, "Tonight is the beginning of always . . . *Amore e'l cor gentil sono una cosa.*"'

NINE

'Come on Boswell, are you a real man or are your stories all made up like mine?' cried Mamoon, always keen on a little lethal competition after a morning keeping culture alive. 'My nuts are not even sweating! Make me run! Don't you want to kill the jumped-up wog who has stolen your white women? Take your chance with murder at last! What risk have *you* ever taken?'

Harry found it amusing to knock balls around for Mamoon to hit, and Mamoon enjoyed the vigorous sessions; they cheered him up, particularly the bullying part.

Thwack – Harry hit the ball, calling after it, 'There, Fred Perry, practise your backhand on that, if you can! Go, go, go, grandad!'

When Mamoon did run, he coughed; he hawked, retched and spat, his whole body shuddering. Then he wanted to play again, to push himself.

In the kitchen, as they were leaving, Liana had wagged her bejewelled finger at Harry. 'Whenever he insists that you kill him, that he would love to be murdered by you, I do not want you to provide him with a heart attack, okay? This may be a labour of hate, and I don't know the incidence of biographers actually murdering their subjects, but let's not begin a trend.'

Harry soon wondered if he had indeed begun a trend. He sent across a strong but not-too-strong shot. The old man was lumbering after the ball when he suddenly pulled up as if he'd been shot, yelling out in pain and falling onto his knees.

Harry ran to Mamoon, turned him onto his back and told him to remain still. He would fetch help.

'I've never been still in my life,' said Mamoon. 'I will rise up and walk!'

Despite what Harry reckoned to be a pulled muscle, Mamoon began to crawl across the court, insisting they restart the game. Holding onto the fence, he scrambled to his feet, bent to one side, and presented his racquet.

'Serve! I'm ready! Come on, you English public-school bastard!'

Harry gently patted the ball towards him. Mamoon hurried for it and keeled over once more, falling onto his face while clutching his side.

Harry hadn't brought his phone. He had to get Mamoon to his feet and more or less carry him back to the house. It was quite a hike, and Mamoon was heavy, sweating and cursing. At last Harry asked Mamoon to climb onto his back; after some consideration, it seemed to be the most efficacious position.

As they went, Mamoon breathed into Harry's ear, 'I bet you wish you were writing another bad book about Conrad. Tell me, what is that story where a man has to carry a corpse on his back? Or perhaps I have become Kafka's authoritarian insect?'

Having to conserve his breath, Harry was unable to reply.

Liana glanced out of the window to see the groaning two-headed, two-legged creature staggering towards the house. Out she rushed, demanding to know what Harry had done to her husband. While she ministered to him, Harry waited for Mamoon to explain, but the old man just yelped, cursed and refused to lie down until Liana threatened to spank him. She sent Harry to the woods to make a stick for Mamoon.

Since Liana was preoccupied organising Mamoon's birthday dinner, for the next few days Harry was deputed to take care of Mamoon physically. He dragged the old man into and out of chairs, got him to the door of his work room – though, like everyone else, he was allowed no further – and helped him return to the house. Liana had strung a mobile phone around her husband's neck with two numbers in it, those of herself and of Harry. A writer is loved by strangers and hated by his family. As a young man, Harry would have been amazed, thankful and flattered to have Mamoon Azam call him five times a day. Why would such a distinguished man, with whom everybody, surely, would love to converse, want to talk with *him*? Now, as 'family', he was too close, and dreaded hearing that languid voice. 'Please, Harry, dear boy, if you're nearby, would you be so kind as to fetch me a book – the one with the green cover, I think it's green, greenish or perhaps turquoise, but I can't remember the title or the author – from near the television . . . At least I think it's near the television. Also, I can't locate my glasses exactly. These are the ones with the blue *not* the black frames. Do you have any idea . . .'

It was unfortunate that Mamoon's back injury, which rendered him physically incapable, as well as more irascible than usual, coincided with Liana's desire to impress Harry with their friends. Liana had become particularly engaged with and, indeed, somewhat manic about the dinner – 'the beginning of always', as she referred to the evening.

With Julia flying behind her being shouted at, Liana hurried into town on numerous occasions, bearing lists, to organise the menu, drink and seating plan. She was keen to ensure it was the perfect mix of people. Apparently, most of the diners would be local, but friends were coming from London; others would be driving across the country. There would be witty talk and laughter, drink, and good food. It would be useful for Harry too: he would see how a successful man lived and was loved. It would be a rehearsal for the sort of thing Liana anticipated happening regularly in London, once they raised the money to buy a place.

Alice, now at work in London, had heard about all this from Harry. She had been in Paris with people from the office, but had promised she would get on the train and join them if she could, depending on how things went in town.

On the evening of the dinner, one month after Harry had arrived at the house, he and Mamoon were sitting at the kitchen table waiting for Julia to finish helping Liana to get dressed. The two women, with Ruth's assistance, had been at it for some time – since yesterday morning, in fact. Mamoon had compared it to redecorating Chartres. Meanwhile, the men, having taken only a second to get their suits on and jiggle their hair, had already had a number of bracing Martinis.

Harry asked Mamoon if he was okay. 'If you don't mind me saying, you have the alarmed look of a man who has just noticed he's boarded the wrong train.'

'It's not the juice making my hands shake, Harry. What could be worse than a dinner in one's honour, my friend? I'd have preferred to stay in and self-harm. The wife, as you would call her in the faux cockney you must have learned at public school, seems to be having a mad spell, even for her.'

'This dinner is making you both tense. Liana is wonderfully kind—'

'I must say, you're a sparky lad to be erecting one's effigy and bringing drinks. I'm getting rather fond of you. You might have to do me a slight favour.'

'I wondered if something along those lines was in the offing—'

Mamoon leaned forward. 'Keep an eye on Liana tonight – you know how good you are at making conversation about brassieres, ley lines and other female interests.'

'Sorry?'

'You're smart enough to recognise that the subjects of migraines and cats never fail with the women. Lead the old girl towards the mint tea.'

'Okay.'

'Mind you, you could do me another favour by fetching that bottle of vodka for me, please. The one in the freezer, where Liana keeps her cashmere sweaters.' Harry got it, and two crystal shot glasses. Mamoon poured two hits and drank one off, replenishing it immediately. 'Drink that. It's better nude. The vermouth was confusing us.' Harry drank his and Mamoon refilled his glass. Mamoon said, 'I know you have a lot of experience in this area.'

'What area, sir?'

'Women.'

'You know more, sir. You were with Peggy for years. I'm studying it.'

'Harry, please do not omit to point out to the eager reading masses that she was a perfectly nice woman, but no one should have had to marry her. One falls in love, and then learns, for the duration, that one is at the mercy of someone else's childhood. One will real-ise, for instance, after a time, that one is actually living in one's wife's mother's armpit. I made a mistake. Per-fectly understandable.'

'How?'

'I believed sex and work could take the place of love. I have to say, when Peggy died, I was relieved and perhaps a little exhilarated. For a while I didn't know what to do. Really what I needed was what I have now. A girl, who is knotty – very damn knotty, without doubt – but one who is a man's woman.'

'What sort of woman is that?'

'A woman devoted not to herself, to her children, to a cause or to alcohol, but to the man she idealises, and to his pencil and his genius. And that man, where pos-sible,' Mamoon sighed, 'should be me.'

'You are lucky, sir. Soon to get even luckier.'

'Why?'

'Wait until you see your wife tonight.'

'Has she had a facelift?' Harry shook his head. 'More expensive? Tell me, please.'

'One minute.' Harry stood at the back door and lit a cigarette. 'I will tell you.'

That morning Julia had come into Harry's room, shut the door, and almost cried. Not that she was usually the crying type. When Harry asked her what was wrong, she reported that Liana, having become particularly frantic and anxious in the past few days, had vehemently reminded her that she, Liana, was in charge and that as she had everything and Julia nothing, Julia should watch out. Julia was on notice.

'Girl, you should be more grateful and better behaved,' Liana added. 'Then, *inshallah*, perhaps Mamoon and I will help you progress in this tough world.'

Harry learned that there had been an accumulation of hurts: Liana had accused Julia, on an earlier occasion, of having greasy hair and of being slovenly. Exasperated by Liana's high-handedness, impatience and one more threat of a slap, Julia had thought and thought. She had come up with a plan to get back at Liana without being fired. Not that Harry thought Liana would get rid of her anyway; he knew Liana was not paying Julia for all the time she spent at the house and that Liana was trying to make out that the two of them were 'friends'.

Julia didn't see money as the essential thing here. She

had found some purpose at last, and had been working to insert herself indispensably into Liana's life. First thing in the morning she prepared her mistress's wardrobe by laying out her clothes, crystals and accessories for the day. She ensured Liana's bathroom was as scrubbed as an operating theatre. Then she drove her, shopped with her, brushed and fed the animals, and put out her vanilla ice cream when she became anxious. Julia was turning Liana into the grand lady Liana had always assumed herself to be, while seeing all. From the other side, Harry had heard Liana say, without embarrassment, that working 'as experience' for the couple would 'look good' on Julia's CV, at which Julia smirked. 'Why do you make that face?' Liana asked, to which Julia replied, 'But miss, we don't have careers down here. Sometimes we have jobs. But not often.'

It was no secret to Harry that Julia prefered Prospects House to her own home. She had first come to the house as a child, when her mother was employed by Peggy. Julia's brother Scott, who tended to take care of her, was away often, and in the past few months her mother's carousing had been accelerating in intensity and frequency. Barely a night passed when Ruth didn't go to the pub and bring several men back to the house for a further session. 'I deserve a bit of company at this time of my life,' Ruth insisted, dragging in a crate of lager. 'I might have been unlucky in love, but it's never too late to live! Look at you for instance,' she went on. 'You bring that posh boy back here and do I say nothing?'

'But why should you say something?' asked Julia. She said to Harry, 'So, Mum has started to hate you.'

Harry said, 'The other morning as I scoffed my scrambled egg I noticed her turning the evil eye on me. But have I been anything but polite to her?'

'It's just you,' she said. 'She does a hilarious imitation of you flirting.' Julia was about to repeat it, but thought better of it. 'She says you're snobby, middle-class and patronising, and you're everything she hates about this country. Someone's going to teach you a lesson one of these days.'

'I am eager to learn, as you know. But I hope to God Scott isn't my teacher.'

With Ruth, on one of her 'nights', there'd be dancing, and boisterous copulation, followed by fighting, and blood on the floor in the morning. Julia stayed with her friend Lucy when she could; occasionally, when she thought it would be terrible at home, she'd creep into one of the barns and sleep on a sofa, unbeknown to Liana and Mamoon. But mostly she was at home, sleepless behind the bolted door, wondering whether, or when, she should intervene. If the shouts were desperate, and the punches too hard, she dressed, went down and yelled at the maniacs. She smashed the boom-box with a hammer. Another time she called the police. Although Ruth wore glasses and was thin, if not emaciated in the scrawny manner of some alcoholics, the mother fetched Julia a tremendous blow across the ear which seemed to concuss the poor girl, leaving her with a relentless buzzing. Not only that, one of the men seemed to have moved in, taking up residence in a cardboard box under the living-room table. When Julia sat down, a clammy hand would reach out and caress her ankle. 'It's like living in a pub,' she said.

In her time off, she didn't go home, but swam in the narrow, cold but fresh, almost concealed river at the bottom of one of the hay fields. She and Harry rode down to the river on the quad bike which Scott had repaired. While Harry strummed his guitar, singing her a slow blues, she considered the lavender sky and the countryside and the future.

She had begun to walk more vigorously, and soon she wanted to jog lightly, sometimes with Harry. She had dyed strands of her hair red, so the colour seemed to dance when she ran. To relax she'd sit on a kitchen chair at the bottom of the field with her face up to the sun. She said, 'A lot of my friends have had kids. I know how they suffer. And how they go on suffering, long after the baby is born and the man has gone.' Many of these kids she'd looked after; she was kind and patient with children. She said that girls like her were called 'prams' by the middle-class locals, but the only regular entertainment in the area was copulation.

One evening after he'd kissed her, she pulled an envelope from her bag and gave it to Harry. Inside were three stained, scuffed reporter's notebooks full of Mamoon's almost illegible notes, in faded pencil and biro. She had been keeping them under her bed. Harry thanked her and slipped them into the pockets of his combat trousers; later, when he had time to glance through them quickly, he saw they were gold dust.

He and Julia avoided eye contact in the house. But convinced there was an 'eternal' connection between them, she texted him often, sending him kisses and instructions as to what he should do to her later. One time she came into his room with a bucket and mop while he was working. When he turned, she pushed her hand down the front of her tights, licking her middle finger and rubbing herself while he watched her in the mirror.

Harry liked the fact Julia was plucky; the flare of her mischievous and dissenting smile always cheered him. He liked her even more when she was schemingly smart enough to recognise that an appeal to her mistress's paranoia would work a treat.

This was her vengeful riposte. 'Liana, you are the chief, organising everything here, thank Jesus in heaven. But there is something I *do* have more than you.'

'You joke with me, surely. *What?*'

'Guess.' After a little giggle, Julia continued in her humble but dogged way, 'You have less jiggy than me. Less than most people.'

Liana stopped and stared at Julia as if she'd never seen her before. Julia flinched, wondering whether Liana would sock or sack her.

'Yes, well . . . Do people talk about this?'

'They do.'

Liana pursed her lips. She didn't describe herself as a witch, mystic and clairvoyant for nothing. She thought for a bit before saying, 'My hands still dampen when Mamoon walks into the room.'

Julia said, 'Does any part of *him* dampen?'

'Yes, that's the question. You're absolutely spot on and right, I must increase my power over him.'

'You have to, miss.'

'Otherwise he will become bored and very dangerous, as he did with Peggy and Marion. In my country we women are very forceful and recognise there's only one way to keep a man – and that is to satisfy him. I will leave him with not a drop of juice or scrap of energy even to say hello to another woman.'

Liana would make sure that everyone knew that she could use her 'wiles and guiles', to turn her husband on – that very night. 'Then the gossiping village dagger-tongues of those who think my husband doesn't desire me will be zipped shut for ever.'

'Good shot, Julia,' confirmed Harry. 'Dangerous, but subtle. I can't wait to see what sort of wiles and guiles Liana has in mind. She can have no better helper than you. Let's hope this little plan doesn't backfire.'

Now Harry stubbed out his cigarette and poured Mamoon another drink. He said, 'Liana, with Julia's kind help, is going to some trouble to please you. It goes without saying that the ideal woman you refer to – a man's woman – needs to be kept occupied by the man.'

'You will be thrilled to hear that I increased Liana's allowance last month.'

'What did you allow her?'

'It is true that a man has to catch a woman by the ears, by talking to her and, occasionally, even listening. But this time I got her head. I seem to have bought her a wig.'

'She certainly needs to be walked out, and shown off. Otherwise it is like keeping a Velázquez in a cupboard. Be nice: get her some new titties for Christmas. She'd love the attention.'

Mamoon laughed. 'Dear boy, your prick is so hard you can barely walk straight. But I can barely walk at all – you know why. Besides, my blood has cooled at last.' He went on to say that he had a good friend in Paris, a wonderful poet older than him. 'Think of two old men sitting in a cafe, watching the world die. He is either weaker or more persistent than me, but he is still playing the game of love. He said the other day that the only thing to be said for ageing is that you don't come quickly, if at all.'

Mamoon said that his friend's eyes would suddenly focus; he would stand up and follow a woman down the street, quoting Stendhal as he went: 'Beauty is the promise of happiness . . .' Mamoon's friend set the women up in apartments, made love to them – at least at the beginning – and paid for them to study to become lawyers. It broke down when the women found someone richer and younger. One day he was apprehended by the police on a balcony, this old man, trying to look in on one of his lovelies who was with another man.

'Then – Harry – he comes crying to me – no better therapist when it comes to comforting the lovelorn.'

'You envy him?'

'My friend might need to learn, as I think you will, when it's too late, that rather than a big bang, the whimper of a companionate marriage, an *agape*, a warm conversation, could be the model union, and the target of all love. Kind, nurturing, even-keeled, dispassionate – such a love will make for contented days when one can think freely. Plus: one's supper will be on the table when one wants it.'

'Parental, or pseudo-sibling, rather than adult?'

'Why say it would not be adult?'

'There's no sex.'

Mamoon knocked back his vodka. 'I have to acknowledge, you might be on to something.' Harry smiled, pleased to have interested Mamoon at last. 'You're almost, but not quite, the fool I like to take you for.'

Harry leaned forward. 'You put your penis on the page.'

Mamoon looked at him quizzically. 'Sorry?'

'Mamoon, you made your women into fictional characters rather than loved them as real people.'

'Think what you'd achieve, Harry,' said Mamoon sorrowfully, 'if you didn't always go too far.'

'It's only when I go too far that I think I'm getting somewhere,' said Harry.

Mamoon had just closed his eyes when there was a cry from elsewhere in the house. 'I'm alive and ready to boogie! Prepare, people!'

'Boys, she's coming!' trilled Julia.

Mamoon came to, and reached for his stick. 'It better be worth it.'

Supported at the elbow by Julia, Liana stepped carefully down the stairs. At some physical cost, Mamoon turned around to see his wife. Harry didn't know whether it was the style Mamoon's wife had selected for his birthday, or the fact that she appeared to be wearing all of his money at once, which made Mamoon resemble a man about to have an electric fire dropped into his bath.

'Help me,' he said to Harry, raising his arms. 'Please, help me up – my bottom half has gone.'

TEN

There was a swish and a sizzle: Harry thought the world would catch fire. Liana was crossing her legs.

'If this doesn't do it, nothing will,' she leaned across and whispered to Harry in the car, tugging her skirt down.

He said, 'I'm getting a twitch in the trousers myself.'

'I'm looking forward to tonight. I so much want to touch him.'

'May you have many soft orgasms.'

'I will do, later,' she said. 'Just between us, I come easily, sometimes two or three times in a row – if I like the man. If I don't, it's just the once. Does sex make life worth living? Didn't you say, the other day, "Our lives are only as good as our orgasms"?'

He giggled. 'I hope so.'

He glanced at Liana again, and complimented her on her short A-line leather skirt, sheer top, and what he recognised as Louboutin pumps with heels. As for her handbag, he had to admit he had always been a fan of leopard print; he wore pyjama bottoms in the same pattern.

'Stop and park – it's here,' she said to Harry at last.

'Mamoon,' she said loudly. 'Please listen, we're getting out.'

'Here?' Mamoon was peering anxiously out of the window. 'Are you sure?'

'Absolutely.'

'It can't be. Drive on, boy!'

'No, no,' she said, getting down from the car and going round to let Mamoon out. 'I'm serious.'

Harry was surprised, too, that the dinner was to be held in the back room of a standard Indian restaurant with seventies ersatz-colonial decor. It was certainly a shock for Mamoon, who began to quiver like a pensioner about to be left in a care home.

'You said you won't travel, and it's our own Pottapatti, where we used to moon over one another for hours, talking about our childhoods, the colour we wanted the library to be, the future and what we would do together. You know you love the food here, *habibi* darling,' pleaded Liana, caressing his hands, while trying to prise them from the seat he was holding on to.

'I do?'

'You said the keema was God's ambrosia. There's plenty to drink, and look – there are our friends!'

'I hate those bastards—'

'Don't be silly. They've read your books. Let's be grateful for the royalties.'

'My publisher sent them free copies.'

127

Harry and Liana had some trouble hauling Mamoon out of the car and onto the premises, particularly as he had to stop to stare at Liana in disbelief, while she informed him for the first time that it would be particularly kind if he made 'just a little speech', later on.

'Speech? Here?'

'Please, darling, just for a moment, a few kind words for your dear friends. You just have to put your Nelson Mandela face on. That comes easily to you.'

As Mamoon intuited – 'Oh God, it's going to be like one of Charcot's Tuesday lectures' – a succession of somewhat withered, demented people soon arrived. Mamoon, sitting low in his chair at the table, and un-inclined, if not unable to get up, greeted the line of un-dead with the indifference of a billionaire Indian contemplating his servants. A wealthy American couple from London who'd always admired Mamoon's work and wanted to meet 'the great man' had also been invited by Liana, to provide 'variety'. Despite the woman's outpouring of praise over his last book, on Australia, which she described as a stellar classic of the 'personal journalism' genre, without the American exhibitionism, Mamoon did not want to speak to them.

During dinner, when his friends asked Mamoon what he was doing now, and when he had shrugged and said, 'Nothing, it's all too late, the work is there, the work is done, I am finished and only eternal darkness awaits,' Liana made conversation about dual carriage-ways, bypasses and 'the green belt', as they do in the country.

Having been asked for his views on this matter, Mamoon cleared his throat and said with some decision, 'I love you all, and I love England – the countryside, the people, even the food, particularly when it is Indian,' before shutting his eyes.

Liana tapped her glass to bring people to attention; they all looked reverently at Mamoon, waiting for the old man's lips to begin moving once more.

Finally Mamoon opened his eyes to say, 'We live in a country which has only a past, but no future. If I am a conservative, it's because I want to preserve what I consider to be the character of that past, of England and the English people. I am an immigrant, but England is my home. I've spent more time in this wilderness of monkeys, this democracy of dunces, than anywhere else, and I prefer its village atmosphere of freedom and fair play to that of anywhere else. I have, too, followed its tragedy and comedy with much interest. When I was a child, Britain was the most powerful country on earth, its representatives both feared and admired. I adore the cynicism it developed in the sixties, the way political figures, far from being idealised, as they too often are elsewhere, are mocked and ridiculed without fear.

'Apparently now, though, we writers and artists are

not allowed to give offence. We must not question, criticise or insult the other, for fear of being hounded and murdered. These days a writer without bodyguards can hardly be considered serious. A bad review is the least of our problems. Every idiot believing any insanity has to be humoured: it is their human right. The right to speech is always stolen, always provisional. I fear the game is almost up for truth. People don't want it; it doesn't help them get rich.

'We are staying, to adapt György Lukács, in the Grand Abyss Hotel, which has every service and facility: it is beautiful, well lit, comfortable, with keen staff. There is an incredible view, because it is perched on the edge of a cliff. And with its inhabitants burrowing beneath it, looking for oil, it could collapse at any moment. We are surviving, in this pleasant liberal enclave where people read and speak freely, on borrowed time. But for those not inside – the dispossessed of the world, the poor, the refugees and those forced into exile – existence is a wasteland.

'This increasing separation is deadly. We in the Hotel are the lucky ones, and we must not forget that. Even I appreciate it. I will never go home. It is here that I will die.'

'Not in this restaurant, I hope,' said Liana.

Mamoon went on, 'The news I bring is to say that, man being the only animal who hates himself, the likely fate of the world is total self-destruction.' He raised his glass. 'All the best then, my friends. Here's to a happy apocalypse.'

'Happy apocalypse,' murmured the other guests, obediently, raising their glasses.

'Total self-destruction,' said Mamoon.

'Total self-destruction,' repeated his friends.

'And death,' added Mamoon.

'Death.'

'Death.'

They sang 'Happy Birthday'. Then, before the kulfi, one of Mamoon's acolytes, a young Indian who sometimes did research for him, stood and made a speech praising, as would anyone, Mamoon's talent, humanity, compassion and understanding. The scholar also referred to Mamoon as a revolutionary, and compared him to Derrida, Fanon, Orwell, Gogol and Edward Said. Fortunately Mamoon had become incapable of facial expression; only bemusement and bafflement remained as the words washed over him.

Harry, realising it might be a good idea to feature this scene of summing up and farewell in his introduction, had been making notes all the while. Once the speeches were over, he went outside for some fresh air and, sitting on a wall, added some information and colour about the guests. He wouldn't present only the 'facts'; he wanted a more novelistic, personal tone, presenting the writer in his later years, puffed with success and honours. Coming back in, Harry was pleased to see the guests were being served coffee, though most of them were hopelessly drunk by now. He hurried to a corner of the restaurant and checked his phone. Had she called?

He missed Alice but he didn't believe she missed him, or anyone. Being low-temperature, she wasn't like that. Without parents who had time for her, at an early age she had made herself self-sufficient. But since Harry had been at the house for almost five weeks, and was beginning to think he was losing his nerve and becoming depressed over the slow speed of things, he had insisted, and even given a cast-iron guarantee, that if she joined him in the country, no one would say anything pretentious, incomprehensible or even intelligent, while near her. On this basis, Alice had finally agreed to visit. But Harry had received a text message, which he opened now to find that Alice wasn't sure she'd make it tonight. She wouldn't know the other guests and, anyway, she was busy. She kept him, as always, 'on hold'.

'Darling, help me.' He felt a hand on his shoulder and an arm around his waist. Liana whispered, 'We must get out of here. I've had enough. Look.'

Harry saw that Mamoon, who after his paean to England had appeared to withdraw into himself, had now dropped from his chair and was sitting on the floor like a bewildered child. Some of the other guests tottered towards him, and helped him up to his seat. Meanwhile Liana was informing their friends that she thought Mamoon had had enough.

It took Harry and two of the staff, their bow ties discombobulated, to get a more or less unconscious Mamoon out through the restaurant and into the back seat of the car. They removed his shoes, put a cushion under his head and a blanket over the rest of him.

'If I'd known that biography would turn out to be such physical labour, I might have thought twice about it,' Harry told Liana, once the job had been done and he'd tipped the staff.

'Let's go,' she said. 'Forward, please.'

ELEVEN

She told Harry to drive carefully and let Mamoon sleep. He'd wake up in an hour or so and they would have sexy fun later. From the car window, she made her last good-byes and waved at some of the departing guests, one of whom was vomiting in the gutter.

Since Liana was pouting and swaying ridiculously as if she would burst under some inner pressure, Harry removed one hand from the steering wheel and pressed it against her chest.

'Careful,' she cried. 'I've got a rose quartz crystal in my bra!' When Harry said idly that he thought her guests had enjoyed the food, she said, 'If you think that, you're a fool who knows nothing about Indian cuisine. You'll never be constipated again. Didn't you see it was a tragedy? I don't want to be around these grotesques.'

'What you really want, Liana, is to be a great lady, a fashionable society hostess, with a salon, where Somerset Maugham, Arnold Bennett and, on rare occasions, Thomas Hardy, drop by for tea and talk about what's on at the theatre.'

She said, 'I would have to be in London to do that. Have you ever noticed how little Mamoon does for me?'

'But you're Tolstoy's wife,' said Harry. 'Aren't the consolations of status and respect enough?'

'I only arranged that unappreciated dinner because Mamoon takes me nowhere. You know Dirty Ben, my psychic with the filthy mind?'

'The short-term psychic? Is that the one you said is a tranny?'

'Darling, with those nails he must be.'

'Liana, can I ask, what is the point of hiring a psychic who can only see a maximum of six months ahead? Isn't that like having a blind surgeon?'

'I asked Dirty Ben,' she said, 'can't you set Mamoon on fire? During the next six months do you see any sex for me? No way – he thinks I've been cursed by my ex-husband, and asked for seven hundred pounds to lift the evil intention.'

'No chance of a loyalty discount?'

'Harry, I'm asking you, what choice did I have? Mamoon hardly talks to me. I wrote about my need in big handwriting and left my diary out. What sort of husband walks past his wife's diary without a second glance?'

'Does he touch you?'

'Not even on my birthday! For me the sacred lives inside the profane. Can a person go mad for lack of passion and love? Aren't I still touchable? I guess you might know, Harry.'

He glanced at her. 'You are a succulent woman, juicy as a dolphin, and at your sexual peak too. A woman of unused potential with much life ahead. Particularly during the next six months.'

'Though I tried, my forties were not fulfilling,' she said. '*Tesoro*, dear, divorce and all that rather dries one out.'

She described her literary admiration for Mamoon, and how, in a moment, it had turned into love. For her, it had been an 'awakening' – sexually, spiritually, emotionally. She saw the point of the world; everything added up and her soul filled with light and life. This went on for the first three years. Then the light began to flicker. 'At the moment he has nothing to give me and no intention of giving it.'

Harry said, 'You were slipping books into paper bags, Liana. Now you have the house, the land, and dogs that wag their tails at you. When Mamoon goes, you'll get the money and you'll be regarded with wonder as the keeper of the eternal flame. You have a lifetime's work ahead of you, refusing permission for this or that, and attacking whichever journalist has called your husband a charlatan faggot.'

'Harry, it is worse for women, Harry, you don't understand. You could find a wife when you're seventy-five. He will be my last lover. Perhaps my last man ever, and I will never be loved again. What man will go near me after Mamoon?'

'You will have had a great artist for a husband. Liana, do you still get horny?'

Although Mamoon was snoring, Liana turned to ensure that he was truly asleep. Harry's iPod was on low, playing Brazilian songs and Nordic jazz – soft trumpets and mellow slow pianos. Harry could hear Liana breathing rapidly. He let her listen to the music, and concentrated on driving through the dark narrow lanes overhung with bushes and trees, dimming and raising his lights as he went.

She leaned across and whispered, 'I'm rabid, dear, rabid. I said to Julia, ideally I wouldn't want to go without love for more than a month.'

'What did she say?'

'She screamed – more like a week. She informed me that a woman who doesn't have an orgasm a day will get dry skin, and lines. According to her you should rub your lover's semen into your forehead.'

'She does have a milky look.'

Liana went on, 'I shouldn't admit this – don't include it in the book – I put out my arms and hugged a tree.'

'Dogs piss against trees, Liana.' He said, 'Would you like me to talk to him about it?'

'Would you? And, if you don't' – and here she looked at him hard – 'I might start asking you where you go at night.'

'What?'

'When it's dark.'

He knew she was watching him. He said, 'When it gets dark I like to relax, Liana. I like to drive. Sometimes I go across to Stonehenge, climb over the fence and press my cheek against the ancient rock. The relaxation helps me think about the book. My paperwork, as you call it.'

'I'm saying this kindly, Harry. Be very careful. I respect your secrets, but save such Stonehenge nonsense for your girlfriend. I'm intrigued to find out what she's like.'

'I'm annoyed because she said she'd be here for Mamoon's supper.'

'Is she always elusive?'

'Her whole life's a no-show.'

'I hate to say it, but you remind me of the Tarot Magician. You've got a lot of spiritual power. You deserve better.' Liana said, 'I'll tell you what we'll do. I'm from a puritanical, Catholic background. In my day we were punished for doubting God. I kept away from chemical experimentation. But I have read about it in modern novels. Have you ever tried cocaine – or whatever it's called – ecstasy? Do you have any?'

'MDMA? It's not good for you.'

'Then why, according to the papers, do millions of people take it?'

'It's enjoyable in the short term.'

'That's what I want,' she breathed, 'enjoyment in the short term. I'm beginning to feel like an old woman. My knees ache. And so does my heart.'

'My father always said that illegal drugs are better for you than the legal stuff. How many artists have created while drunk, high on laudanum, opium, chloral or amphetamines? What have antidepressants ever done for culture?'

'Good. If you don't get me some of the good stuff to try, I'll go to that nasty pub in town you have taken to drinking in.' She touched his knee. 'Just a little, please Harry.' He told her she'd have to promise to be nice to him. 'You must ask Mamoon to give his blessing for me to interview Marion. Okay?'

'But he's very wary of her. She was full of hate and promised a terrible revenge.'

'What sort?'

'We're waiting for it to arrive. All he did was fall deeply in love with me. He won't have her sniping at him. Don't take the risk: if you mention her he could smash you in two.'

'I've got to take that risk.'

At the house, it was a familiar difficulty for Harry getting Mamoon out of the car, into the kitchen, upstairs and onto his bed.

Liana had gone ahead of them and, in the bedroom, she turned off the lights and lit candles. Then she collapsed into her favourite yellow armchair, decorated with exotic birds, let her hair down and removed her shoes.

'You should know,' she said, when he forced and stumbled Mamoon through the impasse of the door and onto the bed, 'that the arch of the foot in this shoe is the shape a woman's foot makes in orgasm.' She reached into her bra, took out her crystal and caressed it impatiently. 'Wake him up.'

Harry said softly, 'Mamoon . . . Mamoon . . .'

There was no response. She said, 'You're the Muscle Mary – slap him. He'll thank you later. We both will.'

Harry tapped Mamoon on the cheek. 'Come on, old fella.'

She told him to do it harder. 'Start his engine. Splash him with water.'

Harry gave the old man a light backhander and tipped a little water over his forehead. Mamoon raised his head, opened his eyes and stared straight at Harry for a moment. Then he fell back, and closed his eyes.

Liana snorted and gestured at Mamoon's silk pyjamas. 'The bastard's gone for the night. We'll have to make our own fun. At least try and get him into those.'

'Why am *I* doing this, Liana?'

'You wanted to know him, and aren't I dead on my

feet! Don't you think my ankles are looking puffy?' She said, 'To be serious for a moment, you've given me hope. Do you really think I can win Mamoon back in the way we've discussed?'

After several outraged snorts and gasps, Mamoon had returned to a deep sleep even as Harry embarked on the considerable process of getting the old man out of his trousers and into the pyjamas. Meanwhile, Harry glanced towards the window. Outside all was dark; thin rain fell. Harry went to the window: he believed he'd seen the light from a mobile phone in the distance.

He said to Liana, 'You'll have to be determined and use all your tricks of seduction.'

She was caressing the arm of the chair with the crystal. 'You're right. I've been too inactive.' Elaborately, she crossed her legs. 'I see you looking at me. He used to look at me. He loved my legs, though I think he was a bit surprised, on that wonderful day in Venice, that he had to marry the rest of me too. Harry—'

'Yes?'

'You've been very inspiring tonight . . . Are you going to go where you go at night? Suppose I become frightened? What if I must cry?'

'Don't cry.' At last Mamoon was done. Harry went to the door and saluted her. He thanked her for the evening and told her to sleep well. He retired to his room and locked the door. A few minutes later she came and tried it, crying out, 'Don't reject me like everyone else!'

He didn't believe her heart was in it, and she soon gave up. He went to the window, climbed out and jumped down.

Julia was waiting for him in the yard, holding her raincoat over her head in the midnight rain.

TWELVE

'They're not for me.'

'Of course not.'

'They really are not.'

'I know what you think, and I've said already they're not for most people, Alice. These pompous, authoritarian old men are more than an acquired taste – a perversion, perhaps.'

But it amused Alice to insist that he must be in love with Mamoon. It was 'obvious'. He asked her where she got that idea from.

'The other day, when you called me in one of your miserable states, I had to endure a description of his lips and eyes.' She repeated Harry's fruity and ironical upper-class drawl. '"His eyes, dear Alice, will appear to be dark and impenetrable, but they contain the heat of chestnuts boiled for a hundred years—"'

'Yes, that was for your information only. You will be thanked for coming here.'

He reiterated that credit would be racked up; a bonfire of money burned in Bond Street for her. And so, after much argument, evasion, as well as the promise of a trip to Venice, a great event had occurred:

Alice had not only consented to visit, but he had found her waiting impatiently on the platform at the little station earlier that morning, tapping at her phone.

Now the couple were driving through the maze of the narrow lanes to the destination where all local roads met: Prospects House. Her fine head on its long neck turned, and, at the perfect moment, the hedges parted: cows grazed, birds sang, deer stood. While she drank in the restful beauty of the landscape, as he knew she would, he said he had to apologise for not exactly inviting her to the department of sangfroid.

'But my body is uncoiling,' she said. 'This is almost a yoga mat moment. Why didn't you say it was wonderful?'

'Glance across. Tell me, how do I look to you?'

'Did you shower? That T-shirt is gone. If I were you, I'd wax your hair now to make it look fuller. Did you enjoy last night's dinner? Tell me all.'

Harry told her that before Mamoon passed out, he had introduced him to his friends as his *darbari* – meaning courtier, or catamite. Then Liana asked him for drugs and insisted he strip Mamoon. She hinted Harry might want to strip her too. Soon, he'd be qualified to work at the Old Vic as an actor's dresser.

Alice said, 'Have you been flirting? Oh God, Harry, I begged you to behave normally down here. Are you buggering everyone about?'

'I assure you it's her. Even her pasta is black. She smells my blood, my fear and weakness, and she's at me, over-intimate, nosy, sneering at my background. When she calls me mediocre and uncreative, as she does most days, I shake with fury and cry alone.'

'Does she whisper a truth?'

'I have to smile and smile.'

'Because Rob insists on it?'

'I'm here to progress spiritually and materially.' When Alice asked him how the interviews were going, he said, 'As you advised so wisely, when standing outside Mamoon's library, I count back from ten, before I can go in. But then, fearing my subject will insert the head of a spiky fish into my anus, I start to shake and have to get to the toilet before he begins to talk.' Alice questioned his masculinity, as she often liked to do, to which he said, 'If you read Mamoon's essays, which you won't, you would learn that he has eaten human flesh.'

'Please—'

'Not a large amount. Not an arm or throat. But at least, as they say about children, he tried it – fried, with salt and pepper. I do scare *him* a bit, Alice. When he spies me approaching with my notebook he looks perturbed, like a shellfish about to take a shake of lemon juice on the nose.' He went on, 'A lot depends on whether I can meet the former lover, Marion. Rob said I have to get Mamoon's permission because if I make the old man any more hostile, he'll throw me out.'

'What scares you?'

'His disapproval. His temper. You will see it all, and grasp the gravity here.'

'Will I?'

'I can't help provoking him to consider me a worthless person.'

She wrapped her arms around herself. 'Is he going to think that of me?'

'Not at first. He will charm you. Later, he will rip your face off and feed it to the pigs.'

'Oh for God's sake, Harry, please take me back to the station. Why on earth did you invite me to this shit?'

'My blackness is spreading, Alice. I've been seeing and hearing things that can't be there or anywhere. At night, when I'm not hallucinating mad women, I can feel depression starting to burn me around the edges. If I sink into it, I'll have to give this thing up and write a novel.'

'Then we will be poor.'

'Worse. Despised by my family. Indeed by all families.'

'I hate to say I warned you.'

'But you will see me come through the fire with most of my hair and at least one intact testicle.'

They passed the garage, the church and the pub, and turned into the lane. Soon they were bumping down the track towards the gingerbread house.

She leaned across, kissed him and told him he was sadistic. 'I sense you looking forward to this. You won't make a fuss when I disappear, will you? You know I like to run away.'

Pulling the numerous cases she'd arrived with from the back of the car, and carrying them to the house, he informed her the locals called the place the Overlook Hotel, and that the exits were padlocked. She would not disappear.

Just then there was a shout: Liana bustled out to greet, look over and embrace Alice. Alice loved the dogs in particular, and Liana was immediately keen to give Alice the tour.

But first Harry and Alice went to their room, and he lay down on the bed. Half asleep, he watched her look through her clothes. Alice changed at least three times a day, and spent most of her money, and a good deal of his, on clothes. She obtained a lot of them cheaply from friends in the business, and looked good. Her favour-ite items were the ones she'd never worn – those which were waiting for the 'right occasion' – of which there were a great many. Clothes and accessories were a per-son's creativity; how someone looked was always a free decision, like a brushstroke on a painting. He would enjoy women more, she had informed him, if he under-stood their clothes.

When she moved in, the parade of dressing and undressing was frequent and regular. They both liked women's shoes, and could fill many an evening with her feet. His tiny study had become a cave of her dresses and coats. Her clothes covered his books. That was the least of it. 'I'm in debt, Harry. I can't stop spending. A tea set, an espresso machine, jewellery, Milan – all those little necessary things have done for me.' She wanted to borrow money from him, but unless Rob advanced *him* a bit more, Harry had nothing himself. If they were to buy a house and start a family, they had to be prudent, like everyone else in Europe.

He knew no one who was not mad, and he recognised Alice was not different from anyone else at the moment: there was no shame attached to debt; in fact, the debtless and thrifty were considered foolish losers. However, he had to urge her to cut down, as one would with any dependency. But she called shopping her 'outlet', and was worried that if she did cut back, she'd require another means of assuaging her anxiety.

Today, once she'd settled in, Harry thought it a good idea for Alice to spend time with Liana. With her ferocious but enthusiastic mind focused on food, furniture and the mood of her man, Liana would set a good example to the young woman.

'Liana, darling, tell me, what do you think of my girl?' whispered Harry, when, later that morning for a moment, he was alone with the older woman. 'Should I send her packing?'

'Seeing her bright face has cheered me up. She is a little haughty, as you said, but fresh and delicate. I loved her from the moment she showed taste. She said a wonderful thing. "Liana, this is definitely a feminine house." She so reminds me of myself before I had hangovers and met Mamoon that she could be my daughter. Is she a model?'

'People used to stop her on the street and tell her to go do it. So she was, briefly. But she's too quiet to show her ass for money.'

'She's so skinny I can practically see through her. And her hair, what an extraordinary colour.'

'It's natural.'

'Did I say it wasn't? Platinum blonde, I suppose you'd call it. It's almost white.'

'Please, Liana, don't give her any clothes. Why are you giving them away?'

'What point is there to them, down here? Women only wear beautiful clothes so that men will want to remove them.'

Harry said, 'Poor Alice, she was almost shaking this morning, Liana, in terror of you.'

She clutched his arm. 'Of me? Never say that! I only want to scare Mamoon – and you, of course. Why?'

'She's afraid. Your depth of experience and sophistication was intimidating.'

'The darling child, I must help and guide her. She lights this house up.'

Alice appeared. Liana shouted and waved, the dogs rushed to the car, and Liana whisked Alice into town to shop for lunch. Afterwards, Liana showed her the kitchen, and cooked with her, the two of them drinking a bottle of wine, while Liana talked continuously. Soon Liana was calling Alice her 'pretty long-lost daughter', and dragging her off with the dogs for a tour of the house, barns and grounds, and then of her clothes and shoes; these things, being of an Italian vintage, interested Alice.

When an older woman met a younger one and liked her, she gave her clothes. This cemented something between them, a hierarchy perhaps, as well as understanding. Liana also gave Alice Indian and Italian jewellery, so much so that when Harry next ran into Alice in the kitchen, he did a double take because Alice – who at the station had been wearing a simple orange jacket, denim shorts and strappy shoes – now resembled, as she jingle-jangled about the house, an actress from a Bollywood film. On closer examination Harry saw that Liana had in fact fashioned Alice into a younger version of herself.

Liana said, 'What a creative girl your Alice is. She took one look at this dying place and threw out a dozen good ideas about how to buck it up. I will speak to my agent. We could set a TV series here. I see how you look at me as if I were a vulgarian. But we are conspiring together to get the house earning its living. We will fill it with young artists.'

'How young?'

'Do not risk your life by telling Mamoon this. He is already scorching in his room because lunch is delayed. But, thanks to Alice, there is asparagus, figs, red snapper, ice cream and the best mozzarella in the world – burrata – sent by my sister. Oh, but I am tearing my hair out with fear that he might be rude to her. Lately he's been wild, because of you.'

When Harry asked her if she'd prepared Mamoon, as promised, for Alice, she was unconvincing. 'Well, I did some ground work.'

'What did you say?'

'I insisted that although she'd never heard of Mamoon the writer, she would come to think highly of him, as she did of the great designers.'

He shivered. 'You compared them?'

'It was the context.'

'What if he says something mad to her?'

'I've warned him not to start talking about his dream. Hurry now, bring the minotaur before he blows up in rage.'

THIRTEEN

It was the middle of the afternoon when Harry crossed the yard to Mamoon's room to fetch the sequestered old man, who was still bent over his stick. After the incident on the tennis court, Mamoon's doctor had diagnosed a herniated disc rather than a pulled muscle, and advised Mamoon to have an operation, not that he could guarantee that it would work at the old man's age. While Mamoon discussed his dilemma at length, he gobbled handfuls of painkillers and, according to Liana, had become more ornery and truculent than usual over what he saw as a future of helplessness and decrepitude.

'Another morning of nothing,' he said as Harry brought him into the kitchen and led him to his chair. Julia bustled over with his favourite sparkling water without ice.

Alice went to him, sat down, took his hand, and looked into his eyes. 'Thank you for having me here,' she said. 'What a lovely place.'

'My dear, we've been waiting for you,' he said. 'Tell me, how is the world of fashion?'

'It's in not bad shape, thank you.'

'Could you explain what the point of it is?'

'Sorry?' She shook her head in disbelief. 'It's business. We buy and sell and stop people getting cold. What is *not* the point of it?'

'Don't think news of you hasn't reached me already,' said Mamoon, looking her over. 'Liana here told me you compared me to a tailor.'

'Which tailor?'

A vein, which ran from Mamoon's hairline to his brow, was throbbing. 'A tailor or cobbler, or some such handyman. Am I mistaken, Liana?'

Alice glanced at Liana, who was watching them, holding her breath. As Liana had no idea what to say, Alice said, 'Have you ever seen an Alexander McQueen jacket?'

'Of course not. What are you talking about? Has this queen read my work? Can he read without moving his lips?'

Alice said, 'Perhaps I did mention, to help me locate you, that you are a maestro like the maestro Valentino, beloved of many, including Liana.'

'You located me, did you? You *did* compare us.'

'It is an honour, perhaps.'

'In what possible way could that be an honour?'

'Well, it is, to me.'

Mamoon was beginning to look irritable. He said, 'We are talking about appearance only with these people.'

'I'm not sure.'

'Sorry?'

Alice said, 'It's more than that. We are discussing how something should be made. How it looks. How it is. An attitude.'

'An attitude. How do you mean?'

She said, 'A kiss . . .'

'Speak up. I'm almost deaf.'

'A kiss, a curse, a cup, a shoe, a hem, a cardigan, a watch, a joke, an act of politeness – and of course a sentence, a paragraph, a page . . . Don't all have to have style, grace, flair – and wit?'

'Of course.'

'Art isn't only in a book?'

Harry whispered, 'Flaubert wrote, "Style is life."'

Mamoon said, 'A more universal beauty might be something to strive for.'

'Good,' Alice said, sighing. 'Yes.'

'Good. Thank God, good,' said Liana. She held up the wine. 'This is the Guigal 2009. Or would you prefer the Chablis?'

'Quiet please, Liana.'

'Sorry, Mamoon?'

'Unlike you, maestro, I read magazines,' went on Alice. 'And didn't you say to a journalist that an artist has to sprinkle a little magic dust on what he does? Doesn't that apply to every object? Look at this simple platinum ring.' She offered him her hand, which he held and stared at. 'Can you see what I mean? The ring has it.'

He said, 'Yes, all right, it *is* a form of sensuality. Some people call it Eros, who was hatched from an egg, setting the whole universe in motion. The luminous radiation of love.'

'You see.'

He looked up at her. 'You almost cheer me up, my dear.'

'Only almost?'

Mamoon said, 'You remind me that language – indeed all real things – have to vibrate with sensuality. I see that. But if I seem slightly gloomy, it's because I've been having this damned recurring nightmare. It's a dull, common one, nevertheless it is persistent, and I want it away for good.'

'Are you naked in the dream, sir?' enquired Julia suddenly. She had been listening while serving.

'The maestro is never naked,' said Liana. 'Now, Mamoon, please—'

Mamoon said, 'Are *you* naked in your dreams, Julia?'

'Never a stitch on, running wildly through the fields singing, with everyone looking at me.'

'You silly thing.' Mamoon wiped his brow and said, 'Harry, if you're imposing yourself on us for a bit longer, you could be of use. I believe you have set yourself up to be something of a dream reader.'

'Have I?'

'Liana informed me that you can see through a dream at the drop of a hat. You learned it from your revered father.'

Harry shook his head and said, 'My father also warned me that you should no more tell others your dreams than you would give them your bank details.'

'But you're brilliant, Harry,' said Liana. 'Mamoon, won't you tell us, please – can we hear where your soul has been travelling? Its wanderings have been paining us all for a long time.'

FOURTEEN

Mamoon said, 'They have? Let me speak for once, Liana.'

'Go forth,' she said.

Mamoon cleared his throat and adopted what Liana referred to as his Nobel-Prize-acceptance-speech face.

'I am in a large hall with shapely, curved walls, for some reason. There I am taking my finals but I haven't prepared. I sit there staring at the blank page until the horror of my failure increases, and I know I'm going to implode. I wake up in a sweat, and, as you know, Harry, sometimes screaming my head off. What's it all about, Harry?'

'I've said before, Harry, no need to hide your light,' said Alice, squeezing his hand. She giggled, 'Dance, monkey, dance.'

They were all looking at Harry now, who, hesitating to expose his light or to dance, hummed his anxious Pooh Bear hum, while wiping his hands on his jeans.

'It's very common, that dream—'

'Yes, but why?' said Mamoon.

'Because it is about that which we can't be prepared for – the great test we men have passed before, but have no way of knowing we will pass again.'

'Thank you, Madame Sosostris,' said Mamoon. 'What test do you refer to?'

'Potency. Phallic male effectiveness. And whether this time, as opposed to all the other times, a man can satisfy the woman. Or will fail to satisfy her. What does the man actually have – a fallible phallus? No wonder you're sweating. Our dreams are always ahead of us, sir.' He went on, 'Very kindly, you let me see your beloved father's letters. He insisted, repeatedly, that you bring glory to the family by succeeding – at everything. I was shocked, he was so tough. Worse than my own dad, with his insistences.' Mamoon was staring at him. Harry recalled that Rob had suggested that a quote, real or imagined, from an ancient author always halted and impressed the writer. 'We know that the wretched Christians want to renounce desire, but as the great Petronius puts it so well, "How can you be a soldier without a weapon?"'

There was a pause. 'I see,' said Mamoon.

Liana said, 'Stop staring, Julia, and wipe that expression off your face. Get on with your work. Why do you stand there like a plum?'

'What should I do?'

'I've never been more filthy. Run my bath.'

'Yes, miss.'

'By the way, what are you doing with that book of Mamoon's in your hand?'

'This? Reading it, miss.'

'You're reading me, Julia?' Mamoon said. 'Are you really?'

'I am – again,' she said. 'My favourite: the story of the five dictators – two from Africa, one from the Middle East, another from China, and the last more local – all in love with the girl. You show the soft improving quality of love, and the man in the monster. It's beautiful, sir. It makes me laugh and cry every time.'

Mamoon blushed. 'Good, good. You used to read a lot.'

'When – when did she read a lot?' asked Liana.

'When she was little, and a lot of trouble and fun she was, too,' said Mamoon. He reached up and pinched her cheek. 'A sweet thing – eh, *beta*?'

Julia said, 'Mamoon gave me books. He threw them all at me, like a test, thinking I'd never read them, but I sat down and got through them, and showed him.'

'You did,' he said.

'Like what?' said Liana.

'Erm . . . Harper Lee, Ruth Rendell, Muriel Spark—'

'*Grazie a Dio*, you are more than ridiculous,' said Liana.

'Don't accuse me!' cried Julia. 'Don't ever say I'm stupid. Are you saying that, miss?'

'Liana wouldn't dare say that, *beta*,' said Mamoon.

'She's shouting in our house, Mamoon,' said Liana. 'Hear her!'

'It's all right,' he said.

'Don't stand for it!'

'I'm not,' he said, calmly.

Julia sat down beside him and said, 'It must be an amazing thing, sir, to have the skill to tell a story like that. You must wake up proud.'

'Thank you, dear girl, I am proud now,' he said. 'I wake up sweating in the night with relief. I got away with it. To have once been a writer is something.'

'Once?'

'You mock yourself, sir, surely,' said Harry.

'Why?'

'A friend of my father's, a film-maker of your generation, has increased his output as he's aged. He sees the necessity of getting on with things, of honouring the talent he has been blessed with.'

'What the damn fuck for?'

'Why should a man's desire for potency and work diminish? After all, what other dignity is there? There is certainly none in feigned helplessness. "A man must follow his path even in the midst of ruin," says Sophocles in *Antigone*. Titian did his best work after seventy. Goethe, at the age of seventy-four, asked for the hand – at least the hand – of a nineteen-year-old.'

'It is uplifting to hear there are forms of satisfaction available to someone like me. I like – I really like – being a writer. But is work enough?'

Liana had been staring at Julia, before banging the table hard. 'How dare you! Why are you sitting still like that? Have you forgotten you work here?'

'Would you like me to continue clearing out your shoes?'

'Yes, and don't take anything without asking. I can't run into you in town again wearing my purple Marc Jacobs. I asked you to wear them in for me, not wear them out.'

'Sorry, miss. It won't happen again,' Julia said.

'And do not fail to place orange peel in them overnight,' called Liana. Then, when the girl had hardly gone, she said, 'A skivvy who thinks she's in the Bloomsbury Group – what attention-seeking rubbish that girl talks. It's about time we replaced her with someone ignorant. Suppose she joins a trade union, Mamoon?'

'I should have discussed it with Mrs Thatcher,' he said.

When Julia had run out and Liana had gone into the garden to find the dogs, Mamoon, clutching the arms of the chair and groaning, attempted to get to his feet.

'If only you knew, Alice, how an artist grunts and strains to keep the language full of beans, and how much my back hurts since the tennis incident, making me stiff in all the wrong places. I could be semi-crippled for good now, with your boyfriend steering my wheelchair.'

'Maestro, why didn't you say before? I can help you.'

'How?'

'Didn't Harry tell you that I trained briefly as a masseuse?'

'You did? No one has ever spoken sweeter words to me,' he said. 'Your darling Harry is no use at all, but only asks stupid questions about things that happened forty years ago!'

'That would make an athlete ache.'

He wriggled. 'Dear girl, are you sure you can bear to touch me?'

'As a teenager, I worked as a geriatric nurse.'

'Perfect.'

'Let me find some almond oil.'

'Try Liana's bathroom. Hurry: we can retire to my barn for privacy. While Harry redrafts my history, you can realign my spine – if Harry gives permission.'

Harry said there would be nothing he would like more. He took Alice out into the hall, and they hugged and kissed, falling against the wall. He whispered, 'You goddess, how did you do it – taking him on like that?'

'I don't know, Harry. He was like you said, tough, and he was at me and I was cornered. It was so quick and I couldn't breathe. But I knew I had to fight or I'd be done for. It came out like that.'

'You tiger, if you massage him, he'll calm down, and we might get somewhere.'

162

She kissed him. 'I'll do it, and leave the rest to you.'

When Harry returned to the kitchen, Mamoon murmured, 'Thank you for your dream interpretation.'

Julia: 'Sure.'

...on said, 'The lovable, country child,
lieve, within my hearing, who is naked and once, I be-
...u were playing pool
in the afternoon, called you Fizzy Pants. While others
talk, you look at her with some interest and amusement.'

'I do?'

'Why would that be?'

'I guess in London you never see white people working.'

'I agree it is a wonderful sight, and not something
you see down here much either. I've long said it's over
for the white races, an obvious truth which caused
much agitation amongst the journalists. The rich will
rule as usual; they come in all colours, particularly yellow.' He said, 'But I admit it is good to watch people
work.'

'You feel superior?'

'Not at all. It reminds me of my humble duty to con-
tribute, which is what I want to get back to, once I'm
free of this pain.'

'Why have you been unable to work?'

Mamoon said, 'I can listen to Bach, just about, and

Schubert I can bear, because I am melancholic. Everything else depresses me – Beethoven, and particularly over-cheerful Mozart, chirruping away. The other day, when I pretended to dismiss Forster and Orwell, your little face looked upset. You still li[...] be impressed. In my teens and twe[...] my thirties, I loved to [...] weeks, reading all their work, everything. Now I've forgotten it, and, besides, it's all gone.'

'Gone?'

'Consider them, Bertrand Russell, A. J. Ayer, D. H. Lawrence, Aldous Huxley, Anthony Powell, Anthony Burgess, William Golding, Henry Green, Graham Greene—'

'No, not *that* Greene. No – *never*.'

'Good, plucky of you. But otherwise – unread, unreadable, discarded, departed, a mountain of words washed into the sea and not coming back. Popeye the Sailor Man has more cultural longevity. Only women and poofs read or write now. Otherwise, these days, no sooner has someone been sodomised by a close relative than they think they can write a memoir. The game's up.'

Harry said, 'Some of *your* books will remain.'

'They will?'

'Probably about four—'

'Four?'

'No, three big pieces. The first novel and a couple of long stories, which are top-drawer lasters. And, probably, the early essay on Ibsen's and Strindberg's women.'

'So much?' Mamoon said. 'It's done, and it's too late. I shouldn't complain. What is there left for me? How many older artists have made significant works?'

'But sir, that was the true meaning of your dream: the desire to fail.'

'Why?'

'To infuriate your father, who never let you go with his expectations.'

'Go on.'

Harry said, 'To renounce work and women's love for a pointless equilibrium or retirement is a destructive self-betrayal. The way you describe yourself is a far more limited narrative than anything I might say about you in my book. And look what happens to Lear. He allows others, indeed encourages them, to humiliate him. Surely a man can remain vital and alive if he feels strong.'

'How does he do that?'

'I have to say, sir, that while I've been here, I've learned something. You taught me that it's frustration which makes creativity possible. You wrestle with the material, and become inventive, even visionary.'

Mamoon was holding his head. 'You give me vertigo

as well as lumbago. All I think is that I must continue, making words which will then be forgotten. I want that; I can do that. At the same time, it's not enough. There must be something else.'

'What is it – that something else?'

'I don't know. I will think now. This conversation has drained me.'

Harry helped him up. Not long after, Harry watched from the kitchen window, as Mamoon, in his slippers and stripy dressing gown, eagerly padded out to his barn with Alice. He was, Harry noted, resembling more and more the ever demanding question mark he had seemed to become. A moment later the barn door banged closed. It was the very place Liana – and everyone else – was forbidden to enter. All Liana was able to see of Mamoon, through the window, was the top of his head, which remained throughout the day in the same position. 'The king is in his counting house,' Liana liked to say. If she needed him urgently, she had to phone, though with the attendant fear that he would let the call run onto voicemail while he was whistling a tune by Stéphane Grappelli. Mamoon's room was, Rob had said, full of generous gifts presented by perverted power freaks, kleptomaniacs and crazed killer dictators. Mamoon, it was said, had never met a dictator whose arse he didn't want to kiss. But Alice was the only other person Harry had known to enter the room since he'd arrived.

Ninety minutes later, when he heard the dogs barking, Harry returned to the window, with Julia sweeping around his feet, to see Mamoon come back to the house looking cheerful and taller, like an inverted exclamation mark.

'She's got the head of Jean Seberg and the hands of Sviatoslav Richter,' panted Mamoon. 'With every caress I felt myself becoming a genius.'

Alice clapped her hands. 'I made him more creative!'

Mamoon said, 'If only I were sixty-five again . . . Harry, you're a lucky man.'

FIFTEEN

'I swear, this is the first refreshing night's sleep I've had here,' Harry said when he and Alice woke up the next day and were making love. She was the only woman he liked to look at first thing in the morning; kissing her then was what he was born to do. 'Thank God you came, and you're with me. Didn't the noise madden you?'

'What noise?'

'The animals outside. The screaming foxes trapped by Tories.'

'That's just the country, Harry. They are natural sounds. But there is another noise.'

'What is it? Where?'

'Why are you so jumpy? Has something disturbed you?'

'Yes, I'm disturbed all the time here. I think Mum is calling to me through the walls. Dead mothers talk even more than live ones.'

'What does she say?'

'She asks me what I'm doing here.'

'That's what mothers are supposed to do.'

He said, 'Keep holding my penis.'

'Just a minute. Come,' she called. 'Oh big, big wow. Wow.'

The door opened and Julia came in bearing a breakfast tray.

'Good morning, ma'am,' Julia said, placing the tray on the low table at the end of the bed. Harry shrank under the sheets. It was the only time his penis had contracted in Julia's presence. 'And sir. Sorry it's me – Mum's not well. She had a fall onto her knee.'

'Not a push? I'm sorry to hear that, Julia. I hope she recovers soon.'

'Thank you, sir. Can I pour the tea for you?'

'That would be perfect, my dear.'

'There's toast and eggs downstairs. I'll run your bath for you, ma'am.'

'Thank you,' said Alice. When Julia had gone, she whispered, 'Is it like P. G. Wodehouse every day?'

'Oh yes. I haven't lifted a finger all the time I've been here. I've found the indolence utterly enervating.'

Alice and Harry went down to join Liana, while Julia and her mother moved slowly around them waving rags and squirting unguents. Although Alice had asked Julia for an ironing board, Julia had somehow found their clothes and elected to do Alice and Harry's washing and ironing, explaining that not only would she be offended if Alice did the work herself, but she even might lose her job.

'I beg you, Alice ma'am, it's my only livelihood,' she said, 'since they closed the abattoir.'

The closing of the abattoir had generated many knock-ons in the area, most of them deleterious. Working for Liana and Mamoon at the weekends, Julia had also put in some hours at the abattoir during the week, in order to increase her earnings. Now, since she was aware that Liana was becoming fed up with her, not only did she take care of her and Mamoon, she cleaned and tidied Harry and Alice's room and bathroom, and organised Harry's papers, notebooks and stationery. Harry felt slightly oppressed by Julia's ever-presence, but there was nothing he could do about that, nor about the way her eye watched over him and Alice from a suitable vantage point, usually near the skirting board.

After the long weekend, Alice realised she was owed some annual leave and decided to stay on instead of fleeing back to the city, as she had said she would. She had become almost romantic about the place, despite the fact that, as Harry complained, it took an hour to buy milk and you had to wear wellingtons most of the time, if not rainwear and a vest. Alice said now that she loved Mamoon and Liana, who felt like parents to her, and that spending this intimate time with Harry – witnessing his anguish and hearing him worry, the exposure of his need – was one of the best things to have happened to their relationship.

While Harry worked, Alice helped Mamoon choose his clothes, before taking him on drives and walks, where she was beginning a series of photographs of him in the countryside, leaning against trees, 'for the book'.

'I thought he hated being photographed?'

'Not by me. He listens to a woman,' Alice said later, when they took a canoe down the balmy little river. Alice sat sedately in the front in nautical stripes and a floppy hat, steering occasionally by dipping her paddle into the water like someone stirring their tea. 'I feel he wants to understand and help me.'

'Help you what?'

'Live more successfully.'

'What is that?'

'To have more pleasure.'

Earlier that morning he had watched her walking ahead of him, in the sunshine, slow, dreamy, sensual, almost vacant and outside time, a creature in another dimension, and he thought, guiltily, that that, for him, was a woman: always other, and a provocation. Now he handed her a peach from a basket at his feet, and watched her bite into it, the juice running down her chin.

'What a beautiful pussy you are . . .'

'Thank you.'

'I'm surprised to hear you say he listened and was in- terested,' said Harry, handing her a napkin. 'Friends of his I've interviewed say he's self-absorbed. He had a tantrum the other night because a tomato was too cold.'

'I'd hate it if he had a tantrum. I wouldn't know what to do. I'd probably just cry. How did Liana deal with it?'

'"Cold, *habibi*? Oh dear," she said, picking up the relevant tomato, sticking it up her dress and placing it between her thighs. "A cold tomato. That must be the worst thing in the world. Why don't I warm it up for you? Is that better?" When she replaced it on the plate he took a bite. "That is indeed better, memsahib," he said. "You know I need to spare my teeth."'

Alice, for whom vulgarity and humour were a portal to madness, said, 'There's nothing in it for him with the men. With the women he really gives us the gaze. He makes anarchic jokes and hums the songs by Dido I've introduced him to.'

'Dido?'

'The Stéphane Grappelli was getting me down.'

'Me too. But he hums Dido? The two of you listen to *White Flag*?'

'He la-las along. It'll be Tracey Thorn next and then I'll slowly manoeuvre him all the way to Amy Winehouse. What would you say, Julia? Does he listen to you?'

'Yes, he does,' said Julia, who was waiting at the little jetty with an armful of towels. Harry and Alice had learned that you merely had to say her name for her to materialise, like a spirit. 'He doesn't treat me like a servant. He never has, since I was little. He sits there and talks to me about what's in the paper when he reads them in the morning, asking me who the people are.'

'You see,' said Alice, moving towards Julia and being helped up the bank. 'Go to him, Harry, and talk. Take your chance. I wagged my finger and said, "Harry's getting insomnia and depression. Do not upset my partner, Mr Writer, or you'll find that things will not go well."'

'Did that go down a treat?'

'He will give more to you now. He seemed to be bubbling over, earlier, and may say you can meet the other woman.'

'Marion?'

'Now, go,' she said. 'I want to spend some time with Julia.'

'Why?'

'We have similar backgrounds. And similar interests. Come on, my dear,' she said to her. 'Let's get together. Let's talk about men, babies and how fat we were as children. Let's frighten Harry and then go shopping with Liana this afternoon. I want to buy perfume. And perhaps later we could dance in the barn.'

Harry said, 'Can't I come with you?'

'Of course not. You have important things to do.'

SIXTEEN

'Would it be possible for us to chat a little today?' whispered Harry, pleased to have found Mamoon in the library.

To Harry's surprise, Mamoon said, 'Yes, why not, I am keen,' though he did glance at Harry's clipboard as if it were his death certificate. 'Do you have any exciting questions for once?'

'I wondered if you might feel invigorated after your morning massage?'

'My skin is singing. And you have put me in the unfortunate position of having to think about you, something I've been reluctant to do.'

'Think about me in what way?'

'You're surprised.'

'Gobsmacked, sir.'

'Good.' Mamoon said, 'Your fascination with the female body isn't unnatural or unusual. In fact the body of the young woman is the world's most significant object, admired and desired by homosexuals, of course, as well as by other women, babies, lesbians, children, fashion designers and men. No wonder Muslims hide the woman like a filthy picture, while their fundamentalists

174

remind us that female sexuality is the biggest problem of all. For these people the woman is already a whore. They're right to be so concerned,' he went on. 'The young female body is at the centre of the world, and usually at the centre of most elections – abortion, single mothers, maternity leave, prostitution, incest, abuse, the hijab . . . The woman is where we all come from, and where we all want to go. The woman's body makes knowledge disappear. It's amazing that anyone has time to think about philosophy, literature, psychology or history. Women know it too, which is why they hurry on the street. No beautiful woman is a slow walker.'

'When did you first get interested in this?' Harry asked him, adjusting his digital recorder but not pressing 'record' yet.

'I can remember as a young man in Madras reading something by Bertrand Russell, who was famous for knowing everything, and a huge passion of mine then.

'He wrote somewhere of his emotional life being "irrational". By God, he disapproved of the "irrational". Russell's loves, hates, desires – the entire bodily caboodle, and all the greatest philosopher in the world could say was that it was "irrational". It made me want to say my say, as if the whole thing still required explaining, to hunt down these irrational people, the ones so powerful in the world, and hear their speech.'

'What is the cure, sir?'

'Halt your naughty finger before I crush it. Do not record this: it is between us. You ask for the cure – I presume the cure for excessive appetite?'

'Yes.'

Mamoon laughed. 'All religions have concerned themselves with the weaning of individuals from their desire. Who, after all, can live with their own wanting? Let's think about endurance, as the Stoics would have it. I like to read Seneca, who says it can be borne. Or self-knowledge, as Plato preferred it, which might dissipate it. But appetite is all we have and we cannot or should not be cured of it. I'm no Freudian, yet no one can deny that desire is the motor of our existence, as it is for any child who wants to go on living. As your enthusiasm indicates, it is usually out of control and it is tied to madness, unfortunately, because the object – the woman in mind – can only be elusive, and will evade one. She will, naturally, have other preoccupations, other lives. This will create jealousy, the belief that the other has what we don't have. Proust made a mint out of this simple idea. Still, more desire, less punishment, I say.'

Harry said, 'You mention Bertrand Russell and his horror of disorientation.'

'So?'

Harry glanced at the clipboard, noticed a question and looked up at Mamoon. 'Isn't it the case that when you met Marion for the first time you experienced a physical connection you'd never had with anyone? That you experienced, at that time, a large bout of irrationality which de-centred you?'

'You are creating a history for me, one that is parallel to my life. But why don't you ask her?'

'Obviously, I need to do that. Would you approve? Can I say that, sir?'

'That would be up to Marion. But darling Alice with her massages and photographs – and how lucky you are there – has convinced me to be more co-operative with you.'

'She puts my case?'

'She is kind, you know, and has pleaded for you. She has thought about my suffering, too, which will be over quicker if I let you in more. Go to Marion and see. I am so looking forward to her giving you a flea in your ear, as she has done to other snoopers. One begging scribbler she tipped a bottle of ink over.'

'Why?'

'You will see – ha – she is chilli hot!'

'Is that why you didn't marry her?'

Mamoon laughed and said, 'It would be true to say there are occasions when certain pleasures can be so strong that you might have to rethink your life entirely, as a way of taking them in – or avoiding them.'

Harry said, 'Pleasure can knock you right off your

feet, it is true. Do you mean that a series of orgasms can be a new beginning?'

Mamoon got up. 'Whatever Marion says, I will always be the stranger in your book.'

'Thanks for your blessing, sir,' said Harry. 'A final question, one which has just occurred to me, I don't know why. Do you regret not having children?'

'Not having children has been the one bright spot in my life so far,' said Mamoon. 'Now, pack your bags and fuck off out of my damn sight. I need peace again.'

'Thank you, sir.'

'You will thank me a thousand more times,' he said, giggling. 'Particularly when you sneak back here with your soul bleeding. I can't wait.'

SEVENTEEN

After almost ten days, Alice and Harry went back to
London. Lotte, from Rob's office, had sent Harry airline
tickets and a busy itinerary for the next few weeks. Rob
also wanted Harry to push on with the book; he needed
to see at least a couple of chapters by the end of the
month.

Harry was relieved to get out of the claustrophobic
atmosphere of Mamoon's place. In town, he and his
father and brothers watched Chelsea and ate; afterwards, their father liked it when they took part, as a
family, in the local pub quiz. The prize could have been
£10 million, it was taken so seriously by the men. The
twins were good at sport and music, and their father
had science covered. Harry did literature. They came
second and were not happy, Father castigating them as
if he'd just received a unpleasant letter from the school
head.

Harry was reminded who he was. His brothers
weren't impressed or intimidated by Mamoon. There
was a cold severity in Mamoon's work, and, because he
had never written a book the title of which everyone
could recognise, and he rarely appeared on television,

they didn't give a damn who he was. What they didn't like was their little brother being run ragged by a manic egotist who wanted a flattering portrait of his big head. Harry saw that, in the shadow of Mamoon's personality, he had allowed his identity to be attacked; Liana and Mamoon seemed to be able to do or say anything they liked to him. And his father had said, 'So far you've been the mirror he needs, Harry, and why wouldn't he be happy?'

'He's benign.'

'Are you sure? Why don't you mess with his mind a little, twist his penis, confront him, and see what happens? Sometimes a little disorder can be creative.'

Harry and Alice went to Paris for the flim-flam of the fashion shows, before taking the overnight train to Venice – Harry's mother's favourite city – where Alice had never been. When he and Alice woke up in the morning, in the bunks of the sleeper, it was a hop, skip and jump to the Grand Canal. They were barely off the vaporetto, exploring. Harry was keen to see Alice seeing things, to watch her as the world unfolded. One evening she took his hand. She had taken a pregnancy test. It was positive. They hadn't exactly planned things, but they had discussed them a little, and she was pleased; was he?

Yes, yes, and maybe. They were joined for good now. He was shocked, and confused and afraid. Suddenly the future had a shape and an inevitability. There would be duties. He would become a different sort of person, and they would know one another in a new way. 'Christ,' he said to his father. 'I'm done for.'

'About time. Welcome to the world,' Father said. 'Do you know how to think about it?'

'No . . . Not yet.'

'Does she?'

'She has her friends. They are gossiping and planning already. I feel alone.'

'It will join you to the world, Harry. You can't run all your life. I love being a father, and I suspect you will too. You're a better man than you believe you are.'

After a few days, Alice went back to work, and Harry, with this new knowledge growing in him, flew to India to look at the places Mamoon had lived as a child.

For two and a half weeks he met family members and acquaintances of the old man, along with those Mamoon had supposedly snubbed, insulted, exploited, or fucked. He discovered what a good scholarship boy Mamoon had been, as well as the fact he'd been aloof and appeared to consider himself superior to those around him. 'The cut and strut of him in his blazer with shining buttons!' Harry was told. 'The looking down of it!' He heard from several older people that Mamoon had not been a 'real' Indian, and was as alienated on the subcontinent as he would be in Britain. He spoke English at home, except with the servants, read only English and French literature, knew little about Islam or Hinduism, both of which he considered to be the opium of the masses, and had rarely visited the countryside.

Mamoon's mother was religious, and stayed in her room praying, leaving only to consult experts on the Qur'an. The father had sponsored the boy's ambition, Harry believed, but not his pleasure, which he opposed. He had had no intention of producing a womanising, hard-drinking, cosmopolitan playboy, sitting in the cafes of European capital cities in worn shoes, borrowing money, stewing in self-pity and debt while discussing Bernard Shaw and Trotsky.

But the father hadn't entirely succeeded. Harry heard, from a decent source, something stranger and more intriguing, and began to see what the father had been up against. Mamoon had been a seductive teenager, apparently pulling both older men and women – the mothers of school friends; the school nurse; a policeman's wife, and, it was said, the policeman himself – into his sphere.

Like many Indian patriarchs, Mamoon's father, in his pride and hope, was determined from the start to send his son to the hated mother country to be educated. The son remained the father's dream, though, and the father had only a little idea of how wrenching the move would be for Mamoon, and what snobbery, contempt

182

and difficulty he would face. The father couldn't think of his despairing son wandering the London streets evening after evening, nearly mad with loneliness and anxiety, relieved occasionally by a beer and a whore. Even if it was a bit tough, it wouldn't be for long, since the boy would return home a better man, and continue to be his lonely father's prop, his mirror, his *chamcha*. 'Remember me,' reminds the father, endlessly, colonising the son's mind. And not only that, 'live with me.' Mamoon refused. In his suffering, Mamoon wanted to join 'the larger or complete civilisation', as he put it later. He dismissed his dad and never lived at home again. The father ensured his own death through grief because of it.

It might appear now that Mamoon always knew what he was doing, that his progress was almost inevitable. Harry learned what determination and strength Mamoon showed, not only in remaining in inhospitable Britain to earn money by his pen, but to make himself into an original writer, one not seen before, speaking from the position of a colonial subject or subaltern, but one without hatred, and with fascination if not identification with the colonisers' culture. Eschewing contemporary causes and attitudes, Mamoon fashioned himself into a considerable and successful artist from a background which had enabled few before. For a time he did an essential thing, bringing the new into culture, speaking from where no one had spoken. He was rewarded too, and not only that. Any fool would recognise that a successful 'bolter' would always inspire recrimination and the radiation of envy. But, at home in India, Mamoon's rise and achievement was accompanied by a level of resentment, scrutiny and criticism which could have bewildered if not destroyed a lesser man.

Some of it was self-engineered: Mamoon's insolence, arrogance and the insanity of some of his statements were no secret. But much of this envy was born of bitterness towards the white man. His former friends and allies believed that Mamoon had become 'white'. For them any betterment was betrayal. Those he left behind said he had made a pact with the devil and violated his forebears and family. 'I hope that turns out to be true,' Mamoon remarked to a friend, waving goodbye. 'Particularly the violation.'

Harry had learned much about all this in India, and had also had time to study the notebooks Julia had given him. With renewed enthusiasm for his subject – *how do you write such complication?* – he flew with some relief to New York. After three days he went to see Mamoon's former lover Marion, who lived in a small flat in Portland.

Characteristically, Rob hadn't exactly 'organised things'. For the last few weeks Marion had been making it difficult for Harry, cancelling proposed meetings, phoning to ask him more questions, and generally acting like a coquette. All the while she ensured that he was aware she had something valuable to give him, and that there would be a price, though he hadn't been told what it was. She also insisted on various agents and publishers vouching for his good intentions and honesty. It wasn't until Mamoon had spoken to Rob, and Rob to her, that Marion gave him a firm appointment. At last he could go to her flat.

The door opened.

With long white hair halfway down her back, and moving slowly and unsteadily on sticks, Marion led Harry into the small, overheated apartment. Relieved to meet her, Harry had tried to take her hand but she insisted on pushing her face towards his, and he kissed her cheeks. She gripped his hand as if she'd touched no one for some time.

She told Harry that as she had cataracts she was unable to read much, watch TV, or clean. What she wanted was conversation, but her family had long deserted her, and she had few visitors now, apart from some nosy students and a secretary who helped her with her writing by taking dictation. There were few creatures on the earth of less interest than a woman in her mid-seventies, but some people were interested in Mamoon Azam. He was the one card she had left.

'Please, before you interrogate *me*,' she said, bringing Harry tea and biscuits before sitting down with a blanket over her knees, 'would you be good enough to answer *my* queries?'

'Of course.'

'Do you have anything of his I can touch?'

'What sort of thing?'

'A tie. A book he gave you.'

He gestured helplessly. 'No, sorry, I didn't think.'

'He didn't send anything?'

'Only me.'

She said he was never particularly thoughtful. 'But I have his reading glasses here, which I polish every Sunday, while recalling the smell and touch of his skin, remembering his smoky voice – gravelly, harsh sometimes, but caressing – and his careful timing when he made me laugh.'

She could imitate Mamoon well, and appeared to enjoy conversations with him, playing both parts. She asked about Liana without agitation, wanting to know how tall and wide she was and whether she was able to deal with Mamoon's moods and tantrums, how her cooking was, whether she liked to shop, if she had indigestion, how well she slept, and whether she could cope with his nightmares and whether she made him laugh.

She wanted to hear what Mamoon was working on, whether he dyed his hair now and how his health was, particularly his back, and his stomach and bowels too, as well as his teeth. She needed to know if he still did this or that with his head when you asked him a difficult question. She wanted also to know about the house and its land – the place she'd only seen photographs of, but where she had believed, at one time, she'd spend the rest of her life with the man she loved.

And then she laughed shrilly, before, inevitably, weeping. He wept too, as it seemed participatory and kind, and they called one another soppy. He looked for tissues, and she went to the bathroom to wash her face.

When she was ready, he turned on the tape.

A Colombian with an English Jewish mother, Marion told him how she met Mamoon at a reading, and how they fell in love. Over a period of five years he had visited her often, and they travelled together in India, the United States and Australia. She had left her dull husband soon after meeting Mamoon, and had taken a little place in New York's West Village, because Mamoon was thinking of setting a novel there. 'Don't forget,' she said. 'He was a Muslim man, and basically thought of women as servants. I advanced him, but there's only so far you can go.'

They had always had plenty to say to one another and, like the most attractive men, Mamoon was amusing and sharp – about literature and politics, about others, and primarily, about himself. He was self-absorbed, but too anxious and insecure to be self-admiring. He worried all the time, she said, and could become absolutely frenzied about his work, which kept him sane, just about. He would show her drafts of what he was doing, and she would help him, sitting across the table with a pencil. He listened to her opinions and replied seriously. He made her feel valued and creative, and she knew how those famous books were made.

'Some of the interviews in *Evenings with the Killer* were fabricated, of course. That must be well known.'

'No one else has said that. Didn't he tape them?'

'Yes, and they were transcribed, sometimes by Peggy, sometimes by me or a secretary. When he sat down to write up the material, considerable work was done. He was never at that famous execution. He admitted to me that he was only "almost" there.'

'He's a creative artist who made—'

'Or made up,' she said. 'He omitted material, altered other things, fudged and even rewrote quotes, to suit the piece. He wrote about places he'd never been, and things he'd never seen.'

Harry shrugged. 'That's novelists for you. Bastards.'

She said, 'No doubt you'll find yourself doing the same.' She was looking at him. 'It's occurring to you that that would be a good idea.'

'"Stolen-telling", Joyce calls it. And Mamoon did say, rather wisely, "I hope you're not going to be one of

those fool writers who thinks the facts are sufficient."
He thinks that originality is the art of stealing the right
things. He's an entertainer . . .'

'How cheap and nasty you are. I suspect you might be
something of an argumentative nuisance. Is there really
any point in us going on with this? If I could stand up,
I'd stand up right now,' she said, and turned away.

Today would be difficult. Would he get anywhere?
Should he walk out? He waited in silence, as his father
would have suggested.

'You gave up a lot for Mamoon,' he said at last.

'Yes, yes, everything.'

'How could it not be difficult for you to speak about
it?'

'Exactly.'

There was more silence; then he sighed in relief as
she went on. Her husband was no loss, but her beloved
children had been furious that she'd traded her family
for what her ex-husband called 'personal excitement'.
But Mamoon, like Omar Sharif, whom she believed he
resembled, was a man a woman could give things up
for. Marion loved him, he was her destiny; she thought
that love was the only game in town. Although he came
to America less often because of Peggy's incapacity, she
had taken it for granted he would look after her for life.
He had said he would.

Marion had had no reason not to believe Mamoon.

Their love life had been more fulfilling and stronger than anything she had encountered before, and they had been together properly. Apart from her, there had only been Peggy, and, at the end, she found they were both waiting for poor Peggy to die. She had nothing against Peggy – though she did refer to her as a 'bed-blocker' – and she admired Mamoon for sticking by her. He had fulfilled his 'futile' duty.

'Futile, you say. Why?' Harry asked.

'As far as I could see,' she said, 'because the two of them had lived in such a closed circle, with very little outside influence, she had hypnotised him into believing that not only was he the cause of her suffering, but that he was the only cure. I freed him from this false belief.'

Not that she'd been thanked. At the end, Marion hadn't seen Mamoon for more than a year. The day came when she learned that Peggy had died, and she'd readied herself for Mamoon's call. At last she would leave New York and move to England to be with him in his house. She had already been thinking of how she'd furnish it. The windows would be opened, Peggy's things put away immediately, and everything rearranged. She didn't want to live with a dead woman.

She rang Mamoon. The woman who picked up the phone – Harry guessed it had been Ruth – said she would take a message. This happened a number of times; Ruth had passed on the message, she said. Days passed and Marion heard nothing. She guessed Mamoon was busy with the funeral arrangements and other mourning matters. More time passed.

When she didn't hear from him, she went to Bogotá, and travelled in Colombia, suffering and seeing him everywhere. It wasn't for some months that she learned from a magazine that he'd married Liana, whom, she also learned, he'd met about eighteen months previously, promoting his work in Italy. Apparently, Mamoon had returned to see Liana several times and they had rented a flat in Paris together. He'd eventually taken her to Venice, where he proposed. Marion examined photographs of them together, and everything she'd tried to forget returned.

Desperate for an explanation, Marion wrote to Mamoon often; she rang repeatedly. Then, unusually, Mamoon did pick up the phone, as he might do occasionally if he happened to be sitting near it. He said he was surprised to hear from her; he informed her that of course it was too late. Everything between them had died some time ago. Hadn't it been obvious to her? She had nothing that he wanted. You had to fail people at the right time, he said, memorably. As a good deal of her past and all of her future suddenly dissolved, Marion screamed and raged. Mamoon said she'd cooked up ridiculous fantasies, and shouldn't contact him again; he was a happily married man and that was that, for him. He put the receiver down.

Harry watched her weep again, and flail at a cushion on her sofa. He was embarrassed and uncomfortable; he'd wanted to write an informative book celebrating a good writer, not lead an elderly woman through a psychodrama towards a nervous breakdown.

This initial conversation with Marion had already taken up most of one day, and he needed to think through what she had said. He returned to his hotel, checked his tape and made notes.

He called Alice to let her know how exhausted he was. To his surprise, he found that she had been with Liana and Mamoon all weekend.

'You're there now?' he asked.

'Yes. He knew you were going away, so they invited me down,' she said.

'Cunning.'

'Kind, in my condition. I need rest, and I needed to bring some ties, shirts and other things for Mamoon.'

'Did he like them?'

'He was delighted. He wants to update his look.'

'Makes sense.'

'Anyhow, they love my company, and I find it restful here. Mamoon wants to regain his strength; we've been taking long walks.'

'You have? Talking about what?'

'It's just chatter. It's amazing, Harry, I can say anything to him and he doesn't judge but always has something intelligent to say. His brain is massive. It's so good for me to relax here, particularly now I'm so anxious.'

'Why don't you write down what he says when you get back to our room?'

'Whatever for? You know I believe in living in the moment. It's a private conversation about everything.'

'What is everything?'

'Life, fathers, art, politics, sex.'

'Does he know anything about that?'

'He has thought deeply, Harry, more than the average man, you know that, and everything he says is interesting, which is why you study him. He's psychoanalysing me and looking into my problems with debt. I'm terrified he'll find me superficial or narcissistic, as your father did the last time we went to the house.'

'My father did what, Alice?'

'Your voice has gone castrato. Don't be oversensitive on that subject.'

'Sorry?'

'You said you never take women to meet your father.'

'They have to be very special. It was a big thing for me, Alice.'

'I was having palpitations. Surely you remember, after we'd sat down, how he looked around the table, banged it with both hands and said, "Tell me, what are your views of the financial crisis?"'

'What were they?'

'I was so intimidated I had a panic attack, which was why I fled to the loo to splash my face with cold water. It was like suddenly being on television.'

'I know you prefer invisibility.'

'Was it always like that at home?'

'He's very democratic, Dad, he listens to every idiot. That's his job. He certainly didn't find you superficial. He said you'd come far. And I know for sure that Mamoon will hang on your every word. I thought you didn't like old men.'

'You know how my mind scatters at the sight of a novel, but I've started one of Mamoon's books.'

'Do you like it?'

'Don't worry, there's no chance of me becoming an intellectual. Do you prefer me stupid? Do you feel threatened?'

'Darling, writing this book is doing my head in. India was difficult. I'm exhausted.'

'Mamoon has been very sympathetic to you.'

'He has?'

'He's desperately hoping Marion isn't misleading you too much.'

'What did he say about her?'

'That not one word she says is true. He hopes, for

your sake, that you aren't taken in.' She went on, 'You know, I'm beginning to understand how brave Mamoon has been, attacking those corduroy-wearing Maoists when it was fashionable to be one. He broke the cult of silence. Wasn't your dad a Maoist?'

Harry laughed. 'Did Mamoon say that? I'll have it out with him.'

'No, please don't, otherwise I won't tell you what else he said.'

'Why, what else did he say?'

'He said his friends and acquaintances were as hypnotised by Marxism as some people are by fundamentalism. Everything they did was calculated to "benefit" the working class. And didn't it turn out that Marxism was hardly a system which sponsored the freedoms they're suddenly so keen on?'

'Yes, he wrote a lovely essay about it, "The Superstitions of the Secular".'

'But that was incredibly foresighted of him, wasn't it?'

Harry snorted. 'Mamoon has always thought everything's a lot of rot, and that anyone who believed anything was a deluded idiot. You can't go wrong if you start off as a cynic.'

'Are you still a socialist? He said you were.'

'He did? A liberal democrat, Alice, and no more harmful than a glass of sparkling water with a slice of lemon.'

Alice asked, 'What does your father think of Mamoon?'

Harry thought for a moment before saying, 'Dad considers Britain's finest post-war achievement, apart from the NHS, to be a multiracial society. Yet Mamoon wanted to be an Englishman, just when they were becoming obsolete, when the mongrels were taking over. Dad considers him deluded for never speaking about the contagion of British racism, particularly in the seventies, when it was at its most virulent. Mamoon liked to pretend it had never happened to him. He was also a risible snob, according to Dad, for identifying himself with a defunct class. At least, later, he criticised the Islamists, those heroes of the seventh century.'

Alice said, 'You know, Mamoon said this lovely thing about me – I could become an artist.'

'An artist?'

'Why not? Perhaps one day, when our future child is asleep in his Moses basket, I'll start to draw seriously. Mamoon says that if I find it difficult to speak, I should express myself more in other ways.'

'Good idea.'

'Mamoon's wicked, too,' she went on. 'I shouldn't repeat this: apparently a fan asked him how he created, with which pen or computer, and he replied that he liked to insert his finger into his arse in the morning and write directly onto the bathroom wall.'

Harry said, 'Do you love me?'

'Yes, of course. I've told you a thousand times.'

Harry asked, 'How's Liana?'

'I haven't seen much of her. She's been gardening, then she rushed to London for a manicure. She saw her beloved psychic, and met someone else on business.'

'How long was she there?'

'Just three nights, I think.'

Harry immediately rang Julia, who claimed to have been tracking things. It was all eating and talk between Mamoon and Alice, she said. They sat up for hours in the late evening, by candlelight; next door Julia was reading Mamoon on the divan, his voice in one room, his words in another. She drifted off contentedly, dreaming of him. In the morning she was under a blanket. She couldn't recall everything Mamoon and Alice had said; how important could a few murmurs be?

Harry said, 'It wasn't important! Just talk, you say! Talking is the most dangerous form of intercourse!'

'Liana is okay with it, so I think it's probably harmless. Otherwise, she'd kill him and then Alice.'

'He got me out of the way, though. At least tell me if Mamoon has said anything notable.'

'Only, "Anyone who gardens is lost to humanity."'

Harry asked, 'Do you love me?'

'Yes,' she said. 'More and more. I so look forward to

seeing you. I'm wearing your T-shirt.'

'You are? Where did you find it?'

'In your room. I put my face in your clothes.' She said, 'Do you love *me*?'

He was morosely silent, listening to the sea between them. 'Whoever you are, Julia, I'm yours.'

'Did you read the notebooks I gave you?'

'Yes, I'm going through them again now.'

'What do you think?'

EIGHTEEN

Harry had arranged to visit Marion again the next day, but as he walked around the block before going in, he wondered if it was worth returning. Alice's enthusiasm for Mamoon was annoying him, and he wanted to take a cab to the airport, fly back to London, shove the old man away and remind her of his, Harry's, existence. He needed to put more into his relationship with Alice otherwise it would slow down and end. What could Marion add now? He was reluctant to re-enter that tent of grief, regret and despair. But he spoke firmly to himself: although Mamoon had deliberately got rid of him, this was still business. He forced himself to buy flowers for her; he rang again at her door.

She was more lively, flirtatious even, today, in a skirt, plunging top and jewellery. She was brandishing photographs of herself and Mamoon together.

'Harry, look how he holds my hands. How he needed me! In that house in the country they lived in an atmosphere of fear and anger. Does it seem haunted, that place?'

'Yes, a bit.'

'That's her, Peggy – haunting but not living! His

original home life had never been like that. Her wretchedness was corrupting him.'

'How did you tell him that?'

'I showed him the possibility of love. And sex. He was, you know, *caliente*. Steam came off him. But he hadn't had proper sex for some time. Mamoon thought that needing a woman was like wanting a cigarette. The wish could be great, but you waited until it passed, you could get back to more important things.

'To give her credit, Peggy was kind, she thought of him only. She led him through society, introducing him to people who might be interested, explaining to them that the world was bigger than Britain. But he was—'

'What?'

'Well, underfucked.'

'I love the way you say that, Marion. The rolling tone.'

'Darling, she had no sexual hold over him. Sad woman; hysterical. When it came to making copulation she was a plate of cold spaghetti, chattering inanely and forcing poor Mamoon to live as if passion didn't have a place in the centre of the heart of every being. You have no idea how naïve he was, when it came to some things.'

He asked her what she meant by 'naïve'.

'In some ways he was like a teenager. As if he expected the other to take the lead. As you must know, his adolescent adventures were many and multifarious. The adults couldn't keep their hands off him. He had been such a beautiful youth, with the dark hair and body of a film star, with a long thin cock. He was almost as beautiful as you, darling boy, but altogether more of a nuisance, with a stronger character and, obviously, more talent. I would imagine that you're only a minor nuisance, though you have a haughty look.' She'd been watching *Teorema* the other night. 'Pasolini would have gone for you. Did an older man ever take you?'

When he said nothing, she went on, 'Try and imagine this. When I first met him, Mamoon had anticipated being properly married for the rest of his life. He didn't think he and Peggy would ever separate. But he did take to sex, when he refound it through me. It gave him a new confidence. He liked it. He liked it too much. He'd regained a part of himself, so that he wanted it the whole time. Then he wanted more. More extremity.'

When Harry asked what sort of extremity, she said, 'If I tell you, and you put it in the book, it will come to be the only thing anyone ever knows about me.'

'You've considered that?'

'Of course.'

'At the same time, you want to give your side of the story?'

She said, 'He will deny me, I know that. He will laugh and shrug and accuse me of being mad, a common strategy of men. Recently, to a journalist, he accused me of being a balloon of unbound fantasies, a magical realist even – stories for children! This from someone who makes up people, and has them speak and then die, for a living! But I will have spoken before *I* go.'

Harry pushed the recorder closer to her. 'What are you referring to?'

'Turn off that damn machine.' He pushed a button on it. She smiled, grabbed it and tossed it out of the room into the corridor, before asking him to shut the door.

She told him there were a couple of clever, attractive married women she'd known, good friends for years, whom she'd introduced him to. One night he said they were attractive. He was bored with her. 'I couldn't make his penis smile. He would go with them, it would put some lead in his pencil.'

He said he had become a utilitarian, providing the greatest happiness for the greatest number. He had also become despondent. His father had died and he was reproaching himself. He'd physically fought with the dad, plucking him from his chair and flinging the old fellow against a wall.

'Yes, I heard. But what are the details of that?'

She told him that the headmaster of Mamoon's school, and also the headmaster's wife, had been dear, lifelong friends of the father. And the man – 'who, incidentally, had only one leg' – had been kind and let Mamoon attend the place at a cheap rate. It turned out that Mamoon, at fifteen, had been screwing the headmaster's wife, the school nurse, in the medical room, most days. She had also loaned him books and read his early stories, editing them for him, encouraging him, telling him that he had it, that thing that everyone wants and most people don't have: talent. He saw that as soon as he wrote he was loved and admired. Literature was the leg-opener. A good paragraph was better than a few glasses of wine.

She said, 'The headmaster didn't find out about any of this until Mamoon was in his mid-twenties. The headmaster then hopped across to see the father, after the woman died, to say his wife's infidelity had be-smirched the last years of his life. The woman had said she'd loved Mamoon. The headmaster was shamed.' Marion put on a paternalistic Indian accent. 'The fath-er said to Mamoon, "You dirty bastard, you shamed us all by fiddling with the very woman – a family friend – on the actual school premises while we were getting a generous discount! What other deceptions are you capable of?"

'"She was very enthusiastic and grateful at the time," replied Mamoon. "Why is it exercising you? Are you jealous? She said she was lonely. I was the 'second leg'. I had a body to die for, and she opened my fly with her teeth. Your friend bored her to death. You should have sent me a telegram of congratulation for cheering her up."' Marion went on, 'As you can imagine, it was here that the father, becoming more and more incensed, struck Mamoon across the face. And Mamoon, being quite strong then, having taken up weight-lifting, picked him up and tossed him across the room, towards the litter bin, like a basketball.

'In his later life Mamoon was ashamed and regretful, and worried over the father a lot. I'd brought up the subject of whether his father was gay.'

Harry almost choked. 'How exactly did that go down?'

Mamoon had taken it seriously. The pieces were falling into place. Mamoon's father had had an arranged marriage, fought with his wife continuously, gambled most nights, and drank ferociously. But he never went with women and repeatedly told his son never to marry. Mamoon began to wonder if *his* weird adolescent sexuality was a picture of his father's confusions.

Marion said, 'Mamoon, as you might have found out, was something of a Nietzsche jukebox, with a quote for every occasion. And he particularly liked this: "That which is silent in the father speaks in the son." We discussed it very intensely. At detumescence, after all, there is conversation, that is where love begins. Over a bottle of wine or three, we spent entire evenings talking, working everything out. We were very close, and living together, because he had been teaching in America.'

He asked her what that was like.

She laughed. 'It was wonderful to spend time with him. But it was not unconflictual. Nothing with Mamoon was unconflictual. There had been the inevitable run-ins with the authorities, culminating in the accusation of misogyny and so on.'

Harry said he'd heard something about that and was going to look into it. He asked her what the details were.

'I'd been living with him outside the university for a couple of months,' she said. Mamoon made sure he was too maverick for the institution. But he knew how to interest people in ideas. 'Then, unfortunately, there was the incident with the black feminist lecturer to whom he said, at a cocktail party, "Surely, being black isn't an entire career these days, is it?"'

'What happened?'

'Big flatulent row. That, along with his remark that there was a high incidence of psychosis in the Afro-Caribbean community because of the fathers' absence, did for him. It turned nasty. We had to pack up and get out of there fast. It was like being run out of town.'

'Did it bother him?'

'Of course he said he didn't want to be deprived of the *jouissance* of racism just because he had brown skin and had suffered it himself. Clearly, he said, it must be one of the great pleasures to hate others for more or less random, arbitrary reasons.'

It meant he was never able to teach again. It cost him

money. He was more bothered than he could own up to, because he had important things to say about the craft he had devoted his life to. Somehow he got himself tangled up in these fatuous debacles. He couldn't understand it and needed 'comfort', he claimed.

'Female comfort?'

'I told him that as I had sacrificed so much to be with him, I couldn't have him taking off with my best friends in front of me. He called me a bore, and sulked. He had the temerity to say I was no good at sucking cock.'

'Oh dear. You have to take care with your teeth,' said Harry. 'I guess you know that. Perhaps you could have practised.'

'Believe me, baby, I could suck your brain out through your ass and blow it down the can.'

He asked, 'How was he at cunnilingus?'

'Enthusiastic, at times. But inaccurate. And then—'

'Then?'

She said, 'When a man doesn't want to eat you out, he's done with you.'

'That must be one of life's hardest lessons.'

She went on, 'Mamoon could really freeze you out, until I couldn't bear the anxiety. Threesomes weren't my thing, I had tried them. Men think they like them, but their eyes are bigger than their dicks. It's rare for a man to satisfy one woman, let alone two. Still, I decided these women could join us, if they wanted to – one at a time. Why not? Hadn't we had the sixties? Why be conventional, why say no to everything? And they were free women. We did it a few times. He said it was the most exciting thing he'd done.'

'Why did the women do it?'

'It was the first time, I guess, that he'd seen that he could use his power, position and charisma to seduce and use. As he said, being famous, witty and good-looking made him catnip to the menopausal. He was so interested in some things that the world seemed to vibrate around him. And these women were curious. But they had husbands, children and lives, and weren't always available when he wanted. He had the bright idea of inviting professionals to join us.'

'How many times?'

'Almost every night, for a few weeks. We were so overtaken by it, we blew a big hole in his income, not that he cared. Why would he? I guess a lot of it was Peggy's and he believed she owed him.'

'Were you drinking and using drugs? Were there other men involved?'

'He was very keen.'

'How do I know this is true?'

'There are letters.'

'If we're to skewer him, I have to see them.'

'You do?'

'Otherwise he can say you're only a mad fantasist.'

She hesitated for a moment before getting up and leading him out of the room. In the corridor, she pushed open her bedroom door.

Ahead of him, framed on the wall, was a large print of Richard Avedon's photograph of Mamoon, which Harry had only seen previously, the size of a postage stamp, on a book jacket. In a suit and tie, and wreathed in cigarette smoke, Mamoon must have been in his mid-forties, dark-haired, black-eyed, anguished, a man with the strength to endure, with a poet's soul, an Asian Camus. In time, Mamoon, the radical transgressor – for whom accurate language was always revolutionary – would argue and fall out with fellow writers; he would be banned from various countries for political or religious opinions, pick up a clutch of fatwas, and numerous prizes and awards, at which he would chuckle; and he would write good books.

'You see?' said Marion.

With her behind him, Harry continued to stare: if he had forgotten why, as a young man, he'd loved Mamoon – the tough-guy, hard-living artist who looked into the dark without flinching, and spoke what he saw, putting truth and authenticity before safety – this picture of pride, self-knowledge and glamour should remind him.

It had to be true, as Rob liked to reiterate, that the writer, indeed every real artist, was the devil, rivalling God in creativity, trying even to surpass him. God was surely man's most fatal creation, the devil's kitsch bitch. It was God, with his insistence on being worshipped and admired, who made the argument of art necessary, keeping the fire of dissent alive in men and women. This dissident was the artist, who spanned with his imagination reason and unreason, the under and the over, the dream and the world, men and women.

Plato, along with the latest pope, recognised how dangerous it is to have an artist around making mischief, stirring things up with the spoon of truth and intoxicant of fantasy and magic. And so, for crossing the line, and for stealing God's fire, artists were banned, imprisoned, condemned, silenced, killed – they always would be, these sometime Christs of the page.

It must have been the Faustian idea of Mamoon as hero and holy transgressor, as the one who took on God and the righteous, that Harry had fallen in love with, an image which had brought him to this room today, followed by this woman who had slept every night for years beneath the picture. It was, also, a picture of the man Harry had, at one time, wanted to become. Yet now he was only the illustrator, not the subject. In what way, he wondered, could he become more like the image? How brave or daring had he ever been?

Marion kissed her fingers and pressed them against the photograph.

Harry noticed there was nowhere else to sit except beside her on the narrow single bed. On the undusted shelf there were photographs of her children when young. He told her they were lovely kids.

'Women must not bolt,' she said. 'The children punished me. When I went, one of them attempted suicide, and is still mad in an asylum. The youngest refuses to let me meet my grandchildren.'

She asked Harry to pull a shoe box from under the bed. Out of this she extracted the letters, of which there were about fifty. She opened two of them, and let him see the date and the 'Darling Marion' and 'all my love, Mamoon', in his familiar minuscule writing.

She said, 'During this period he kept saying I bored him, and he didn't feel alive any more. If I didn't think of new things for us to do, he'd go mad. He was fascinated by styles of love-making, by how different women respond, move, kiss, and how he was new each time. It was almost forensic for him.

'I suggested we could ask men to join us, and he could watch, if he wanted to. He did watch; he wanted to take part. He seemed to join forces with the other men. There were too many of them. He started to make me do things I couldn't bear to do to please him. Scenes so depraved it makes me sick to think of them. Tiger burning . . . burning . . .

'He wanted an accelerated ecstasy, as he nominated

it, what Poe calls an "infinity of mental excitement . . ."
He claimed, oddly for him, that this extremity, this repeated transgression and sacrilege, was the closest thing
to a religious experience he'd had. Here, he said, he
could fruitfully lose himself entirely, and betray his
father over and over again. He understood the point of
the crowd, and how it could pull you away from yourself. And this from no keener follower of individualism.

'I made love to people I wouldn't otherwise have
touched. This was dangerous at that time, but I would
have done anything to keep him. *Anything*.'

'Did he hurt you?'

'Now, looking back, I feel abused. I *was* used. I was
a fool to think he would love me always, that he would
marry me.' She said, 'He was strong then. He grabbed
my face and forced it into a man's crotch and I remember thinking, "You've hurt me for your pleasure. It
matters more to you than I do." There's a lot of degrad-
ation in sex, isn't there?'

'When it's done right. Are you saying he was a per-
vert?'

'Are you a serious writer, or are you working for the
National Enquirer?'

'The *Enquirer*.'

'I learned that real sex is mad, mad, mad,' she said.
'It can overrun everything else, particularly sense and
intelligence. And you must remember, he loved me so

much, even as he hated me. I had captivated him, sexually, and he was mine. Fortunately, he was travelling a lot at the same time and wrote to me with various "requests" I should fulfil when he came home.'

'He did?'

'In the end, Peggy, who was not well in mind or body, requested him to return. He hesitated for days. Suppose he just walked out now. What would he lose, what would he gain? What about her? Duty or love? I'd never seen him so anguished. I was foolish: I said I'd stand by him whichever way he went. He kissed me goodbye. I believed he would marry me. I didn't think for a moment I'd never see him again.' She went on, 'I suspect he went back to see another woman – not Liana. It wasn't her turn yet.'

'Another woman? Do you know which woman?'

She shrugged. 'Do you? Yes, obviously. You do know.' When he said nothing she continued. 'I learned later, from reading him, that the experiences we'd had together had traumatised him. He could only process all that raw experience by sitting in a room for months. I even think he still believed he could turn his back on his sexuality and sublimate it entirely.

'Peggy kept going for eighteen months. She created the environment he needed, where he wrote that horrible text, one of the ugliest books I've read, with a sadism which I believe is quite unconscious, since he actually loves women. He was the most conscious of artists, but he knew there were some things you had to leave alone when they occurred to you, which were the essence of something true.'

Harry said, 'I need to ask you something. Are you sure I can't see his letters to you? Could I copy them? I could photograph them with my phone. I could help you arrange for them to be purchased by an American university. It goes without saying that you could do well out of them.'

She laughed. 'I'm aware of that and I need the money badly for healthcare. I'm not so stupid, Harry. This material will make a chapter in your account. I'm hanging on to it for now because for me it will be an entire book. Mine will be far more spicy, passionate and vulgar than yours. I know the other women involved and they will back me up with their recollections, while remaining anonymous. And I have started my book. Are you and I racing?'

He said, 'Coming from me, this will sound a bit rich, but why would you want to expose this private material?'

'Suppose Flaubert's lover had written a book about him? Or Kafka's fiancée? What would it be like to be a writer's companion? After my story of my life with him, he and I will be side by side for ever.' She added, 'He loved and exploited me. Now I can do the same to him!'

'Very tabloid.'

'Isn't it usually the women's voices which are suppressed? You envy him, and will never know what it is like to love him. I will give the view from the bedroom, the intimate picture. If you want to know a man, see how he is in love. Isn't that where the truth lies?'

'Yes, the truth always lies. It might be in the complexity of the work.'

'That's the cover story.'

He said, 'And if he wanted you back?'

'I'd be there like a shot, even now. Will you say that to him? He was cruel, handsome and brilliant, everything a man should be. Harry, will you say my name in front of him and watch his face? He knows very well that he is still mine, that he will not escape me.'

At the door she put her face up to his. He kissed her cheek, and saw she wanted to give him her mouth. Perhaps it would be her last kiss. For a short time he gave her his mouth. Why not? She tried to pull him towards her, but he removed her hands from his body.

'I still have physical feeling,' she said. 'If you help me, I'll show you the letters.'

'What do you mean?'

'I'm tired. Come back tomorrow? Would you – for one more day? I will have something important.'

The next day he learned that he could read some of the letters on her bed, where she would lie next to him.

214

He would wear a T-shirt and trousers, and she would be permitted to touch his upper body only: chest, shoulders, head and hair. He didn't object to her caresses; he believed he was glad to be of use, and he was, anyway, tense for a number of good reasons.

As her hands worked on him, Harry took in the material: they were love letters, with requests for assignations disguised as wishes for others to accompany them 'on walks'. Despite her promises, and sentences about how much 'the other evening' had meant to him at his time of life, and how 'revived' and 'interested' he was, once more, in what he referred to as 'the human scene', there was nothing substantial to count as confirmation.

All Harry could do was thank Marion, kiss her, and say goodbye. He would write to her if he needed anything else.

'Please come back again – whenever you like,' she said, taking his hands. He wondered if she'd ever let him go. 'Please, I'll try to find other pictures and notes. Tell me, do you pity me, an old woman alone, with nothing except a few memories of a writer?'

'I admire you, Marion.'

'For what?'

'For being a fundamentalist, for giving up everything for one idea – love. And you still live it.'

'Would *you* have sacrificed so much?'

215

'For me the world's full of women. Many of them – too many – are nice.'

'The serial loves keep you safe, and that's the most dangerous thing of all. You never miss anyone, and if there's no sacrifice, there's no love.'

He asked her how she read her love now, as devotion, or the siren call of masochism?

'Until you said it, I thought it was the first. Now you tell me.'

Self-sacrifice would be the hardest addiction to shift. He said, 'Mamoon felt uneasy, with all that relentless love and possessiveness coming at him.'

'That's what *you* would feel. I know some puny men are afraid of women. But why would you say that about him?'

'He fled.'

'So he's the victim here, after all.'

He said, 'I guess it's wonderful to fall in love, but falling out of it, losing the illusion – now there's a necessary art, which might profitably be learned.'

'I suppose that is what you will write. I must do my book then.' She sighed. 'I seem to have ruined my life, and you appear to have saved yours.'

'Not so fast,' he said. 'My girlfriend and I did a test back in London, and she's having a child. We talked about children, but never agreed on anything definite. Myself, I still feel I'm an adolescent.'

216

'You're mis-recognising yourself,' she said. 'That is very dangerous.'

'How to see straight?'

'That is the thing.'

'How, how?'

'It's been done already, the straight seeing,' she said. 'You've seen. Now you cover it up. You hide yourself from yourself.' She kissed him. 'Don't forget, conventionally, you actually have what most people want. Send me a picture of the little one.'

NINETEEN

Harry guessed there was something wrong with Rob when, the afternoon after his return to London, Rob suggested they meet in the frantic bar of a railway station. It was not the case that Rob was intending to take a journey: he said he only liked 'anonymous places' or 'non-spaces' now. As soon as they met, Rob commented on the number of anxious bodies rushing around them, saying how the limbs had lost contact with their owners and resembled electrified stumps.

Rob had been drinking and was sweaty and shaking excessively, even for him. He appeared to have shoved most of his clothes in a kit bag that didn't close, and Harry could see a slew of manuscripts, Bulgarian, Albanian and Tunisian novels, and poetry books. As there was the stench of the grave about the editor, Harry got down from his stool, saying it was awkward, and insisted they sit at a table where Rob was further away.

'Don't I look a hundred per cent?' said Rob. His eyes widened and he glanced around furtively, as if he were about to be attacked. Harry remembered how gentle his father was with paranoiacs, speaking to them quietly, and without intrusive questions, often just repeating what they said in a whisper. He managed this until Rob informed him that he was intending to accompany him to Mamoon's place in the country.

'You are? Why?' asked Harry.

'Don't you think it would be a good place to detox? We can talk through the material while strolling about the woods. I can help you organise it.'

'Rob, I'm not ready for that,' said Harry. 'All you need to know is that India was terrific.'

'And America?'

'I had to beg for it, but finally it turned out to be good stuff, with Marion. She's very similar to Liana in her brashness and confidence. Mamoon must know that people go for the same types without seeing it. But she's more intelligent and shrewder than Liana. She knows him better. However, it turns out she loved the curmudgeonly old cunt non-stop for years, and still does, remarkably enough. She even fetched other women for him.'

'There's no accounting for taste. Particularly with literary giants, Harry, you will find that the women fling themselves into the fire head first. We fans are on the wrong side of literature.'

Harry said, 'She gave him everything he wanted, and plenty of what he didn't want. There was so much of it, he had to run for his life, even if it meant going back to the moaning lush Peggy who'd swallow anything, except his semen.'

'No wonder he hid in the shed writing.'

'He regrets the hiding, I suspect. It did him no good to miss out on the kisses. Still, it cheers me to think what a torment the bastard endured with both of them. It must have been a relief when Liana turned up, his escape from the labour of love. He must have believed everything would get easier.'

'Did it work out for Mamoon? What's it really like down there in the country with him? I guess I'll find out later tonight.' Harry must have looked surprised. 'But I'm already packed. And this is juicy stuff, Harry. I can't wait to hear more!'

'In due course.'

'What the fuck?' said Rob. 'Aren't you going to let me sniff the sock?'

'Rob, you sound a little manic. Your words are too close together. You don't look at your all-time best.'

He said, 'Did you get objective confirmation of the Mamoon violations? You can't just stick any fucking gossip in one of my books: the lawyers will rip it right out.'

'I understand that.'

Rob said he was rereading Mamoon's second book, which was improving with age. He saw it all: how Marxism and fundamentalism both require and enjoin silence, and that where there is silence evil is done. Far from fading, the writer had become a more crucial figure. He and Harry should shout out to the world that Mamoon still existed and people should hear him. Rob went on to say that things were not good for him either. 'The wife's thrown me out of the house. We had an altercation involving violence – on her side. She says I'm a paranoid alcoholic with a personality disorder.'

'Who'd have thought it?'

'I am narcissistic too, apparently, as is anyone who doesn't think about her continuously. I'm going to get treatment for depression. If the pills don't work, I'm going to ask to have electricity put through me to jolt me into full health. Will you hold my hand when I'm plugged into the AC/DC?'

'Rob, it was you who suggested that things were not good for *me*.'

'Sorry, I forgot. They are not good for you. They couldn't be worse, no.' He leaned towards Harry. 'Watch out all around – from behind, the side and the front.'

Harry laughed. 'For what? I've just been in New York discussing the book with the American publisher. I'm full of ideas. He was pleased.'

Rob leaned towards him. 'There's a young gun, just out of college, more businesslike, less drippy and dreamy than you. When you left the country Liana hopped off to London to meet with him secretly. She told him how difficult you are, with your unusual hard-on for the truth, and she gave him encouragement.'

'She did that to me?'

'The young gun was guaranteeing he could turn the biography around in a year, and give Mamoon a lovely fresh gloss – the last of the post-war literary geniuses, there being only blogs, trolls and amateurs from now on. I could hear Liana's vagina clapping with enthusiasm.'

'You're joking, Rob. I signed a contract.'

'If Liana gives the word, you're gone like a used condom. Me and Lotte, my super-soft sidekick, are making a superhuman effort to hold you in place.'

'How?'

'We're using threats – among other things. Liana has to trust me: I said the young gun doesn't have half your brain or ability. It sounds as if you've been doing good work. I bought you more time. You must press on, friend. Without my protection it will get dirty. I wouldn't want to see *you* on antidepressants. What's up? Your coat is going on. You're looking away. You're dashing off tonight – but, please, not without me.'

'Sorry, Rob, I don't want to be rude, but I need to see Alice properly.'

When Rob said he did too, Harry got up, paid the bill and started to walk away. Rob followed him, still talking. 'I say – let's meet soon, with the material in front of us. Perhaps on site. I could feel purified down there amongst the goats, fish and dung.' He went on, 'And if I can't confirm the material's decent, it's curtains and creative writing for you, dude. You get me?'

Harry got away from Rob, and hid a bit. At last Alice, who'd been shopping for two days, came to the station with the car stacked with gifts. After tea, they drove to Mamoon's.

'You're in a good mood,' said Alice. 'I haven't heard about the trip in detail. Did you get what you wanted?'

'I might have a story. Let me talk it through. There's some kind of centre to the book. Similar events to the ones Marion described occur in two of Mamoon's later novels. One of his guilt-filled terrorists likes the same stuff, degrading the woman with other men and so on. Mamoon describes him as "moral filth", which confirms it for me.'

She asked if that was enough, and he told her that 'the Marion time' had been a crucial period for Mamoon. After temporising over the matter for weeks, Mamoon deserted Marion in America to return to Peggy and help her die. She had begged him; she had no one else, apart from Ruth, who'd supervised the house for years and was her only friend nearby. A nurse came in every day, and Julia, a girl then, not yet a teenager, ran errands. But it was lonely.

Peggy had also made it clear, at Ruth's urging, that a Mamoon no-show would ensure that he forfeited the property, which was in her name. His belongings would be dumped in the yard and the house would go to her sister. Mamoon owned nothing. He'd never had to think where he should live, or what he should have for supper. Peggy was maternal, at least. She'd enabled him to become an artist. What was marriage but sex plus property – property being *the* thing here.

So, corpse-tied, Mamoon slunk back. It was toxic; a fateful, blackmailing wrench for him and an interrruption of the new life he was exploring. He had promised Marion he would go back to her. He thought and thought about her, but he didn't return, and he didn't ask her to join him. He let it go – for a bit. And then for longer . . .

Peggy's diaries were sparse here, unsurprisingly, but she noted how kind Mamoon was, when pushed. She had been alone too much, and now couldn't bear it. The moment he walked back in through the door her heart leapt. He had come home, her prince. She praised and thanked him, her husband, a thousand times. He put down his bag. She had him where she wanted him.

While she rested and slept, he sat with her and wrote at the desk across the room – and he kept on writing: fiction, diaries, and notes on his life. Harry told Alice he'd discovered several of Mamoon's scruffy notebooks among Peggy's things in the barn, which he was going through. These notes, given to him, in fact, by Julia, were a fascinating insight into his method, as Mamoon served her: the description of a body shrinking into death, her hands, her mouth, how he washed her, and her suffering and humiliation. Also – his memories of India, political and philosophical ideas, characters, ideas for essays, and so on. For a time he became a zombie, to survive. He had stopped loving her a long time ago, and she knew it.

Mamoon confessed that Peggy's whole being made him ill. Her voice turned his stomach; the way she pulled at him made him cringe. The terror was that she wouldn't die. The combination of hate and duty did him in: he was out of control, passionately unhappy, half mad, drinking, wondering why he was so loyal to her. Shouldn't he have stayed with Marion and let Peggy down?

Peggy did die. He went into his room, eating and weeping at his desk, crying for Marion too, with whom he had also broken – at least in his mind. So: he was done with her, too. But what did it mean to be 'done' with so many people? Who, or what, was left?

He wrote about the hell within him with a new honesty and seriousness. This was when he became an 'authentic' artist. He was no longer standing to one side of himself, but said everything straight out. Harry said that no one described death as well as him, and how the mourning, isolation and deprivation made him mad.

Harry said, 'Mamoon saw no one for eighteen months.'

'No, no—'

'Except – except what he describes as "his new family". And he writes a lot about them in the journal I have.'

'What? Who do you mean when you say "family"?'

With Peggy gone, Harry explained, it was the local woman, Ruth, attending to him. Because Mamoon couldn't cope, and Peggy had insisted on it, Ruth moved into the house with her children, Julia and Scott, who was a teenager. He'd known the kids for years, of course. Peggy had always been aware how cruel Ruth was as a mother. So, when she was a child, Julia lived there for weeks on end during the holidays, hanging out with Peggy, making cakes, taking care of the animals, seeing the place as her home.

But now Mamoon became fond of them in a more adult, responsible way. He had never wanted crying babies or whinging toddlers. But now, to his surprise, he found he liked being a paternal figure. He enjoyed having authority and being relied on. The children taught him that the inside of his head wasn't the only interesting thing in the world.

He discovered that he could be good fun, joking

around as his parents did with him. But he was solicitous too; he saw what the kids needed as they got older.
They ate together and watched sport and movies. The
kids were used to seeing him sitting on the sofa scribbling in the notebooks. Ruth asked him if he wanted
some peace. But no, he found he liked the everyday
noises and the voices.

He even had a swimming pool dug for them and
their friends, the locals, who came over to splash
around. He drove Julia to school. She was moany, sullen, excitable, but perhaps he pitied her, or even liked
her. He talked to her as he thought – his usual free
association, about politics, his childhood, reading and
writing – and she listened. He wrote a story and read it
to her. He and Scott boxed together in the garden. Scott
built bikes, and played with engines. When Scott was
in big trouble with some of the locals, Mamoon went
round and faced them down. Ruth kissed his feet.

Julia was the one Mamoon adored more and more.
Appalled by her ignorance growing up in the country,
he paid for her to have piano lessons, and to attend
dance and art classes. He started to teach her Greek,
and – quite mad this – made her read Homer and the
Bible. He bought her classical records and sat with her
while she listened to Mahler, and he was pleased when
she wept, since it showed 'sensitivity'. He promised he'd
send her to college, but it didn't happen. 'I guess be-

cause he was with Liana by then,' said Harry. 'But I suspect he never stopped paying for her.'

'Why would he do this?' Alice said abruptly, 'Oh no, he wasn't going with Ruth, was he?'

'He might have been. I don't know yet. Though she wasn't as far gone as she is now, she was drinking, and capable of violent despair.

Ruth was not entirely awful, or a halfwit, then. She was mightily enthusiastic at that point. She wanted everything, of course: love, the house, a future . . . She thought she might get it if she served Mamoon. Then she made a mistake: she was not entirely self-serving. Maybe she understood what he really needed. Perhaps she cared for him. Harry said he thought she did. Maybe even now.

'What happened?' Alice asked.

Ruth had told Mamoon that enough was enough. There was no money coming in. He had to clean himself up and get on with his career. 'My mother', said Harry, 'gave herself to her demons. They devoured her.' But Mamoon resisted: he got up, he shaved off his long beard. Ruth cut his hair and kissed him. Instead of continuing to lay out his clothes for him every day, she packed his suitcase, and shoved him off to London to see his agent and his publisher. Meanwhile, he gave the family money, allowing them all to stay in the house while he was away. They loved it there: the space, the quiet, the isolation, and Julia regularly began to sit in that lovely library, leafing through books on art.

That was where the notebooks finished.

Harry told her that he'd worked out from Mamoon's friends that under Ruth's instruction Mamoon headed for London, where he found people talking about the new Britain made by immigration, and a younger generation who wrote about multiculturalism, ethnicity and identity. Mamoon had never thought about his identity. He had always been who he was. That was, conceivably, his problem. In London he couldn't find anyone new to get along with, and his friends bored him. He tried to pick up women, but the charm was intermittent; he was too old and didactic, too needy, out of practice.

Because he couldn't go back defeated, he pushed on. He travelled in Europe – Prague, Vienna, Madrid, Budapest, Ljubljana, Trieste – writing in hotel rooms, sitting in cafes alone with the newspaper and a notebook, as alienated as he had been as a student in Britain. He got on a train to Rome.

One day he found, at last, a woman, and brought her back – Liana. It was instant, magnetic, their attraction for one another. Their excitement was high.

Now, you can imagine it, Harry went on. Liana charging around Prospects House, amazed by everything she had married into, shouting, brightening the place up, throwing things out, putting up new curtains until everything was transformed. A new woman, a new world. An opening out. Ruth, Julia and Scott became 'servants' or 'staff' again. Mamoon had written ahead, instructing them to return to their house. Mamoon was no longer the surrogate father. He just dropped the family; everything was different. Mamoon was not a great explainer.

Scott was devastated, but what could he say? He still came to work in the garden, and did all the odd jobs. He slashed his legs until they ran with blood. He chased and beat the father of a Somali immigrant family with a cosh. But Mamoon continued to see Scott and listen to him; he was interested and firm, giving him guidance, but no money.

Liana, even today, had little idea of the family drama which took place before she arrived. Mamoon knew she would be too jealous. She would never have allowed the family to work at the house. 'No woman would, frankly,' said Harry.

'But Harry, what you're doing is forcing her to see all this – you're pushing it in Liana's face.'

He said, 'Alice, I promise, this book will introduce her to things she had no idea about.'

'But Liana is happy. Why disturb her? This is much too dangerous, Harry. I've said it all along.'

Harry told her that there was a peaceful passage

coming up since, for a time at least, back in the house with his new wife, Mamoon was cheerful and optimistic. He wrote well and was happy to be alive.

'Only for a time?'

'Is he cheerful now, or is he restless again?'

'How would I know? Oh God,' she went on. 'This book is going to give them nightmares. He'll blame her. He can be tough, vicious even. Can't we forget it and just be friends with them?'

'I'm not being paid to be a friend.'

'But they're *my* friends now. They've done nothing but treat me with affection and kindness.'

'Alice, I am warning you – keep your distance.'

'What's made you so brutal, Harry? I'm not staying long, but thank God I brought them some lovely things.'

Alice had been rushing around in London, finding tablecloths, glasses, cutlery, good vodka, earrings, hazelnut cake, and a print of a pig for Liana. After Alice and Harry had driven into the yard, and lugged the swag into the house, Alice made a fuss of the dogs. Eventually she and Liana sat down to gossip while examining the presents.

Mamoon didn't come out. Through the window Harry saw the old man watching the news. He was, after all, just a man, and not merely a narrative. Mamoon just nodded when Harry appeared in the doorway.

'All well, sir?' said Harry, striding in with a bottle.

'All it takes to cheer me is a bright smile from Alice, and my favourite vodka, as you well know.'

'Let me thank you for your kind assistance, sir, with Marion.'

'Yes, my spirits rather dropped when I noticed that you seemed cheerful. Is she well?'

'Formidable, but frail.'

'Ah. She was full of life, before.'

'Mamoon, she told me everything.'

'Everything, eh? Did that take long?'

'She showed me some letters and told me how much she loved and admired you as a man and writer. She said you were generous with your time and affection. It was the bitterest moment of her life when you came back here.'

'I feel a *but* coming at me between the teeth of a rabid dog.'

'She said your life changed when you were with her. You refound your sexuality, and developed it. Mamoon, sir, she described events which involved other men, as well as her female friends.'

He laughed. 'Casanova claimed that Dante forgot to include boredom in his description of hell. As you might have heard during your research, I suffer from ennui as an illness, and this can make us sadists. I do recall Marion attempted some feeble tricks to keep me interested. I blame her for nothing. Say what you like about me, Sherlock, but I will question you severely if you condemn her for this nonsense.'

'When you were writing she kept a diary. She's working on a book about her adventures with you.'

'She is?'

'You had no idea?'

'If every semi-literate fabulator scribbles away non-stop why would it be my concern – or yours, for that matter?'

Harry said, 'She says there's a publisher willing to take it if she tells all. I guess', he went on, 'the only way to stop her would be for you to talk to her. To persuade her. I am sure she would love to hear your voice.'

It took a lot to make Mamoon spark up, but this information made his eyes dart about. He composed himself before saying, in his slow sonorous voice, 'As the genius Nietzsche told us, "The eternal hourglass of existence will be turned again and again, and you with it, you dust of dust."' He looked at Harry. 'And you are dust of dust.'

He pulled himself up out of the chair and left the room.

Harry went to Alice upstairs and shut the door behind them.

TWENTY

Harry sat close to Alice and confessed how mad and discouraged this part of Mamoon's story was making him. It was true, you couldn't just say anyone was a sexual sadist. Mamoon, predictably, was already hostile, and Marion wouldn't let him quote from the letters – not that they confirmed much. Unless there was more than Marion's allegations to go on, he would have to drop the material and write a bland book.

'I will pull out of the project if I can't do the sort of intimate, psychological portrait we've talked about,' he said. 'The archaeology of a whole man. He speaks; they all speak. I can't bear the idea of just being mediocre, Alice. I would rather die than be ordinary.'

'What can we do?'

'You could go to him and ask if Marion told the truth.'

She looked horrified. 'Why would he tell me, Harry?'

'The old fool flatters himself he can seduce you. Haven't you been prancing in the woods with him?'

'Not prancing, no. He can't walk far. As we go, we discuss the nature of love and art.'

Harry said, 'Let's turn it around. If you can persuade the old man to own up, you will help me out, and indeed the family we will have. Our future together could be secured.'

She was biting her nails. 'Why are you pulling me into this, Harry?'

She didn't want to be put in the position of having to 'trick' Mamoon, as she put it. He trusted her; she liked him, and it was awful when Harry became so insistent and domineering.

'I need your help,' he said. 'We're in financial trouble. Won't you do this small thing for me?'

Before supper Harry nodded at Alice. She went downstairs to Mamoon and gave him the scarf, cuff links and tie she knew would cheer him up. She offered him her arm, and suggested they take a stroll. She had her phone with her, to use as a recorder. Harry had briefed her about the numerous acts she was to ask Mamoon about. There was quite a number of stories; she'd been shocked to hear them, and didn't believe Mamoon would do such things. 'Are you absolutely sure about this?' she kept saying.

'Just be certain to remember them all. I'll be interested to hear what his attitude to this part of his past is.'

They were gone a long time. When Alice returned with Mamoon, she couldn't look at Harry, but she did hand him her phone which he took upstairs and plugged into his computer. He heard her playfully asking Mamoon if he'd been as macho as she'd heard. Had he ever used his power and position for sexual advancement? Was he as dominant as he appeared? The old man grunted and laughed. She said there were some 'sexual excitements' she wanted to try herself, if she could talk Harry into them. Had Mamoon tried, she wondered, any of the following?

Vaguely Mamoon confirmed, or at least didn't deny, much of what she asked. In truth, he said, Marion had had many strong wishes, and had turned out, to his regret, to be too demanding for him. Female passion was a whirlwind: he couldn't devote himself to a woman; he needed time to ponder and write. Come to think of it, he preferred art to life. Once he'd met Liana everything had seemed easier. As a defence against unwanted excitement, marriage was a prophylactic he would recommend to anyone.

Alice sat on the bed watching him while Harry listened to the recording, nodding and making notes.

'Don't I look pale?' she said.

He looked at her. 'Pale is your colour.'

'Don't you want to know what happened?'

She asked Harry to go outside. He followed her into the nearest field, walking quickly. She was white and shaking. Her eyes were dilated.

She hit Harry several times and shouted, 'Why did you make me talk dirty to a stranger? I kept thinking he was enjoying it in some obscene way. And when I'd turned the phone off, guess what, I had a panic attack – violent palpitations, like being hit in the chest with a rock. I had to lie down on the ground.'

'Oh God, I'm sorry.'

'You're never sorry!'

He said, 'What can I do? This is maddening! You did offer to help me on this project. I never said it would be easy.'

She said, 'Mamoon stroked my forehead until I felt better. He was worried that the things he was telling me would make me mad and ill.'

'He was right. You're sensitive. Are you okay now?'

'I'm not going to thank you for putting me in that position. Are you sure you actually want to take care of me? Liana wonders if you really do. She has reservations about your character.'

'And I about hers. I love you, darling. Can I kiss you?'

'How could you even think about it when I'm in this state?'

She was already walking back to the house. It wouldn't be a good idea to speak to her for a while. His desire for the truth had made him a criminal. She didn't want to eat with Liana and Mamoon, she didn't want to talk at all, but wrapped herself in a duvet on the sofa in the living room and slept there in a woolly hat, sucking her thumb. The next morning he drove her to the station, where she took a train to Cornwall for a photoshoot. Harry kissed and thanked her, and reminded her of his adoration, but there was nothing he could do with her in this mood.

When he returned to the house, he found Mamoon, sitting in the living room, and said, 'Could I ask you, sir, if I'd be completely wrong to think that your experiences with Marion, your *amour fou*, informed the character of Ali in your sixth novel?'

There was a silence, before Mamoon said, 'Harry, you do already know, don't you, that I like to aid your intellectual development by refusing to allow any banal and simplistic correlations between art and experience.'

'I know, sir. About that I follow you as a master. Art is a symbolic dream of life which transcends that from which it derives, and, indeed, everything which is said about it. However, there was an unmistakable outburst of desire and love, even of happiness in your work at that time. Before, your male characters were isolated, naïve even, perhaps book-bound. Then, brilliantly, you made another step.'

'I did?'

'You said, early on, that if every age has its central philosophical issue, ours will be the revival of religion as politics. And so you began to link radical Islam and its weird sexuality with hatred of the body, the body burned in the sacrificial auto-death. This is a gesture of the profoundest obedience. We know that the West attempted, in the sixties, to remove the father, authoritarian or not. That was how we ended up, as you have often helpfully pointed out, with a culture of single mothers. Take Ruth, for instance.

'The father – as fathers do – returned, in the form either of a gangster, as in *The Godfather* or your favourite, *The Sopranos*, or of religious authority. There is also the father's attempt to exclude, if not stamp out, sexuality. At least in others. Perhaps the father, according to this myth, wants all the women for himself. The sexuality returns, as it must, as perversion, as a kind of sadism. The fear, if not hatred, of women, of course, is at the centre of many religions.'

Mamoon yawned. 'I said this, did I? And if I did, so fucking what?'

'You let a woman in, sir. People say that sexuality is at the centre of the human secret, and that the erotic leads us into new experience, both sacred and profane. What is the connection, in your mind, if any, between the women you've been with and the work you've done?'

'I haven't a clue as to what you could mean.'

'Think, sir, please: I'm trying to make you look interesting here. I can make you look good in bed, and out of it! Marion has suggested your mind opened to fresh ideas when her legs did, when the two of you embarked on your adventures in America.'

Unlike most people, Mamoon had more or less complete control over his speech; he didn't like his words to run away from him. But for a moment he looked like someone who had swallowed a large marble.

At last he said, 'Ecstatic as I am to hear Marion's views from over the pond, I have no idea what you're talking about. I wish you weren't trying to peel me as you would an onion. You know, like the general public, I have a passion for ignorance. I want to work in the dark – the best place for me, for any artist. It just comes out, compacted as in a dream.' He was silent, before saying, 'There's no denying she sparked me into a new creativity. The intellect and the libido have to be linked, otherwise there's no life in the work. Any artist has to work with their prick or cunt. *Any person* has to work with their desire, to defeat boredom, to keep everything alive. Anything good has to be a little pornographic, if not perverse.'

Harry said, 'However, the biographer sees the inevitabilities, the same paradigmatic sexual scenarios enacted repeatedly. When it comes to love and sex, the past writes the future. That would be the story of everyone's life. Cannibals don't become foot fetishists.'

'Harry, you know more about my many selves than I do. You're in the remembering business while I'm in the forgetting game, and forgetting is the loveliest of the psychic luxuries, a warm scented bath for the soul. I follow Chuang Tzu, the patron saint of dementia, who advised, "Sit down and forget."'

'Thanks for telling me.'

'Perhaps my wife has hired you to do the little re-membering I do require. I have to say, I particularly like it when you remember things which never happened. You are now making an imaginary life.'

'How?'

'My life, as I lived it, has been a Marx Brothers film, a series of detours, mistakes, misunderstandings, missed opportunities, delays, errors and fuck-ups. I am a man who never found his umbrella. Your life, I expect, is similar. Your ascription of a teleological arrow gives too much meaning and intention. Still, the idea of becom-ing a fiction does appeal. To my surprise, you might have the makings of an artist.'

Harry said, 'I doubt I will ever reach your level, sir. I am impressed that you survived extremity and guilt with Marion, and that you came home to see Peggy through her vile death, sitting with her night after night. Then you carried on. You even had something of a family, for a time. Having repudiated the role previ-ously, you seemed to like being a sort of father. What was that like?'

Mamoon nodded. 'You know one is subject to many distractions and foolishnesses. It has always been my good fortune to have work which has saved me, and to have been able to look at the world through the lens of my ideas. I hope to God that you, one day, achieve that essential stability.'

'In what way has work saved you?'

'You strive to make me look lewd, when the truth is, even Philip Larkin had more sex, and I have been committed to the word throughout. I have always wanted to return to my desk to make something which hasn't existed before. That is my only – meagre – contribution to improving things here on earth.'

Having said this, Mamoon closed his eyes and began to snore gently. He had the ability to nap at will but was most likely to fall asleep when Harry was making an enquiry.

Harry went into the garden in shorts and trainers to do some stretching and weights. He hung a long bag from a tree and kicked and punched it. This was his routine and his release after things got sticky with Mamoon, when he knew he'd have to return to him with more impossible queries.

He wondered how long he'd have.

A few minutes later Liana, in fishnets and wellingtons, came out of the kitchen and settled herself on the bench outside the door with a popular biography of a grand lady, a cup of tea and her reading glasses. 'Bravo!' she called. Feeling more like a member of the Chippendales than a literary biographer, Harry took a breather and Liana poured him some tea.

'Poor man, you must be exhausted. I know I am. Here, I bought you this energising moisturiser,' she said, handing him a little pot. 'You'll like it, you'll see.'

'How kind, Liana. Why did you do that?'

'I heard you complaining about your uneven skin tone. Mamoon said that for you it's more serious than the collapse of the economy.'

'Much more. It's the result of childhood eczema. For years I scratched myself almost to death. I'm worried the anxiety here will make it return.'

'What anxiety? That cream has amazing healing qualities, and you seem agitated.'

'I am.'

'I think you know more about my husband than I do now.'

'That's the problem.'

'Was Marion kind about my darling Himself? Or was she bitter like the other one?'

'There was some bitterness, not entirely unwarranted. She turned out to be rather splendid.'

'Are you sure? You must have flirted all over the place.'

He rubbed the moisturiser onto his arms. 'She had plenty to say about many things. I haven't written it up yet, but I can feel that the book has really progressed.'

'Progressed where, my dear? You are alarming me, Harry.'

'I am?'

'I don't want you to get carried away and inflame my skin too. Let's keep everything gentle in your account, shall we?'

Alice had warned him to be careful; to endure being patronised and even insulted, and not to allow himself to give anything away, sucking rather than puffing, though that attitude had yet to get him very far. Still what he and Rob admired about Mamoon, they both agreed, was his talent as a provocateur, his ability to create anarchy and fury and then sit back to gaze out over the ruins. On occasion Mamoon was more Johnny Rotten than Joseph Conrad. Harry had begun to think that, as his father had suggested, he had been too passive. His fears had kept him too safe. He'd make some mayhem; it was time to go gonzo, and up the stakes.

He said, 'Liana, I guess you already know all about it.'

'About what?'

'The background to the Marion story. How Mamoon humiliated and insulted a young woman at an American university, calling her "a career Negro". He had to get out and quite soon after became violently bitter.'

'Might this be in the book?'

'When I've done the research. It was after this that Mamoon decided to give up on, or pull away from Peggy, while continuing to live with her. He and Marion began something of a perverse relationship, which

made me wonder whether such a thing had been a feature of his life.' Liana was silent. 'Or whether it was just
a one-off, as it were.'

'Perverse?'

Harry said that some might call it that.

'Do you know for sure?'

'He confirmed it. When this material comes out,
people will think about both of you differently. The
hacks and papers simplify things. They might call it
sadomasochism.'

She thought for a moment and said, 'Whatever you
do, don't put this in, but I wondered why, at the beginning, he asked if he could watch me urinate. Being a
lady, I said no. Why would anyone want such a thing?'

'To experience a particular form of intimacy.'

She said, 'Listen, Harry, what the bloody fuck are
you hinting at? Can't you actually be precise? I don't
want to live in the dark like an idiot! As a mature
woman –' she pressed her face close to his, 'and don't
you like to remind me all the time that I am? – I need
to know every detail of the Marion part.'

'Why?'

'How awful it would be if you knew things about him
that I didn't.'

He pulled on a tracksuit top and sat with her. It wasn't
long before she'd turned red, and was waving furiously
at her face with her book as if trying to put out a fire but

succeeding only in fanning the flames. To her credit she heard him out before saying, 'And you say you're going to put this filth in the book we commissioned?'

'If it is relevant to the work, which around that time turns very dark and sometimes brutal.'

She began to cry, and covered her face. 'Poor Marion. I think of her often and how she was rejected. That will happen to me!'

'Why would it?'

'She couldn't do enough to keep him interested. He regrets leaving her.'

'He does?'

'She inspired him, she was intelligent. They loved to talk about Shakespeare. She was learning Arabic and he said she was cleverer than him. He read her letters with a dictionary. I had an intelligent father, so I know men love women who are useful to them, like assistants.'

He asked her if she'd be okay.

She said, 'You did promise, Harry dear, that you'd help me earn his love and kisses. Now you come to me with this *merda*. He will blame me for stirring it up. What have you done!' She got up and walked quickly away, into the woods, stopping only to turn and say, 'I've cursed you. I thought of unleashing the bees on you only I'm too well bred. But a very bad thing is going to happen to you – tonight.'

TWENTY-ONE

That evening, while changing in his room, Harry could hear the two of them hollering, their voices overlapping as they interrogated one another. He had had, he guessed, something of an effect on their marriage. Too bad; he had a book to write. Writing was the devil. Writing was what he was employed to do.

He played music through his headphones and waited until it was nearly dark, although the kitchen light was on, when he crept out of the back door. He was smoking in the yard and about to get in the car when he heard a shout, or perhaps it was a shriek. Mamoon was coming out of the kitchen and heading towards the man chosen to make his portrait.

Mamoon was not leaning on his stick, as he always did now, the very stick Harry had cut for him, carving the head into the rough approximation of a rabbit. Mamoon was bearing it above his head with the genuine intention, Harry guessed, of bringing it into contact with the young writer's cognitive equipment.

Harry turned and jogged across the yard towards the track. To Harry's surprise, Mamoon was behind him, running and tripping, as if trying to throw away his limbs.

'Mamoon, please, sir—' tried Harry.

Harry ran some more, and so did Mamoon. He could hear Mamoon breathing heavily, and thought he must be tiring already. Harry was also keen to use reason and discuss literary matters. He'd had an expensive education and, even now, didn't want to waste it.

'Listen,' he began, and stopped. The writer was on him. Harry dodged the coming stick by ducking and turning away. 'I say, sir—'

Mamoon struck him across the back with the stick, as hard as he could. Harry fell down, and Mamoon followed up with two more blows. 'See, Judas – I've still got the forehand!'

'Stop that – Jesus! It hurts! What are you doing?'

'You want the cross-court smash with top spin?' said Mamoon, raising the stick again. He was ready to strike Harry across the face with it. 'The horse whip is coming – ha!'

'No, it's not!'

Harry crawled away as quickly as he could, got up, manhandled the stick away from Mamoon, and took it across the yard, placing it on the top of his car. The old fool, full of adrenaline, stumbled after it, and soon learned, after attempting to jump up, that his days as a sportsman were done. He tripped and fell face down, grovelling in the gravel.

'Don't touch me. You blabbed about what Marion

'alleged,' puffed Mamoon, as Harry hauled him to his feet and brushed the dirt off him.

'You agreed, sir, that nowadays not a moment of existence goes unrecorded.'

'How would you like it if you had everyone you'd ever fucked dragging behind you for ever? Perhaps they will, a ghostly crowd of dead souls, howling hostile curses. Then I'll laugh.'

'You've always been dissident, nonconformist, anarchic. Aren't most good books about sexual weakness?' Spying an opening for the intertextual discussion he'd long anticipated, Harry said, 'You adore Strindberg, adapted his work for the stage and wrote an essay on him. Kafka's agonised hysterical letters to Felice have long fascinated you. Let's think about how male writers have characterised the force of female sexuality—'

'Shut it, bastard! Liana's killing me, screaming and raving. She can't believe I've had a good time with anyone but her. She dismissed me from the bedroom into the room next to yours. Now she insists I tell her every detail of my life with Marion. How can I do that? How will I get her back?'

'Do you want her?'

'If I have a terrible dream or become ill in the night will *you* give me the kiss of life?'

'My kisses are soft and deep, sir. But to be honest, this material was going to come out anyway, by Marion's hand or mine. What else am I doing but teasing out the truth, knot by knot – like Goole in *An Inspector Calls*?'

'You're a ghoul trying to play God with me. It was bloody well private.'

'You forfeited that right when you invited me here to tell the story of your life. Why worry, when you know that sexuality makes fools of everyone?'

Mamoon told Harry that he could not confirm his material, but Harry explained that Marion had shown him the letters. When Mamoon asked why Marion would do that, Harry replied, 'The life and the writing make one continuous book. It's the same for all writers.'

'Marion – I mean Liana – said you're the sort to want to appear on television! You're trying to make a career out of me, young man!'

'We're strapped together, sir. We sink or swim as one beast.'

'Yours is a work of envy, and you are a third-rate semi-failure of a parasite who has got by on meretricious charm and fading looks. Did you ever read a biographer who could write as well as his subject?'

As if this wasn't enough, Mamoon grabbed Harry by the lapels and tried to throw him against the car.

'You're fired, Harry. You're never going to finish this work of tittle-tattle and when I come in from work tomorrow lunchtime I want to know this ridiculous misadventure is over! We've got another writer lined up to take over. He wears a tie!' He put his face close to Harry's. 'Remember this, little boy. You know nothing. You *are* nothing. You will always be nothing.'

Mamoon seemed to have exhausted himself and began to cough. Harry led him back into the kitchen and sat him down with a glass of whisky.

'You want me to call Liana?' He guessed she was up-stairs somewhere, tearing at something or listening to Leonard Cohen.

Mamoon shook his head and said, as Harry went to the door, 'Do I look particularly ancient and infirm to you? Have I suddenly aged? Don't leave me – I don't think I have long.'

But Harry hurried outside and sat in the car for a bit, collecting himself, before driving to Julia's and picking up the key she'd left for him.

Sliding up the passage, he saw that Ruth was in the living room, wearing the bright shirt Liana had worn to Mamoon's birthday dinner. She was sitting at the table with two of her paramours, in a smog of dope smoke, drinking Mamoon's champagne in beer glasses and, Harry soon made out, discussing some money-making scheme involving forged signatures, which they were practising. Harry greeted them quietly. He inter-ested them, unfortunately; one of the men stood up and shouted for him to sit down for a bevvy, and Ruth called, 'Harry, Harry, Harry – won't you grace us for a drink?'

Harry was sensible enough to continue to the woman he had come to see.

In the attic Julia was waiting in bed for him.

He stripped off his shirt. 'Look!'

'Gorgeous. Thanks – I've been waiting for this.'

He turned. 'Notice the bruises!'

'Oh my God, who did this? My brother? Is he back?'

'Luckily not. Mamoon.'

She laughed. 'Shut up.'

He took her hand and laid it against his face. 'He's dangerous for an old man, Julia, with strong wrists.'

'Jesus, it'll go a funny colour. You'll look like an aubergine.'

'That is a vegetable I don't like. Here's my phone. Photograph the injury. It's all gone wrong. I've been sacked.'

She photographed him, before pulling the rest of his clothes off and sitting on top of him. Her kisses were calming.

'I need your love, Julia.'

'I know. Congrats, lover boy.'

'Why do you say that?'

'You've been beaten as well as sacked. You must be doing good work.'

'Yes, well, the old boy pretends to rise above the everyday stupidities, gazing into the immeasurable distance with that superior tortoise blink, presumably regretting all the sexual opportunities he eschewed. Then he goes berserk with the stick I carved for him.'

She began to fuck him, knowing he would relax. 'Can I ask you something? I've been thinking about it non-stop. How many times did you have Alice while she was here?'

'Just the once. We were going again when we were interrupted by you, thanks. I know you were pretending to work outside the room, ears vibrating. I added some keen grunts to flush you out with laughter.'

'I wasn't listening!'

'With Alice, it's only ever on her terms, like being granted an appointment with the queen. Her latest thing is claiming to be allergic to semen. She has the rigidity of a hurt child.'

'I was going to say "abuse". You'll get it less and less from her, pretty boy.'

'How soon these things wear out. I'm nearly ready for a change.'

'But you don't like to let people go.'

'Tell me what you really think.'

She popped a joint into his mouth and lit it for him. 'You two might have a chance if she can appreciate you. She doesn't notice that you're funny and sweet. You say fascinating things, and you're good company. Unlike the old man, you're interested in other people. Plus, a gift for cunnilingus puts you in the top one per cent of all men.'

'It takes practice to be such a gourmand.'

'I always put musky perfume there for you, but I won't ask you to do that for me right now, Harry.' She turned off the lights, lit candles, and blew on his eyelids. 'You seem cracked; you look like you're going to cry on me.'

'I'm down. This is our last night together. If I'm really sacked, I won't be that displeased, to be honest. I've had enough of them both.'

'I'll set my alarm. I predict I can help you. I'm your girl, remember?'

'If you save me this time,' he said, 'you're a genius. I'll take you out for an Indian.'

'You will do something for me, Harry. You know what it is. I've asked you before. Take me with you, Fizzy Pants.'

'Where to?'

'London.'

He laughed. 'I wish I could. As it is, I'm done for.'

TWENTY-TWO

In the morning he cried, 'Why have they put floodlights outside the window?'

'Er . . . shut up. It's called the sun,' she said. 'Are you ill?'

'Julia, I'm going to give all this up and go back to London.'

'You're going to Liana now.'

'I can't face either of them. I can't face anything.'

She pulled him out of bed, filled him with food, and got him into his car, giving him instructions all the while; he nodded and shook his head silently. She ensured he was back at the house and in the kitchen hunting for haddock, and running up a Bloody Mary to accompany the Arnold Bennett, before Liana finally made her entrance in a satin dressing gown.

As she stood there, taking in the day, feeling out her head with her fingers and deciding to be jaunty, he dashed across the kitchen to lay her favourite breakfast in front of her.

'Here, Liana darling.'

'*Ciao bello*, you sweetie, this is too lovely, thanks. How did you know where to find this fish? What a treat.'

'And here – for you.'

'What is it?'

'Some of those things you asked for.'

He handed her a saucer of pills. There had been a jar full of Es in Julia's bedroom, as well as some hash, and a bag of mushrooms. She'd told him to take something for Liana. He was kind; he'd taken a lot.

All night he'd been persecuted by the ghost of Mamoon's words, coming at him in sinister whispers: over-educated but mediocre, worthless, parasitic . . .

'You can be a fine boy,' said Liana, dropping them into the pocket of her dressing gown.

'A caress from nirvana,' he said. 'But how can Mamoon resist you when you wear that cream silk dressing gown, and pyjamas with high heels? Even I—'

'Shut it, this early, and take your sunglasses off in here! Are you straight with me or any woman? Do you let any of them in? I don't think you're an idiot, just difficult, evasive, and probably a fraud. Darling, give me a little morning kiss on the lips.'

'Please, Liana, you smell of fish, and I've got a problem that only a diplomat like you can help me with. The day has come – I've been fired.'

'Who by?'

'Your husband. Last night he chased me with his stick. He was a little, let's say, agitated by the Marion material.'

'So was I.'

'Do I leave then?'

'Why not?'

'Okay. I'll get my things.'

She said, 'Not that I believed a word of that filth. Did you? The *puttana* made it all up for revenge and publicity. Can you imagine for a moment him behaving like that? The British public are decent and will understand. It was obvious he would fall out with you.'

'Doesn't he ensure a fatal fight with everyone? Particularly the women.'

'Not with me,' she said. 'I'm the boss here, *tesoro*, don't worry.'

'I'll ring Alice and give her the news that you will help,' he said. 'She's at home fretting about me.'

'She is delicate, we must take care of her. But doesn't it worry you –' Liana said, 'and don't take this the wrong way – that she doesn't find you at all amusing?'

'Thanks for that, Liana.'

'You *are* very funny, you know.' She looked at him, and said, 'As for Mamoon, never ignore him, and never listen to him. You go to work, and I'll speak to him at exactly the right time.' She winked. 'Observe the masterly way I shoot for his G-spot. It's like feeding a lion while keeping your fingers.'

Mamoon came in, with a dressing on his forehead. If Harry had wondered whether Mamoon would remember last night's threat, he needn't have worried.

Mamoon scowled, and said with a ferocity Harry had yet to become accustomed to, 'My spine aches the entire time, I can't see a foot in front of my face and I'm dizzy. My knee feels like an envelope full of broken glass and my penis is like a chloroformed slug—'

'Are you constipated? Have you had the dream again?' asked Liana.

'I am facing this urchin in my kitchen.' He jabbed at Harry and said, 'I rang Rob and ordered that you must stand out of my sunshine, sunshine.'

'No, Mamoon.' Liana pointed the washing-up brush at him, and then flicked it, as she did with the cats when they jumped on the table. 'Idiot or not, we've given him this damn job and he has to complete the paperwork. Your tantrums are ridiculous and interfering.'

'This serpent, the woodworm, insulted me.'

'How?'

'He made allegations against my honour.'

'Are you finally saying they're absolutely and completely wrong?'

'Liana, I've told you, he's beyond a pest.'

'He is. Even Alice has absolutely confirmed the woodworm is a blood-boiler. But he stays.'

'Why defend a fake who actually hasn't written a word? I think you like him a bit too much.'

'Too much for what?'

'It's repulsive in a woman of your age. You resemble a mutton chop.'

She started to laugh. 'Eat me then!'

'Shut up.'

'Watch it.' She repointed the brush in his direction.

Harry wouldn't have wanted that brush pointed at *him*, and could see that a younger Mamoon, at this point, could become mightily annoyed and cranky. He appeared to be looking about for something handy to heave in her direction. Then his breathing slowed, he closed his eyes and caressed his battered forehead.

'Remove him for ever from my sight.'

She said, 'We made a decision, you and I together, and we should follow it through without this mad fatwa against him. Otherwise I won't feed you.' She picked up the saucepan from the Aga and walked to the bin. 'Dal makhani, your favourite. And your paneer – say bye bye, paneer.'

'Liana—'

'And you love my salty raita. It was going to be followed by apple crumble and cream. Choose now – food or mood.'

'Food or mood? Don't throw that away! I choose food.' He was hurriedly tucking his napkin into the neck of his shirt. 'Will there be tomatoes? I love how you cooked them last time.'

'Did you?' she said, winking at Harry. She went and

kissed Mamoon, sliding her hand down the front of his shirt. 'Did you like that, *habibi*, my love?'

'It might be more tasty if you cooked everything that way.'

'I will do it like that – if you make me.'

'One more thing.' He thrust his finger at Harry. 'Where is Alice?'

'Why?' asked Liana.

'She has calming hands,' he said.

Liana rolled her hands over Mamoon's belly. 'Don't I?'

'She's professional.'

'I'll do what I can,' said Harry.

'Looks like you've been given a last chance,' said Liana. 'You'd better get that book done. Soon we will read some of it. And we had better like it . . .'

TWENTY-THREE

Alice and Liana sat in the heat on the lawn, passing a tub of vanilla ice cream between them and conspiring to bring young people to Prospects House. Her face hidden under an umbrella to protect it from the sun, Alice had her feet up on a stool; when she wasn't scooping up Ben and Jerry's, she laid the back of her hand on her overheated and worried forehead, and sighed deeply. Then she noticed Harry and started on the considerable business of sitting up.

Liana was writing lists and thinking aloud; she used the words 'young' and 'artist' a lot, as well as 'yoga centre' and 'writers' retreat'. In contrast, Mamoon didn't look like a man whose home would soon be open to the public. Sitting in the shade a decent distance away, working on the proofs of his collected essays, *Means and Ends*, he couldn't hear his wife. Occasionally, he would interrupt his humming of a tune by Everything But the Girl to groan and complain about his irrelevance, but no one listened. On Liana's instructions, Julia bustled over with tea until he accused her of trying to poison him with lapsang souchong. Despite the sight of Harry pacing up and down outside the back door,

Mamoon was cheerful. He had been active: recently, with a few remarks, he had made a lot happen.

Alice had been there for two days, swimming in the river and resting, while Mamoon was working again. Harry, after his conversations with Marion, had been settling back into his work. It had become difficult and frustrating as he fought to find clarity in the chaos of his research. For days he had read letters and written to friends, colleagues and possible lovers of Mamoon, while considering the work in relation to the life, making links across the decades.

But Rob had been attempting to harry Harry, as Mamoon had insisted he should. Harry might have been reinstated as official portraitist, but only on condition, Mamoon had concluded, that Liana get tough with Rob. It was time, Mamoon had said, for Harry's work to be thoroughly inspected by the editor before Harry became waylaid or dangerous to literature, perhaps going too far in a 'strange direction', or becoming 'self-indulgent' with the book. Mamoon wanted to look like himself.

Mamoon might be annoyed, but it wasn't as if Rob had been unprovoked by the biographer. For some time Harry had been ignoring his communications, claiming he was 'out of range'. However, that morning, waking up late with Alice, Harry had pulled the curtains and stopped dead. Rob was stumbling up the track bearing a large suitcase and rucksack. It wasn't long before Rob had walked into the house, demanded breakfast from Julia, and, when Harry went to greet him, insisted on seeing his laptop.

When he began to read through Harry's work both aloud and to himself, Harry said, 'I'm not ready for this, Rob. These are notes. Why are you doing it?'

'Liana is right. I have got to know.'

'Know what?'

'That man out there is an artist.' Rob pointed out of the window where Alice and Ruth were trimming a tree to Mamoon's instructions. 'He met Borges in Paris in the mid-seventies. They had dinner two or three times. What did they talk about? Kafka? Adjectives? Their agents? Why don't you tell us?' He rapped his knuckles dangerously against the screen of Harry's computer. 'Talent is gold dust. You can pan among a million people and come up with barely a scrap of it. Commitment to the Word stands against our contemporary fundamentalist belief in the market. Have you forgotten that?'

'Rob, I'm telling you, he's vile to ordinary people and charming to fascist monsters.'

'Put that in.'

'He's insane. He attacked me with a stick.' Harry pulled up his shirt and showed Rob the site, still visible. 'Joyce didn't do that to Ellmann!'

'Jesus, that's bad. Still,' he sniffed, 'any simpleton can be good. Mamoon has the balls to be a sinner. Liana has been phoning me. She says among other things that you have inflated ideas about yourself.'

'She said that?'

'It was reported by Ruth: Alice and you – the long, blond boy, with his impossibly tall and thin platinum fashionista girl, strolling with the dogs around town, in fashionable raggedy clothes and scuffed boots, disappointed you couldn't find somewhere that served nettle fettuccine, staring at the tattooed chavs as though you'd just discovered an African tribe. I heard you even photographed a chav's dog. Liana had to personally apologise.'

'To the dog?'

Rob removed his skull ring before taking aim and slapping Harry across the face. He stared at him, daring him to respond. 'Tell me, how come you haven't been beaten up more?'

'Should I be?'

'The party's dead. We're on truth time.' Rob lowered his eyes to Harry's efforts on the screen. 'You sit close enough to inhale every emanation of me, and we will examine what you've been doing. Are you having a breakdown? You look crazed and seem sad and manic.'

It was true: since Alice had found herself pregnant with twins, her anxiety had entered the red zone, as had

Harry's. Harry's father had even summoned his youngest son to London for a talking-to. It was like visiting
a mischievous cardinal and, cheerfully, Dad had been
glad to repeat his homily that a baby in a family, or
worse, two babies, was like a hurricane hitting a crowd.
All that which had been blown apart had to be put back
together, in a new, broader configuration: this was the
work of a man, not a boy. Being a father was not a
given; one had to assume the throne, stated Dad the
throne-sitter. 'There will be difficulties,' he added, dab-
bing his eyes in amusement. But he was also pleased;
Harry, with his easy cleverness and tendency towards
arrogance, dissipation and frivolity, particularly when it
came to women, had given his father good reason to believe he'd achieve zero. In fact Dad had almost become
reconciled to it.

Now, having finished her ice cream, Alice came
across the lawn towards Harry. If Rob had already
wrung him out, it was Alice's turn.

Not only feeling sick and faint, Alice now found Harry
too noisy, overbearing, with his breath too oniony, his
fingers sweaty and his eyes suddenly too beady. Meanwhile he was forbidden, of course, from finding her repulsive though she described herself as 'just sludge'.

She touched him gently on the back and they walked.
Worrying about where they would live, she hadn't been
sleeping at all. They would require, at least, a much

bigger place, a house in a safe neighbourhood with a garden. How would she look after the children? For that she would need help since he couldn't expect her to do the housework and childcare while he was in a library, no doubt sipping espressos with publicity girls who would bring him croissants.

'I am going to be working even harder, Alice. As Mamoon knows, earning a living for life at this game is difficult. We will have to go where the money is – America, where I hope I'll be able to get work teaching—'

'Teaching what?'

'Creative writing.'

'You know nothing about it,' she said. 'I've been thinking we should move to Devon.'

'What would we do?'

'We have to be somewhere quiet. Somewhere we can hide.' She began to weep. 'Not only am I pregnant, Harry, but threatening letters from bailiffs have been arriving while you've been down here. I've gone a bit over with the spending. I'm terrified that someone is going to enter the flat when you're down here and seize your Telecaster and the Gibson.'

For him there was nothing like hearing the word 'bailiff' to evaporate all hope in the world. 'What did you say to them?'

'Don't scold me. I'll cut back,' she said. 'But now he's here, please ask Rob for more money.'

266

'I will. But what have you been buying?'

'Coats, jewellery, dinners with girlfriends and a few pairs of shoes. I'll show them to you.' They were by the front door, and she called out, knowing Julia would be nearby. 'Julia, could you bring out the pumps, please? I think they're in our room.' She said in a low voice, 'Julia's a lovely girl. We have similar backgrounds. Council estates and single mothers.'

'Is that right?'

'I think you've got it from Mamoon, but I wish you wouldn't answer a question with another. It's evasive.'

'Sorry.'

'Haven't you noticed Julia?'

'I've been preoccupied with the book.'

'She and I went shopping together again. She knows where to go in town. Her brother might give me kick-boxing lessons to give me confidence.'

'He knows how to kick, does he?'

'You seem annoyed. Is it because she's a cleaner that you're rotten to her?'

'Rotten?'

'Harry, you can be a snob, you know.'

Julia came out with two boxes. Alice tried on a pair of shoes, and Julia an identical pair. They stood in front of Harry. Rob came out and saw the girls showing Harry their feet.

He said, 'I knew it. This is what you do down here

– look at girls. Now, I've worn out two pencils and I'm done for today,' he said, not giving anything else away. 'Let's talk later.'

Liana drove Alice to the station, where she waited for the London train. Harry accompanied them, promising Alice he would get a lot of work done, while thinking about their future. He waved her off, before Liana dropped him at the pub, where Rob was waiting. Harry would get the money question settled immediately, text Alice and relax for a bit.

In the pub Rob was already in a good position where he could see Julia sitting with friends across the bar. Unlike most of Harry's friends, Rob still felt at ease in pubs where there was nothing to do but drink and talk.

'Thanks for coming down today to see me, Rob,' said Harry. 'I need a further advance, my friend. Cash-wise I'm a bit hemmed in and pressured right now.'

Rob laughed. 'I can't organise another payment until it looks like you might not only complete this but make it original. What work are you actually doing?'

'I'm interviewing and planning. But most of it is in my head.'

Rob shook his head. 'I'm fighting hard to keep you in place here. Mamoon thought you'd run up an innocuous *Reader's Digest* life to increase his standing. He didn't understand that not only would you be wearing his pants on your face, you'd tell him about it.

I might come to regret hiring you.'

'Looks like you made a mistake.'

'Anything to do with art is always a risk.'

'But you over-idealise artists, Rob. There are more interesting and useful people.'

'That is a blasphemy.'

'I'm working well, but you're undermining me. I feel pretty disturbed by this. Look at my shaking hands.'

'Don't drop the drink you're going to be kind enough to get me. You know I never carry any change.' Harry got up. Rob said, 'By the way, can you do me a favour while you're at it? Please ask that girl—'

He pointed across the bar.

'Julia?' said Harry.

'Ask her if she'd copulate with me later. I put it crudely to save time. Rustle up some smoother words, word-wanker.'

'Where should she go for the aforementioned copulation?'

'How about on a coat thrown down on a moonlit field? Being in the country makes me come over bucolic. But it might be draughty. How about your luxurious car?'

Harry said, 'Consider, Rob, think for a moment how you might appear to her, not having shaved or washed for some time—'

Rob grabbed his collar. 'What are you talking about?

It's like Iceland here, they haven't seen an outsider for decades. They queue up to fuck Londoners.'

But Julia had left and Rob was delayed by his drinking. Harry listened to him for too long about interesting events in the world of literature before saying he was going back to the house. He needed to phone Alice and talk calmly. She'd be at home by now; sometimes she could be kind and would listen to him.

It was arduous getting Rob to his feet. Having been consuming duff speed to enable himself to drink for longer, by now his brain appeared to have been drowned, like a Ferrari driven into a pond.

Harry was helping Rob along the lane when Scott and some mates, with their heads covered, stepped out in front of them. Harry and Rob stopped. Scott was in shorts and, as they were near a rare working street light, Harry was able to notice that he had a grey police tag around his ankle.

'You went too far. You banged my sister and stole my stuff,' said Scott. 'You laughed at me. What's all that about?'

'Who is this?' said Rob to Harry, in a low voice.

'The brother of the girl you were going to fuck.'

'Ah,' said Rob, leaning forward to vomit.

'What stuff?' said Harry to Scott.

Scott and his mates made a move towards Harry and Rob. Harry fancied giving the little shit a slap; he thought it would help the kid see straight. But Rob was swaying and the boys probably had knives; Harry wouldn't be able to take the three of them on. Anyway, his legs were trembling.

Scott was swinging a piece of wood. 'I'd love to kill a nigger tonight. I'm in the mood for a dune coon. Failing that – there's you.'

'Look here, chaps,' said Rob. He took another step forward and dropped his phone, which one of the thugs stamped on.

Harry said to Scott, 'I can't imagine you'd have anything I'd want to steal.'

'Them drugs. In our Julia's room. You think you can come down from London and take our stuff?'

Harry put his hand in his pocket and offered a couple of twenties to Scott. 'How much?'

Scott spat on the ground and rubbed his trainer in it. 'I'm going to remember that you are a stupid boy.'

In the car Rob said, 'No chance with the girl then? You're well embedded down here. It's racy, innit? I haven't had such a good time for ages. It's not England or Britain, but another place altogether. Ingerland they call it, and Ingerland it is.' Rob sang, '*Ingerland, Ingerland, Ingerland . . .*' all the way to Prospects House.

TWENTY-FOUR

Everything good in art came from seeing a new thing and saying it, Harry said to himself. So when it came to the book, what mattered most was that *he* liked it. And despite the fact the world seemed be exploding in his face, with everything suddenly shifting and moving in ways he couldn't comprehend, Harry knew that to write he needed time and regularity. He worked all day and, at the end of each afternoon, had taken to running in the woods, illuminating his way, when it got gloomy under the heavy trees, with the light of a miner's helmet Julia had found in a market.

By the late evening, Harry was glad to get out of the house. He'd meet Julia at the top of the track. Smiling, she'd rush out from the woods, jump into his car, and they'd go for a drink – she knew all the local high spots. She liked it if, after, he accompanied her to her bedroom. Increasingly under siege from her mother and the agitated suitors, she would ask him to read to her, or to play her guitar while she sang.

Having issued a severe warning, Rob had gone, flinging his rags into his suitcase and taking off like a Romantic poet, striding through forests and across fields, through streams, across car parks and into pubs. He seemed to believe he would gain knowledge of the countryside if made to suffer by it. To celebrate Rob's departure, Harry thought he'd take Julia out for an Indian. 'What do you say to that?'

She had to say she was pleased about the on-the-way children. She knew her place, shut her mouth and accepted what she was offered. Her family had always been on the wrong side, too. She was, however, slightly bemused by the dinner. Why pay for something when you could have a tuna sandwich and Coke at home? The last time she and Harry had gone out 'formally', they'd taken an E each and gone bowling at a floodlit centre called the Hollywood Bowl, just out of town, where there was a mega-cinema, drive-thru McDonald's and KFC. The evening had been fluorescent, glittering, like a cartoon.

But drugs were fatuous, he found, as he got older. This time they would talk – about what, he had no idea. Why would he worry? If love is loquacity, in bed they liked to discuss her body and its vicissitudes, as well as her weight and hair colour; and, he had to admit, he learned more about present-day England from her than he did from anyone else. In bed, while he thought about the book, she would ask questions, not wanting to waste the resource she had beside her.

'Friendly Harry,' she would say, 'how many prime

ministers have there been since the war? And who was the best? Which is the most interesting newspaper and why? What do you think of Canary Wharf? Will you take me there? Who was Muhammad Ali? Why are men unfaithful to their wives? Will you dump me?'

What tormented her now, she told him, was that he was like a circus which came to town for a while, and then went away. 'When you and Alice go, I'm scared of being left behind. Mum's getting worse. More men come to the house. I'm always in her way. She says I put people off loving her.'

But Julia loved Harry, and there *was* something she wanted to give him, a special treat to remember in exchange for the kindness he had shown her. And, as she said, 'It isn't every day your lover's girlfriend gets pregnant.'

And so, that evening, when they walked into the Indian restaurant where Mamoon had had his party, a girl stepped out from behind a screen. Julia had arranged for a friend to join them. Prettier than Julia, like her she wore eye shadow, lip gloss and platform shoes, as if they were going out to meet footballers. 'This is Lucy,' she said, as the girl went to kiss him. 'We both congratulate you.'

Lucy gave them each some MDMA, and took them to a club where an obese woman vomited over the floor. Julia suggested they go somewhere else – not Julia's, as her brother could be there, no doubt tattooing himself on the forehead with a penknife; and not Lucy's, because of her child. The girls were keen for him to take them to a hotel in town. They bought alcohol and cocaine, closed the curtains, turned off their phones and didn't emerge until the next afternoon.

However, some time in the late morning, while the girls slept on either side of him, Harry, who didn't sleep at all, recalled something Mamoon had said with regard to Marion. 'The truth is, everything we really desire is either forbidden, immoral or unhealthy, and, if you're lucky, all three at once.'

'What follows from that, sir?'

'Don't forsake your desire, even if you're punished. Take the punishment gracefully, as a tribute, and never complain.'

In the afternoon, he and Lucy stood outside the hotel, waiting for Julia, who had misplaced her bra in the room. Lucy kissed him; he held her tight.

'Three's always a party,' she said.

'You are irresistible, Lucy,' he said. 'Last night was so much fun I can only contemplate an eternity of regret and self-recrimination.'

'For not having a laugh more often?'

He fumbled in his pockets. 'Here. Perhaps the closing of the abattoir ruined your life too.'

He gave her almost £100 and she handed it back,

saying, 'You'll need it to buy clothes for the babies. Your partner, Alice, she's having two, isn't she?'

'Yes. Twins.'

'When did you find out?'

'At the scan the other day, the nurse said, "There's your baby – oh, and there's another one. Looks like you've got two there."'

'You'll cope,' she said, putting her phone number in his phone. 'You're a joker, and you're never happier than when you're with a woman. It's like you want to suck us right up. Didn't your mother have twins?'

Usually he said as little as he could get away with. Like his father, he wanted to be a listener: it seemed safer. But the drugs had undone his tongue and condemned him to the truth, at last. When Julia came out and joined them, he found himself telling them that his older brothers were identical twins, and his mother had been a paranoid psychotic. Distracted by voices, she had gone to the river and drowned herself.

' "Fear death by water," the Tarot says. She haunts me, and I think of her floating, like Ophelia.'

'How bloody awful,' said Julia, kissing him.

'It's the easiest death – you can be gone in thirty seconds if you keep your mouth open.' He added, 'What is the desire for death the desire for? Wasn't my mother always going in that direction? We three boys, who would have maddened a stone, were lucky to have her for as long as we did. I'd say she was too obedient.'

'To what?'

'I guess to one fascist voice speaking in her head. Far from being too mad, as some people said, she was too orthodox.'

Lucy banged Harry on the arm. 'Julia told me you're weird.'

'If I've been granted a flicker of madness, I'll be sure to take care of it.'

'She said at breakfast you were making a list of people with a parent who killed themselves.'

'And of those who are drawn to suicides. All Hitler's women – I think there were seven – killed themselves. It is a very particular sort of death to live with. The worst thing that could happen has already happened. I've been wondering what sort of psychology it makes.' He said that if you have a parent who kills themself, you never lose the fear that everything you most loved could be taken from you. 'This morning, as you beauties slept, it occurred to me that I should attempt a small book about suiciders and those who love them. I'll talk to Dad about my mother, meet her friends and the writers she was supposedly fond of. Be *her* biographer.'

When Harry's car rolled up at the house, Julia's brother Scott came out into the front yard and stood there, looking at Harry sitting in his car, the two girls silent and watchful.

Julia whispered, 'He's protective, but he knows what you mean to me.'

Harry lowered the window. 'Good afternoon.'

'All well?' said the brother.

He made a gesture at the girls and they scuttled inside the house. Scott stood in front of the car. Harry went to seal the window once more, but couldn't manage it.

'You have a good one?' Scott asked again, without raising his voice, but unable to resist a little gob on the ground.

'Yes, thanks,' said Harry. He thought he might reverse away fast, but wondered if that might seem impolite. The two of them looked at one another until at last the brother stood aside.

TWENTY-FIVE

'Is there something seriously wrong?' Mamoon said. 'Why are you humming a cheerful tune?'

'Could I pour honey on your yogurt?'

'It would be the first time, but thank you, Harry,' said Mamoon, sitting down at the kitchen table and smiling at the younger man. 'What is the source of your good cheer, my biographfiend friend? Is it because you have discovered I am a homosexual with several love children – thus ensuring you have the scandalous bestseller you require to secure your coming career as a television presenter?'

'I will go for a long walk and contemplate your life, before returning to London to write it all down in as filthy a fashion as I can, with Alice by my side.'

'Thank God I will never read it. And Liana and I shall have some peace at last.'

Julia rushed into the house and flung a large bag onto the floor, followed by another. 'Sorry, had to wait for my brother to give me a lift.' And indeed Harry could see the scowling sibling through the window, before he took off. She said, 'Are you ready? Shall I put my bags in your car?'

'Sorry?'

'I'm coming with you,' she said. 'To London. Didn't Alice tell you?'

'No.'

'She's big and tired now, and I'm going to help her clear out the flat and get you into the new place you're renting. You'll be writing; she says you won't lift a finger and she can't do it herself. Be sweet, Harry. Don't worry, no one will say anything. We get along. We'll have the time of our lives.'

The last time Harry and Julia had gone together, in the fields a few days before, Julia had once more begged Harry to take her away with him. It had to be now, she said; there was not one thing left for her here. Liana was cruel, and Ruth was wild with hatred for herself and everyone around her. She had never liked Julia, and wanted her to leave the house: Julia's 'disapproving' stares were dragging her down, and repelling her boyfriends. Likewise, Julia's spirit was deteriorating; she dreamed people were trying to kill her; she was afraid to go to sleep. 'I'm a blink away from being a cleaner,' she said. 'I'll always work, Harry, I'll never be a burden to you.'

Harry said it was impossible; she didn't know London, which was too fast, big and expensive for her. How would she survive? To her credit, she'd taken no notice.

'What's going on? Is everyone leaving?' said Liana, sweeping in, in her dressing gown.

'Yes.'

'Even you, Julia, surely not? What about the ironing? Who gave you the right?'

'I went and punched my own ticket this morning, Liana. Mum's upstairs, doing the bedrooms. She'll cover for me.'

'No, sorry, won't allow it.' Liana wailed, 'Alice isn't here – both my daughters have left! The place will seem stone cold and silent, and I love the voices and cooking and activity! Mamoon, what will I do?'

'Liana, what do you usually do here?'

'I look after you. I'm a carer.'

'Yes, you're a wife.'

'But are *you* a husband?'

'Now look here, Liana, if you've woken up in one of your moods, you can jolly well go back to bed, after you've made my coffee and brought me two boiled eggs, please.'

'Mamoon, you need to ask yourself some serious questions. All that time alone in your study hasn't been good for your sanity. You've even been singing to yourself in your sleep.'

'Singing? In my study I am working – and only for you. Who in reality puts this damn food on the table?'

'All you're doing is pleasuring yourself, Mamoon.'

'You say that now, after all this time, when you know quite well that it is what I do, who I am—'

'But I am getting tired of that, *habibi*, I need something more as a woman. Both the girls have gone towards more life! Please – let's jump in Harry's car and go with them! Let's run away!'

At first these disputes had made Harry anxious, and he wanted them to be over. Now they were just another country noise. He left them to it and took a calming turn around the orchard, though he believed he could even hear their voices from there. But, more importantly, as he walked out of the door, he'd turned for a moment. While Liana, standing at the sink with her arms crossed, continued to berate Mamoon from a distance, he saw Julia go to him and kiss him just once respectfully on the cheek. For a moment he held her elbows, and his eyes seemed to be wet. It was the only time Harry had seen them touch.

He and Julia drove away up the track, and he thought he'd never return to the house. In the mirror he watched Liana waving, gesticulating and covering her face; he believed she would cry all day. Something had altered in her, and there was a black shadow around her aura.

'How am I looking?' said Julia.

'Alice cut your hair well. And you've been working hard on your body.'

'I like you to admire my breasts. I can't bear for us not to be skin to skin.'

He said, 'I saw Ruth watching us go from the upstairs

window. She didn't wave. Is she pleased for you?'

'She knows I can't stay here.'

'Will she talk to me about Mamoon?'

'I don't know.' She said, 'The notebooks I brought for you. The ones by Mamoon about us as a family with him.'

'Yes—'

'Were they of use?'

He said, 'Put the Little Richard song on.'

'Which one?'

'"I'm in Love Again". It's my favourite.'

They were bouncing their heads. He looked at her. 'Perhaps we could stop on the way. A snog and a feel on the hard shoulder, followed by a quick lunch in the Little Chef?'

'You know how to show a girl a good time.'

He said, 'The notebooks really were of use, Julia. They opened it up. You did me a favour there.'

She said, 'I'm still not happy.'

'Why?'

'You don't pull my hair or whoop me hard enough.'

'I'm a softie, you know that. I love you too much.'

'Thank you. I was dying,' she said. 'I would have died there. Now you'll never get rid of me.'

'No,' he said. 'Somehow I think you're right.'

TWENTY-SIX

'Ah-ha!' said Rob.

Harry was sitting in his almost empty study, hunched over a desk, when Rob appeared at the door like a genie, somehow having sneaked into the new house.

'I like your fresh look, Harry: the short hair suits you. It's given you a new brutality and determination. And I like the new place. Can I move in?'

Harry had sold his flat and paid Alice's debts; the couple were now renting a house from a friend who was away. It was large, but closer to Acton than anyone would want to be. Eventually he and Alice would have to make more suitable arrangements, but Harry couldn't see how they would be able to do it. He was far into it, but hadn't finished the book. His present circumstances were confusing and disorienting. He believed all he could do was continue to work.

'It's a relief to have caught you at your desk,' said Rob. 'I came straight here after discussing you this morning. My poor colleague Lotte, now recovering, told me that a couple of months ago, after running into you, she invited you over. I was impressed by the transport detail.'

Harry whispered urgently, 'Keep it down – the women are in the house preparing for the birth of my bloody children. What transport detail?'

'After a party, she was kind enough to invite you in. But, Lotte noticed, you kept a taxi waiting outside, so you could make a quick escape. That hurt her.'

'She was living in Queen's Park.'

'And you cruelly blamed her for that?'

'I only went that distance because she'd been wearing a yellow dress I loved. She wanted me to see her breasts, and wore a perfume I liked. I have the ability to attribute supernatural qualities to unremarkable women.'

'She is not unremarkable, but one of the best when it comes to intelligence and beauty, with the legs of Venus. This might surprise you, but you make her laugh and think like no one else. But Mamoon's been ringing her, and is now hassling me, insisting on seeing you.'

Harry laughed. 'When I left three weeks ago he was opening champagne and cheering.'

'Please go and talk to him tonight.'

'Psychologically I'm on the edge. And I'm in the middle of a paragraph about his mother.'

'Tomorrow morning?'

'Does he have something specific to say to me?'

Rob said, 'It's been harrowing. He's been having awful death dreams. He has beautiful gifts for both of you, and he wants to talk honestly.'

'It would be the first time.' Harry said, 'If it's important, and there's some material he has, I can drive down in a few days.'

'He needs both of you to go. Alice in particular.'

'Why?'

'Mamoon says the country is a sedative for her agitated temperament, the only place she relaxes. Learn to give a woman what she needs. Look at me – I have no one, and it's dark and desolate at night, when I blub alone.'

Harry looked hard at Rob. 'Alice is busy expecting twins.'

Rob said, 'You're not grasping the gravity, dude. Liana has also been ringing me – Miss Lonelyhearts here – to say Mamoon's becoming savage.'

'How?'

'He pulled her hair. She scratched him. She screamed in his face. He even wept in despair.'

'They deserve each other.'

'I'm not sure they do.'

'Sorry?'

Rob sat on Harry's papers on the desk, took Harry's hands, caressed them and then put them to his lips and kissed them. No one in publishing had done this to him before.

'Beautiful man, Mamoon has always been concerned with the almost impossible task of using real words to describe invisible things. You and I know that language is the only enchantment. Alternative magic – spells, crystals, lamp-rubbing – is a lovely futility. Now Mamoon has developed an old-man crush on Alice. Unlike his wife, she hears him, and he her. He's never touched her, you know that. She is the tasty bait.'

'Why don't I lift you up with my little finger and hurl you through the window?'

'Instead, think of everything he might spit out while he's biting on her. Notice how you fail to spot the opportunities here.'

'I'm not yet a pimp.'

Rob picked up handfuls of recent novels, flung them against the wall and cried out, 'You're not even looking at me! But I'm telling you something, Woodworm.'

'Is that what he calls me?'

Rob said, 'I'm here to discuss what you did to one of the world's greatest artists. And the naked flame.'

'Naked flame?'

Rob told Harry that at home a few days ago, Mamoon, having usefully occupied himself examining his own faeces – something older people like to do – and looking forward to a relaxing evening with a new translation of *The Odyssey* and an as yet unwatched DVD of the Australian fast bowlers Lillee and Thomson, heard musical noises, interspersed with yelps. This did not agree with him. How he wished he could have stopped his ears. He called out for help, but Ruth was at her place, halfway through a bottle of her boss's vodka. Clutching his stick, Mamoon opened the door to his library. It might as well have been the door to hell.

For at least a week Liana had been restless. While Mamoon worked, she'd languished in bed, getting up at night to read, send emails, and roam the house. She had begun to sing and dance, talking to herself in Italian, a certain sign of madness, Mamoon believed.

Now he opened the door to find her 'whooshing up': leaping ethereally in a loose white nightgown, her breasts exposed, with a glazed look of blissful happiness on her livid white face, a goddess or a butterfly. When he asked what was going on she was unable to stop, though she did stare briefly at the interrupter, but without recognition.

He moved towards her and noticed between them on the floor a plate of candles. She bent over to pick it up. Her loose hair fell into the flames and suddenly caught ablaze. In a moment she was a human sparkler, a halo of consuming fire around her face. As she danced wildly, the flames spread to papers on the table; the wind blew them onto his favourite Venetian carpet, which also began to burn. A blanket started to smoke. A book began to smoulder.

The old man hobbled to the table, lifted up a huge vase and poured the contents over the poor, hysterical woman, putting her out. He scurried into the kitchen for more water, which he threw across his beloved room – now gradually igniting – before it all went up. He scuttled back and forth, exhausted, weeping, pouring, cursing.

Mamoon held her at last, wrapping her in cool, damp things until her convulsions stopped. She was singed in places, and would have to cut off her hair, but she was not badly hurt. He comforted her, gave her downers and put her to bed. He sat with her, scratching in his notebook on a new piece. For a time she didn't cook or attend to the place. When one of the spaniels caught a duck and killed it on the lawn, she refused to get up to help, and it made Mamoon sick to look at the bloody smears and innards across the grass. Scott had to be called for.

'You know Scott does the dirty work without complaint,' said Rob. In a terrible black rage and depression, Mamoon had made him throw away the burned carpet. 'And, you know what? Scott rescued the carpet. He scraped it off and cleaned it up as well as he could, and said Julia could have it. She will give it to you, and you will keep it on your study wall to remind you of the months you spent falling through the decades, being forced to confront wonders and secrets, until you grew up.'

Mamoon had been having dizzy spells. He'd been falling down. Only Ruth had been picking him up and taking care of him, bringing him food and tea. As Harry might imagine, her corpse-like Mrs Danvers visage horrified him. 'You wouldn't want her coming at you with clippers and cutting *your* toenails, would you?

'Mamoon hates the phone, but he has started calling me. He is frightened that Liana has gone mad, that it will always be his destiny to be trapped in the countryside with a lunatic. It has become a death drive competition: which of them, remaining sane, will send the other one mad first. They provoke and curse one another continuously. So: good morning, Harry. This is where you come in.' Harry asked if it was his fault. It was. 'Yes, Liana has been mumbling about your influence. She hasn't quite given the game away. But Mamoon has become convinced you've put a spell on her.'

'How would I do that?'

'I know exactly how. That stuff you gave her. Those fragments of utopia: the magic mushrooms and other things. Are you going to deny it?'

Harry put his hand to his face. 'Oh Jesus, Rob.'

'The woman has been bombed out of her skull. What were you playing at?' Rob shook his head gravely and went on, 'The old man's got something else heavy on you.' Rob leaned forward and whispered right into Harry's ear. 'Can Alice and Julia hear us?'

'How do I know? They're sorting out some clothes. Is there more? Is it worse?'

'It's her: Julia. She's the thing here, and the question of convention – the convention being ridiculous, but it exists, nonetheless.' Harry nodded slowly. 'I see you humbled. It is admirable, of course, from one point of view, that you had the nerve to go with his staff right under his nose. Dangerous, but Mamoon would never let on.'

'Why not?'

'He is fond of you. But never push him. You don't want anyone blabbing across the literary world that you behaved like a beast in his house.'

'Rob, I swear, I crept about like a ghost.'

'Ha ha – when you weren't depressed, you were baiting him, cunt-teasing and provoking his wife. You even turned her against him. You screwed his staff while consuming large amounts of his booze, eating his wife's food, stealing his notebooks, slapping him around the head, and accusing him of being a sadomasochist. What is ghostlike about that? You'll be discredited, you'll never get a job anywhere. You might have to give him something – see?'

There was a silence. Rob seemed to believe understanding was coming to Harry like the slow but inevitable action of a tranquilliser; and, while it enveloped Harry and smoked his brain, Rob stroked his author's arm.

'Good boy,' said Rob. 'Think, think. Think hard.

You're my sweetie.'

Alice came in holding her phone. She went to Rob and kissed him. 'Liana has been texting me. Mamoon even rang and said he's been making preparations.'

'For what?' said Harry.

'Our arrival. It would be lovely to go down in the morning. I miss the openness, the views, and the water. We don't even have to stay the night, if you don't want to.'

'Darling, are you absolutely sure you want to?'

'You said there was still one person you hadn't spoken to for the book. And you know my conversations with Mamoon give me strength.'

Harry looked at Rob and sighed. 'Okay,' he said. 'We'll be there.'

'You won't regret it,' said Rob. 'You're not quite done yet.'

'No,' said Harry. 'It doesn't look like it.'

TWENTY-SEVEN

They arrived in the morning, dropping Julia off at her mother's on the way.

Harry had wondered if Liana did really want them there. But when they walked in they saw that she had gone to some trouble to make a fine early lunch of seafood pasta and avocado and mozzarella salad. As always, the table looked welcoming. Liana ran out and embraced them.

The conversation was cheerful and diverting; Mamoon was witty, but he only discussed what he'd been watching on TV. After, while Mamoon and Alice continued to sit in their places, discussing their all-time top five favourite puddings, as well as the places and circumstances in which they had consumed them, Mamoon said he had left a 'special gift' upstairs for Harry. 'Go: you'll be pleased. Keep it,' said Mamoon.

Harry went upstairs to continue with his work, and found his gift on the bed, in a folder: a four-page handwritten early short story of Mamoon's. Not long afterwards, having removed her wig, Liana came to the door wearing a Nepalese woollen hat to cover her singed hair, and asked if she could sit with him.

Unusually, she didn't chatter or boast, but put out her tongue.

'Look at the purple colour of that! Have you seen the circles of hell under my eyes? You heard I caught fire, didn't you?'

Liana had been in astral torment, traipsing about all night like the miserable undead, with her skin shrinking and her bones aching. She had been satisfying herself too much, four times a day on occasion. She had worn away her finger tip in those soft folds, and thought she might rub herself out. But it was hopeless. 'The world is flying around and around in my mind. What can I do to stop it? Even Mamoon insisted you come back. It is the only thing we have agreed on lately.'

'Why did he want us here?'

'To smash our isolation.' She put her head on Harry's shoulder. 'Won't you walk with me? Despite all your trickery and determination, I've always believed you've a kind heart and love women. You listened to me for free.'

She was keen to show him how the walled garden was developing, and eager to have him see the carp and goldfish in the pond. She insisted on taking him behind the barns and via the swimming pool, which they had opened properly at last. It was early autumn, but it had been unseasonably warm, and the day was spectacular.

'I expect we'll find Mamoon there,' she said. 'You

know, though he has hurt me more than anyone else, I still love to turn a corner and see him.'

'I thought he rarely went into that part of the garden.'

'I can't tell you how strangely he's been behaving.'

Mamoon had become interested in their pool. Uncharacteristically, he had even forfeited a day's work to oversee and scrutinise its cleaning by Ruth and Scott, ensuring that it was heated to a temperature he approved of, not something Mamoon would normally attend to himself. Even more unusually, Scott had been ordered to drive Mamoon into town to buy food and wine, as well as garden furniture, loungers and towels, Mamoon insisting that Scott get them to the house immediately. Liana was cheered by this, wondering if Mamoon was beginning to forget the burden of his work.

As they walked, Harry and Liana saw bare-chested Scott with a fishing net, dragging leaves from the pool. Beyond him was the increasingly large figure of Alice, in sunglasses, white bra and pants – she was admirably reckless like that – lowering herself into the water.

Mamoon sat close by, clapping his hands, encouraging her to go in. 'Is it correct temperature?' he was saying. 'Surely it is! Go down! Good. Lower. That's it . . .'

He stood up to watch her swim a couple of slow, elegant lengths.

'Well, well,' said Harry to Liana. 'Thank God Mamoon

is using the pool at last.' Liana asked what he thought they talked about. 'Many artists have had a muse,' he said, 'and with Alice he's found sensuality, inspiration and a pin-up. He hears her dreams and talks about them in relation to her history. She tells him what trousers suit him.'

'He listens to her dreams, you say?'

'Doesn't he listen to yours? In his spare time he's become something of an oneiromancer now. He learned that a dream can make or break a day.'

'He shoos me away.'

Harry pointed towards them. 'He's not shooing *her* away. It looks like Mamoon's ready for the Olympics, the way he dashes to fetch that towel, a frenzied old man hurrying to catch the last bus. "Forever panting", as Keats puts it.' Harry went on, 'But I don't actually believe he'll seduce Alice. He's too nervous. He just wants to pore over her.'

'But why, why?'

When Alice emerged from the water, she appeared to be naked. Mamoon stood completely still, with a towel over his arm.

Harry said, 'Mamoon did say to me, wisely, I believe – and this is advice I've taken to heart – that a man would be a fool to think he had to make love to any woman he fancied.'

Harry went to Alice, shivering on a lounger, wrapped

in a towel, and kissed her on the side of the head. He took her hand and sat down next to her. He patted her stomach and addressed his children inside her, 'Hi kids, how you doing? Was it too cold for you in that water? When are you coming to see us? We want you!'

Liana sat with Mamoon and grasped his hand. 'What a wonderful job you have done. The pool must be cold, but it looks tempting, my dear. I will swim. Won't you join me? It would be lovely if we went in together, side by side, and I could see how strong you are. Mamoon, can you hear me, are you fine?' He shook his head vaguely. 'In that case, will you watch me and make sure I don't drown, my love?'

While Liana changed in the nearby hut, Harry said to Mamoon, 'I'm shocked not to see you in your study at this time of the day, sir. Have you finished what you're doing?'

Mamoon looked away. 'I'll never be finished.'

Alice had closed her eyes and was falling asleep. Harry said, 'I love looking at Alice now she's pregnant. She's even more ravishing – her skin, her eyes, her hair just glows.' Mamoon nodded sullenly. 'You once said, sir, and under pertinent circumstances, "Rather a book than a child," didn't you?'

'You invented that.'

'I think I remember reading it in Peggy's diaries,' said Harry.

'Why did you think such a thing?' Alice said to Mamoon, opening her eyes. 'Did you never want a child, maestro?'

'Don't believe a word you read,' said Mamoon.

'My blood's gone to my feet,' said Alice. 'I feel quite faint. I thought I had more puff. The children are already taking my life.'

Harry stroked Alice's hair. 'Books are traps: rather a child than a thousand libraries. Stories are merely a substitute.'

'For what?' said Mamoon.

He kissed Alice. 'The real thing. The woman.' He looked up. 'Ah, here comes Liana, doesn't she look beautiful in her bathing costume?' He stood up, helped Alice to her feet, and led her away with his arm around her. 'Come on, let's go inside and lie down together before you turn blue. I think it might rain. And Mamoon wants to be with Liana.'

'Mamoon,' called Liana. 'Take my arm, darling, and help me drown – sorry, I mean down into the water. Where are you, my dear husband?'

'See you later, we're leaving you to it,' shouted Harry.

TWENTY-EIGHT

Harry stood in the yard in the rain holding a box. He had the feeling someone was watching him, but what did it matter?

Ruth had come to the house to clear up after lunch, bringing Julia with her to help Harry empty his room. While Julia attempted to sort and order the papers and books Harry had neglected to take the last time they left, Harry carried the stuff out to the car. Lingering there in the yard a moment, something made him go to look over some quotes and take a final peep.

Mamoon had often dismissed and evaded Peggy, particularly around the time of the abortion, not long after they moved into the house. It was then, apparently, that he had said, 'Rather a book than a baby.' For Harry, Peggy's version of Mamoon's early history was authoritative and believable, and the material at the end, when she begged Mamoon, 'If only my dear husband would relent and think to bring me some pages to edit, he knows for me this is the most important thing, our only connection now,' when he had sat at her bedside with his head in his hands in awful silence, was unbearable. The ghost is always the one not admitted. As Harry flicked through the diaries and believed he could hear Peggy crying out to him, he assured her he would tell her story – whatever it was – as well as he could, alongside Mamoon's.

'Harry!' Mamoon was standing at the kitchen door when Harry returned to the house. Mamoon removed the headphones he had now taken to wearing, through which he played music sent by Alice. 'What are you doing in there? Looking at Peggy again? You'd better be done with that,' he said. 'It's all going to the university this week. I should have stuffed it in the grate. Ted Hughes, whom I knew and loved, had the right idea with Sylvia's diaries – push them in the oven after the woman's head. Otherwise those unreadable academics never stop trying to make their careers and a good income out of it, while making the man look like an ogre. They see it as they wish, without imagination. And it is ordinary male sexuality that they hate.'

'If we're talking honestly, as you wanted,' said Harry, 'would you say there's some regret there?'

'Far from being merciless, I was too loyal and dutiful. What do you do with dead desire? I had none for her, and her desire was to suffer. The sensible thing would have been to scarper sharpish.'

'Is that the rule you recommend, sir? When you no longer desire someone, you leave them? I am thinking of *Don Giovanni* here. One's emotional life would be a revolving door.'

'That is one of your caricatures. You do not grasp the truth or difficulty of the thing.'

'But what about guilt?'

'Guilt exists, you damned fool, and has to be nego-tiated and confronted. But who could it possibly serve to live with the corpse of a dead love? It is hard work, betraying others in order not to betray oneself. Perhaps you would be trying to convince the person that they are still desirable. And meanwhile one turns oneself into Proust's poor myopic Swann, who degrades him-self by opening Odette's mail, spies on her house and spends every evening at the awful Verdurins'. Jealousy outlives desire, and Swann uses that ghastly vacant woman to stuff excrement into his own mouth.'

Harry said, 'Can I ask, sir, what makes you so sharp? There's an energy in your eyes.'

'You see me. Yes, I am beginning to write well. I want to do something on ageing. Writing's an uncomplicated pleasure and all I'm good for.'

Mamoon had been unhappy a lot of the time; in fact, he had rarely experienced contentment or been entirely cheerful. The world being what it was, only a fool would whistle all day. He didn't think it mattered, except when he made it rough 'for other people'. What Mamoon wanted was to have been creative and to have

301

caused no more harm than necessary, though often harm *was* necessary, like war and murder.

Harry touched his arm. 'You're a lucky man, sir. At the end of your life you found someone who admires and loves you, and who can't wait to see you each morning.'

'Really – who?'

Harry cleared his throat. 'Liana.'

Mamoon began to speak of renewal. He had always written intuitively – one thing developing from another – which was why he found his art difficult to explain. Now he wanted to be more conscious of what he was doing, of how he planned the material. This new approach excited him, which, he believed, guaranteed a thrill in the reader. The short book he had begun writing was, even at his age, a new direction. He had conducted many interviews, but this was different: conversations between generations, an older and a younger person. He hadn't quite got it into focus yet; an essential element of intimacy was missing.

Not that he knew if the public would be interested. The market had changed; these days there were more writers than readers. Everyone was speaking at once while no one heard, as in an asylum. The only books people read were diet books, cookery books or exercise books. People didn't want to improve the world, they only wanted better bodies. 'But I will say my say, and, since it's not done, it will be published after your book on me. I want to outlive you at least in this sense.' At this, Harry looked at his watch. 'But you are restless. Am I keeping you from some other ecstasy?'

'I want to miss the traffic.'

'You're going to London?'

'I think we'll leave in the late afternoon.'

'Why doesn't anyone tell me anything?'

Mamoon concluded the conversation quickly by dismissing Harry with a wave. He shouted for Julia, telling her to take tea to his study immediately and fetch Alice from the garden. They would, he said, be having 'discussions'. Julia told Alice what Mamoon required, and then she went off to visit Lucy.

Briefly, the house was silent. Harry saw it was 'time', and yet he wasn't finished. He looked for Ruth and called her name. He found her, at last, on the top corridor carrying towels. 'Would you talk to me – would you, please?' he said. She put the towels down. She was afraid, as if this was the moment her sins would be exposed. 'About everything,' he went on. 'Can I take you somewhere close by?'

She was pale and put her shaking hands together in a prayer. But she nodded and hurried out of the house before him as if afraid of being caught. He drove her to a nearby tea shop.

Harry prepared his recorder and notes, invited her to

talk about Mamoon, and then, when she said nothing, passed over £50.

'Nobody asked me anything before,' she said. 'I was thinking, how clever *is* this Harry, that he doesn't go to the most obvious person – the one who saw everything.'

'From day one, please,' he said. 'How you met.'

The talking went on until she emerged, skinned. She had nursed Peggy; she had cared for Mamoon in his despair. He had slept with her twice, after she had got into his bed and he hadn't turned her away. 'He couldn't love me,' she said, 'but I had been celibate in terms of pleasure and feeling. But you don't know anything about failure or having nothing.'

Later, the new bride, Liana, landed in the yard. Ruth knew that if she wanted to keep her job she had to seal her mouth and unpack Liana's bags. Ruth knew that women now had careers 'and all that', but she had never been able to rise above her station. She was where she was before, if not worse, and certainly older; the blacks had more opportunities, the Somalis better housing: they were sitting on golden cushions eating caviar with platinum spoons. Nothing had improved for her and her class, and she liked a drink, that was all.

As Harry packed up his notes, she said, 'Will I definitely be in the book?'

'Of course.'

She clapped her hands. 'And you'll put in that he loved me all along?'

'The two of you didn't get anywhere as lovers, Ruth. He left for Europe.'

'Exactly – because I'd been telling him that Peggy might be the sweetest person to talk to, but she had been a vampire for years, drinking his life-blood and giving him complaints and guilt. And some mornings, after she'd died, he had become so dark, I was worried he would go and hang himself in the barn. I believed I'd find him dead. So he went away. And then Liana infiltrated him, and forced him away from us for ever.' She leaned towards Harry and hissed in his ear. 'He regrets it. For me it was, at first, the best time. Those memories are my highlight. He knows he could have been happy with just us, the family who adored him. I know he still loves and wants us. Perhaps Liana should have an accident.' Ruth took his hands across the table. 'Will there be pictures? If I find one, of Mamoon and all of us together in the garden, so happy, will you promise to put it in? Will Liana try to stop it?'

'Let me see it,' he said.

Alice texted to suggest that she and Harry might stay one more night, since she didn't want to drive back in the storm which had been predicted. Harry wasn't keen, but didn't think it would be a problem as long as he could begin to write up the Ruth material. He drove

Ruth home; she was weeping and he helped her inside, to Scott. 'You've emptied me,' she cried. 'I lost my battles with life, didn't I? Who will look after me in my old age?'

When Harry got out of the car in the yard, he stood still for a moment. He heard a raised voice: Liana's. Mamoon's reply followed, and there was fury in his harsh tone. Harry became sure a number of things were being smashed. He hurried across and found that, un-usually, Mamoon's door was open, and Alice seemed to have backed out into the rain with her hand over her mouth.

Inside, Liana was standing at Mamoon's desk. She had already swept from it soiled wine glasses, cups full of pens, CDs and newspapers, while strongly informing Mamoon that he was a bastard and a son of a bitch.

Mamoon said, 'You're killing me with this destruct-iveness!'

'You seem strong enough to entertain a girl in there!'

'Entertainment? We are talking about important matters for my work, and for her life.'

Liana picked up the stick with the rabbit head and approached him with it. 'Why don't I take your stick and tap out some nice words on your forehead? I could hear you from the kitchen laughing together – while I make your favourite spicy parsnip soup! You disappear to be an artist, and leave me alone all day! You absolutely forbid me to enter the room. Then you let her in.'

'She is like a daughter to me – to both of us! You know that perfectly well.'

'You filthy man, what's wrong with me, why can't I be your daughter? And then you condemn me for talking to Harry!'

'I do?'

'You accuse me of flirting like a fishwife and plumping up my breasts pneumatically! And then, finally, you deliberately and cruelly deny me the thing I want most in the world!'

'What, Liana, please, you know I'll do anything for you!'

'A place in Chelsea! You're too mean to spend the money.'

'Don't raise my blood pressure or I'll slap your fat face, you ignorant bitch, and knock your aura right into the gutter.'

'You're not man enough.'

'Get out!'

'What did you say?'

'No, no, Liana, sorry, you know that though I find you irritating, I love you,' he said, putting out his arms and stretching across the desk towards her.

'If you love me,' she said, moving away from him, 'you will agree to the following. I was dancing with Alice to Abba in the barn a few weeks ago. Julia was the

DJ. We were in something of a stupor. I had a flash of inspiration. I'm going to write a self-help book.'

Mamoon looked startled, but, in the circumstances, could only continue to listen.

She said, 'It'll be about me, my story.'

'What exactly is your story?'

'Don't you know?' When he shook his head, she leaned across the desk. 'An attractive, feisty woman captures the heart of an artistic powerhouse, revives his career while dealing with his impossible ego, and helps turn him into a monument while running a country estate.'

He said, 'The story you describe is a miracle, and its heroine clearly a parasite. Where is the self-help in that?'

'It will include good advice on how to seduce a man and get him to marry you.'

'It's true, you have mainly used me for money,' he said.

'I wish I had,' she said. 'It was what people advised me to do.' Liana turned to Harry. 'Didn't you say the book was a brilliant start, Harry, when I showed it to you a couple of weeks ago?'

'Well, yes, but I only glanced through it, Liana—' Harry began.

Mamoon said, 'Is it true that your filthy stain extends even this far?'

308

Liana said, 'You depress me, Mamoon. What really is the point of you?' She was looking at his desk, as was Harry, who noticed a journal held open by a couple of beach stones. Next to it were some white pages with Mamoon's scrawl across them. 'Give me that diary to read,' she said. 'We'll go through it together. We don't have secrets, do we?'

He snorted with laughter. But not for long. Liana picked up a full cup of the tea which Julia brought Mamoon continuously throughout the day, and tipped some of it over the journal, and the rest over the other writing. They watched the writer's words suddenly dissolve and disappear into a puddle on the desk, dripping onto the floor.

Liana leaned her hip against his desk, and tried to shove it to one side. 'I am not your fan, and I don't want to be just a sucking and shopping spouse! I am moving in here, beside you. You can advise me on the finest words.'

Mamoon said, 'It's laughable, us side by side like school children. I will never come in here again.'

'Wherever you are, I will be next to you.'

'Then I will kill myself.'

She laughed wildly. 'You lack the courage.'

'To get away from you, I will do it.'

She picked up a rock he used as a paperweight. 'Why don't I insert this into the middle of your face?'

She even threw it, and not limply; he put up his hand and it bounced away. If he hadn't laughed, she wouldn't have taken a step forward and struck him across the face. One of her rings must have caught him, because suddenly there was a line of blood and his cry, when he realised he'd been slashed.

She had done it and gone, running out of the barn towards the house. Mamoon hobbled out behind her, his handkerchief at his face, with Alice and Harry behind him.

Inside, Liana flew upstairs, shouting, 'Leave me alone, you deceivers! If any of you follow me I will kill myself!'

TWENTY-NINE

In the kitchen Alice led Mamoon to the sink. She staunched his bleeding cheek, cleaned the wound and applied a plaster. Harry put the kettle on and made tea. He tried to catch Alice's eye to indicate that this might be a good opportunity to leave, but he guessed they wouldn't be able to get out until this dispute was settled.

Mamoon was upset, but not devastated; he had seen this before. Later, he would open a bottle of champagne for Liana. All would be well. Glancing at the notebook which Harry always carried with him, he said, 'I hope you're not writing this down in bad English to make us look like mad people.'

'Maestro, I'll make sure he won't,' said Alice.

Mamoon said, 'I'm sorry that Liana somehow blames you for this.'

'She does?' said Alice. 'Is it really my fault? Harry, please tell me if it is.'

Liana came down, carrying a suitcase. 'I am wearing my necklace of skulls – a piece I hate. But I slam the door and goodbye! Alice, please hold onto the dogs.'

Mamoon hurried across and took her arm. 'Liana, I beg you, this has gone too far.'

'Yes, who will change the batteries in your tooth-brush? Who will rub cream into your injured foot and give you your pills? You will die here alone. Do you really believe these young exploiters care for you?' She pulled the case towards the door. 'I will go to those who love and appreciate me.'

'Like who?'

'You can take Alice, you old fool, but you're too stu-pid to see how she used you!'

'What nonsense!'

'Harry sent her to persuade you to confess to things with Marion that you never did – I heard it from Rob.'

'You didn't do that, Alice?' Mamoon said, in incom-prehension.

'In a way I did,' she said.

'Dear girl, I cannot think of you like that,' said Mamoon. 'Harry must have been behind it. Don't worry, I'll take him down for that.'

Harry said, 'Why don't you sit, please, Liana, and we can talk this through.'

'Yes,' said Mamoon. 'Please, Marion, I mean Liana, you are working yourself up too much!'

Mamoon tried to pull the suitcase from her, but she pushed him away. He fell against the table, turned, twist-ed and collapsed.

'Oh my God, Mamoon,' said Alice, going towards him. 'Your back's gone!'

'You see, you see!' cried Liana. 'Now give me the car key!'

'Never.'

'I will walk across the fields to the station,' she said, disappearing out of the door and into the rain. 'Good-bye for ever!'

'Don't let her go,' said Mamoon to Harry.

'What can I do?'

'It's dark already. Suppose she falls in the pond and drowns! Fetch her back!'

'*I* will,' said Alice, and out she went.

Harry had to pursue her as she headed for the track up to the road. The rain was heavy and the wind was loud, but Harry could hear her yelling for Liana. It didn't take him long to find Alice. She was his priority. He had to lead her back to the house forcibly, while urging her to be quiet. Yet he could hear nothing of Liana.

Alice was soaked through, and when Harry had brought her in, he found a towel and fetched her warm clothes. Then he went to Mamoon with a blanket. 'Please, just lie down on the sofa and wait. Liana will be back soon.'

Mamoon said, 'If you pick up Liana on your way to London, I will kill you straight away.'

Harry made Mamoon comfortable on the sofa and said, 'Sir, I can tell you she won't want to come with us.'

'She talks about you all the time,' said Alice. 'If she

didn't love you so much, she wouldn't be so worked up. She's trying to give you a fright.'

'I've got one, along with a chill and palpitations.' Alice found Mamoon's painkillers and brought him water. 'This time I really will pass over,' he said. He had started to sob. 'I can't take any more. You won't leave me here like this, will you? Where's Ruth? What will I eat? Who will look after the animals?'

Harry had already phoned Julia, who said she and her family would take care of it. Whatever happened, she did not want Alice and Harry out there; two hysterical and confused townies afraid of the dark wouldn't help anyone. She knew the terrain 'intimately'.

It wasn't the easiest evening in Mamoon's kitchen as Alice, Mamoon and Harry ate, made tea and worried about Liana. Julia, Ruth and Scott were scouting for her with torches, shouts and blankets. They didn't believe she could have got far; she was probably going around in circles. Mamoon refused to allow Harry or Alice to leave him alone, and lay on the sofa staring into the distance, or he closed his eyes and seemed to drift off.

While they were waiting for news, Harry reiterated how competent and reliable Julia was. If anyone could find Liana, it would be her. Alice added that it had been helpful to have her staying with them in London. She wanted to make it a permanent arrangement, and Julia had agreed. Julia would look after them and the babies, for at least the next eighteen months.

Harry was surprised at this; his view was that it would be best if Julia returned to Liana and Mamoon, and the rest of 'her community'. But Alice was firm; she'd heard catastrophic stories about au pairs and nannies. She couldn't see any reason why Julia wasn't suitable. She was willing, good with kids, and they knew her and her family.

He couldn't win; he was fated to live with both of them. Mamoon may have been lying there contemplating eternity, but he wasn't so oblivious he didn't find the time for a micro-smirk.

It was another hour before Liana was located. Her fury had carried her quite far, but at last she had collapsed in a ditch and was found by Scott and Julia moaning and whimpering. She was taken to hospital, where she was checked over by a doctor who decided that since she was exhausted and suffering from minor injuries she should stay the night. Harry drove Alice and Mamoon to visit her. She slept well, and the next afternoon he brought her home, where Alice put her to bed. Mamoon was solicitous, kind and quiet.

The day after, when Alice and Harry were finally leaving, Mamoon was still worrying about whether he would have to share his writing room with Liana, and he kept asking Harry what he should do. He wouldn't be able to work with Liana sitting next to him; it was absurd.

Going to the car, Harry found a film crew in the yard, unpacking their equipment. A German TV station, encouraged by Liana, apparently had an appointment to make a documentary about Mamoon. They said Mamoon had agreed, for a nice fee, to give his opinion on many contemporary subjects he knew nothing about.

'One of them has a clipboard full of questions,' said Mamoon to Harry. 'I fear it will be my martyrdom video. Tell them to get out.'

'Only you can do that,' he said.

'You're just clearing off and leaving us like this?'

'Yes.'

In London, mortified by what she believed she'd brought about, Alice went to bed for two days, wearing a woollen cap. Harry and Julia were deputed to bring her carrot juice and soup, hold her hand and hear her complaints.

'It didn't occur to me that they would be so vulnerable,' Alice said. 'I love them both so much. They've become like parents to me. What should I do? Write or phone to apologise? Oh God, she'll never forgive me . . . Harry, why didn't you warn me? You didn't seem to mind me being with him. Or were you just pleased I could fetch you material? Please, answer me. Will you be speaking to them tonight?'

Harry couldn't answer. He was glad to be away from

Prospects House. He had no wish to see Mamoon or Liana for a while; he would go into a room for at least eighteen months and write his book as he wished. Mamoon would remain Mamoon; Harry neither liked nor disliked him. In Harry's mind he was becoming something else, an invented or made-up man, someone who had lived only so that Harry could write a book about him.

THIRTY

At a literary party, Harry felt flat and not at all like talking. Leaning against a wall, drinking and watching seemed a more agreeable idea, until he saw Lotte. She had been Rob's assistant, had left for a while, travelled and had therapy, before going back to work with Rob, this time as an editor, looking after Mamoon's collected essays. Harry was glad to see her, though he wondered if she might be annoyed with him after the Queen's Park incident. She only laughed and said that Rob had exaggerated. She was glad to see Harry and had nothing arranged for later. Might they have supper together?

After two years of serious writing, Harry had time, indeed whole long nights of time, on his hands. He suspected he might have plenty to say to Lotte now. Having worked harder than he had ever worked before, he had at last stopped, and was waiting for Liana to read and sanction the biography, while wondering whether he'd accept the next job Rob had offered him.

He needed the money. The twins had been an event. They were born prematurely, and one of them almost died, remaining in hospital for a month. Alice and Julia were drained. When Alice did go out, it was with other mothers and au pairs, and the women talked about sleep as addicts talked about dope.

Harry's father had liked being a father, as did Harry's brothers, and Harry found that he took to it. He walked for miles across London, pushing the boys in their huge buggy. As their engine, umbilical and life-support, he existed now, mostly, to serve them, as they became flirts and celebrities, getting presents everywhere they went. He loved his boys' mouths, their flesh, the smell of their hair – which might often conceal pieces of broccoli or corn – as he'd loved those of women.

Alice, whose company he'd quite enjoyed once, a long time ago, was only a tense mother, as if she had gained a burden she'd never be free from. Harry's father, in his louche suit at his London club, and always the optimist, had said with a satirical giggle that Harry would become familiar, as at no other time in his life, with the parks and museums of London, while becoming increasingly unfamiliar with his partner and his friends. There were few lonelinesses like that of the new father, as Harry suddenly found himself in places and with people he would otherwise have avoided. It would, his father suspected, be at least five years before Alice emerged from the orgy of motherhood, and only then with considerable persuasion from Harry. The boys, wailing fascist phalluses in nappies, would be the only little pricks she wanted. He would have to wait, if

319

he had the patience. When, after this advice, Harry was told by his father to plod off, his father slipped him £20, as he always did on these occasions, as if he were paying off a tradesman, murmuring, 'Dear boy, do be sure you have female cover. And do make sure, next time, only to go with women who have had good fathers.' Harry thanked him. His father went on, 'And, otherwise, with a woman, be sure to find out what was done to her, because before long she'll be doing the same to you. Ha ha . . .'

'I wish you'd said that earlier.'

'It only just occurred to me where you were going wrong. Glad to be of help.'

Harry's priority and pride, his other child, had been the book. Working twelve hours a day for months, he had completed a decent draft in a cafe around the corner from where they were still living. After delivering it, Harry found that Rob as editor was arbitrary and sadistic. The manuscript was scribbled over with remarks like, 'This is shit', 'Rubbish' or 'Improve a million times'. At first Harry argued with Rob over the changes and cuts, though the stress was awful; then he gave in, and went along with it, but he felt worse: humiliated and bullied. Alice urged him to change what needed changing, and resist the rest. Harry saw how authors could get a reputation for being difficult.

After shoving Harry head first through a grinder,

Rob pronounced the biography lively and authoritative, predicting it would be a little success. It was sold into several languages and Harry would front a television documentary on Mamoon. The publication date had been provisionally set. Rob had instructed Harry to send the book to both Mamoon and Liana, which was the condition he had agreed. Harry knew that Mamoon wouldn't even have a secret peep, but Liana would read it, and would not want for opinions. Harry believed he could hear her pencil violently scratching from here.

While he'd been waiting, he spent time with Julia, who in her time off had become part of a London Harry didn't know, London as an international city of students, refugees and drifters. Her friends were Brazilian, Angolan, Somali, Indian, and when she took him out, he was introduced to night buses, dark new bars and cheap food, crawling around the city in the early hours. He liked being on a bus at four in the morning, when you could see the city and what a wonder it was. He and Julia had the compatibility of fond ex-lovers, and she continued to be devoted to him; he had never seen such love before, resembling madness in its irrational fidelity.

Lotte took his hand, and whispered, 'I'm going to take you out of this dull party. Don't worry, you'll like it much better where we're going. You need to hear what I'm going to say.'

She took his hand, led him through Berwick Street Market, around a corner into a narrow street, and through a black, broken door into a semi-derelict eighteenth-century house. They went up the carpetless stairs and into a large undecorated, peeling room with a sloping floor. An exhausted book reviewer and a minor poet sat at a wobbly table, served by a woman who might have been painted by Lucian Freud. After Lotte had kissed the staff and the patrons, he and she sat close; he stroked her hair while she poured talk into his ear.

Lotte had driven down for lunch with Mamoon and Liana. Mamoon was still weak and distressed after the serious stroke he'd had three months ago, but his speech had improved. He'd even said, 'Death had been avoiding me, but I know that he wants me now, since I have been receiving Lifetime Achievement awards most days.'

Lotte said, 'I don't think you went to see Mamoon, did you?'

'I had to feel free to make him up.'

'He was, as Rob might have told you, in an uncreative state for a while. He hated being flat on his back, and became even more depressed. Liana got him moving. But there's some excellent news: despite his physical setbacks, he's finished a short new book, his first for a long time. You put an idea in his head.'

Harry said the only thing he remembered was nodding across at Liana in the kitchen once, and saying the novel had always been concerned with marriage, and that perhaps Mamoon had been doing research without knowing it. Mamoon looked almost interested, but of course didn't say anything. 'Is it about that?'

'Don't you know?'

'I've concentrated on the early and middle life. Once he marries Liana they just stay home not having sex and bickering, like everyone else. The literary public won't eat that up.'

Lotte said she wanted to show Harry something. She took him back to the flat she'd recently moved into, near Goodge Street. Most of her things were still packed up and her bed was in the middle of the room. She lit candles. As there was nowhere else to sit, they lay down, in their clothes, drinking brandy.

She asked him what he was doing, and he told her he was making notes to start work on another book, about psychosis and his mother. His father had said Harry's mother was liable to fall for mouth-merchants of all varieties. He'd given Harry letters from one of the writers he'd referred to. Harry had pictured some local Vargas Llosa, but this character was living in a dingy flat in a council block.

'Surrounded by piles of mouldering paper, he was a conman full of swanky talk and a mile of continuous bullshit. He said Mum was an enthusiastic and flexible lover, but she talked too much and couldn't listen. One time she grabbed him by the hair and smacked his face against her knee. She wouldn't let him alone, until he had to cover the windows. He was surprised I turned out so reasonable, and tried to touch me for a few quid. I should have learned, shouldn't I, that biography is a process of disillusionment.'

'What will you do?'

'There have been too many fathers and old men. It is the time for mad mothers. I want to get into women's minds, rather than their bodies. Except for you.'

They drank some more, before she patted a slim manuscript perched on a pile of books. 'This is what we've been talking about. Mamoon's latest.'

She put it in his hand. He looked at it and noted the title, *A Last Passion*, and then handed it back. He was tired of Mamoon. He asked her to whisper him the story, briefly.

'Are you sure?'

He said, 'He kept saying I was nothing. He wanted me to feel like nothing. He mocked and almost destroyed me. There were times when I thought I'd lose my mind. Then I had two babies, and I couldn't get out of bed for weeks. I thought something was going to fall on me, and I had a stomach and bowel infection. My mother and Peggy as ghosts wouldn't stop talking.

I could have murdered the world. Our help Julia was kindness itself. Dad fixed me up with a therapist.'

'Where was Alice?'

'She just drifted away, leaving the kids with Julia so she could visit friends. Otherwise she'd go to bed early with a headache and shut the door behind her. She had better things to think about than me. Since I'm a kid who brought himself up, I did the same again. I forced myself to get out of bed, and wrote Mamoon out of me. Pass the brandy: I'm free of him, Lotte. Cheers!'

'I wouldn't go that far.' She was looking at him. 'The new book is unusual for Mamoon. It concerns a young admirer who comes to stay with an older man, a writer, and begins to write a book about him. So, the old writer secretly writes about the younger man as the younger one writes about him. Unusually for Mamoon, it's pretty funny. It's a love story.'

'What does the old guy say about the young guy?'

'Harry, it mostly concerns the older man's love for a younger woman, the hot-but-cold, vanilla-haired wife of the acolyte, whom he describes as having the stillness of a Modigliani. Displaying at least five of the eight fatal symptoms of love, he adores and mythologises her, as one does.'

Harry told her Lotte was going too fast. How did this encounter happen?

She said the old man and the girl began spending

time together, having intense and honest talks, while the young man, who was in something of a panic about the biography, read diaries and papers in the old man's house.

The book was sad, Lotte said, because the old man had fallen in love with the girl. He became angry when she remained in what he saw as a wretched relationship with the young man. This guy had tried to titillate and distract the old man with a pack of lies about women he'd slept with. How the inane kid loved to boast about his potency! Five women in one day, he even claimed. No wonder he was known as Fizzy Pants!

'The writer advises her to break with the horny punk. When she falls pregnant the writer is the only person she wants to tell. For a while she doesn't even inform the young man, the actual father. The old man takes the pregnancy seriously. They discuss it a lot.'

'Discuss it in what way?'

'He struggles over whether he should advise her to have an abortion. It's an anguish for him, perhaps because he regrets the child he and his then-girlfriend aborted years before.'

Harry suddenly said, 'So what? What is going on? Why the hell does he get involved?'

Lotte shrugged. 'Inevitably the old man says the girl should reconsider.'

'Jesus! The arrogance of the man! I could slap him!'

'But the old man has to hit the young idiot with a stick.' She went on, 'The old man says he has lived a long time, and in his own paternal way he wants to know that the young woman he loves has thought these things through properly.'

'As if anybody ever does.'

'The old man says the young man can only have catastrophic loves, for which he takes no responsibility.'

Harry said, 'What a stupid old man. I hope the novel states that clearly.'

'Oddly enough, it doesn't.'

'She has the kid?' She nodded. He said, 'Nice story. I hope that's it.' She looked as though it wasn't. 'Why doesn't it stop there? How can there be more? More of what?'

He went to the window, threw it open, and sat on the ledge, gulping down the night air. Outside, London was humming. They could go back into Soho and drink and dance to jazz music. Why was he bothered about what she said? Why did he have to listen? Couldn't he climb out and never return?

THIRTY-ONE

'Although it's not far down, and you'd probably only break your ankles, you're making me nervous,' said Lotte. 'Come back, darling.'

'Why?'

'To hear the end.' Her voice behind him said, 'You'd think that would be the lot, wouldn't you? But in his eighth decade, and in what the old man calls his "mid-life crisis" or the "Eros of his old age" – she has had a child, and her boyfriend is deep in his book – he per-suades the young woman to begin to meet up with him in London.'

He turned to her. 'To do what?'

'What do you think?'

'How would I know?'

'I'm asking you, Harry—'

'What, Lotte?'

'To please come and sit next to me.'

He did so; she kissed him on the mouth; she em-braced him, and told him that Mamoon had set it up delicately, with his old precision – a lonely couple hur-rying to meet in a friend's almost empty, unheated flat in Victoria. He – the character – was shocked by how relieved and delighted he was to see this woman, his human feeling coming back. How alienated, he says, is the older adult from his desire! He buys her gifts, and loves just to look at her, his new muse. Never out of a track-suit now, she dresses for him. He likes to see her take her shoes off and she's happy to oblige.

Harry said, 'But why is she happy to oblige?'

'A woman who is really wanted by a man is going to find him difficult to resist. How often in a life are any of us so adored? He says that Count Sascha Kolowrat, when dying, had Marlene Dietrich visit him, and pull up her skirt.'

'This woman does that for the old man?'

'Why not? She lies naked in front of the fire as he looks at her. She poses, like an artist's model, while he looks on. She shows him herself. Just this, for them, is electric. He longs to express himself, this word-master, without words. To just "be" with another person. Like a contented baby with the mother.'

'What about his wife?'

'He had loved her. It hadn't occurred to him that after a while they wouldn't have anything to say. He is done with her, and wants to separate, but he doesn't know how to do it because it'll be expensive and will make her mad, suicidal even. She is obliviously contented, shopping in London, while he is having a sort of breakdown.'

'Why? What sort?'

'He was vulnerable, since he could not return to his daily routine, the prison which held him together. He asked himself repeatedly, even at this stage of his life, how can we rid ourselves of old, dead selves and make new ones?

'He calls the two of them Prospero and Miranda, and she attends to him like a good daughter. She draws him, they make tea and talk intimately about their lives, their partners, and the future. They have to.'

'What sort of future could this couple have?'

Lotte said, 'This blank girl, a piece of fluffy erotic nothing, who seems to absent herself from herself, can help him prepare for his death. He knows she is evasive, silly and insipid, but she is sincere, at least, with a couple of years' real beauty left. And he believes he has wasted his time infuriating people, and giving them little, for which he is now tearing himself apart. Like a lot of people, he believes, in his imagination, that he is a murderer.

'The old man had been struck by a story he'd heard about Ingmar Bergman, who, when dying, sat through his own films in chronological order. Mamoon admired this, and wanted to say, in a last gasp of integrity, what it was to be old, what it meant to look unflinchingly at one's life. He was amazed by how labile the past is, and how one rewrites it, and writes over it, continuously.'

Lotte went on, 'The girl with the vanilla hair encourages him to talk through his work, and about the people he'd loved. She even helps him write to the people he has regrets about.'

'Like who?'

'A woman living in America, I think, to whom he owes some kind of explanation or apology. There is going on, in that room, between the older man and the younger woman, a play of reparation and atonement. It's rather wonderful, Harry. He writes about his own sexuality, and that of his father, with a new curiosity and insight, as if he has found a new subject, even at his age. It's the warmest, most moving thing he's done since the early work.'

'I'm sure. Jesus, I'll go mad.' He was silent for a time. 'Can you tell me, please, what's in it for the young woman?'

'A sort of education, a more complex way of seeing the world. For the first time she gets a sense of the whole of someone's life. She begins to read. He has started to write again. One person can develop another, you know. There with her in the room, as they sit by the fire together, he dictates some of the book to her.'

Harry said, 'They keep this secret?'

'This necessity is private.' She said, 'I suspect some of this concerns you.'

She asked him what he thought. He kissed her and

lay back. 'I don't know yet.' He said, 'Was he keen for me to know what it was about?'

'Oh yes. He suspected you would try not to read the book.'

'Was he eager for you and me to meet again and for you to tell me this?'

She nodded. He sat up, looked for his bag and told her she'd done her job. 'Is that why you invited me here? Is that all you want from me? Shall I just fuck off now?'

'I wanted to see you again.' She took his hands. 'So no, please don't cry or fuck off.'

'You want more?'

She kissed his hair, his forehead, his nose, his mouth. 'Yes,' she said. 'Oh yes. I could look at you, and look at you. Lots.'

'And me at you,' he sighed. 'Love is the only damn thing. It catches you when you're not ready.'

'Rob told me you're single, but still living in the house.'

He said, 'I'm reading a bit, thinking about dead mothers. But I'm always optimistic in Paris; everything looks better from there. Shall we go for a few days?'

In the morning Harry and Lotte went to a cafe for breakfast. He walked with her to work. When they kissed and parted, she said, 'I've an idea as to what you should do about Mamoon and Liana.'

THIRTY-TWO

Travelling with the kids was a major operation, and such manoeuvres had to be planned in advance. But they intended to turn this trip around in twenty-four hours, as Lotte had suggested to Harry. Alice was known for her list-making, Julia was recognised in the family for her ability to pack things in the car, while Harry would complain, confuse and eat all the sandwiches before they started out. Having been consulted, Rob considered it an excellent idea for them to 'complete the process', and by the late afternoon they were gaily bowling down the motorway, the kids vomiting.

Liana heard the car and came out into the yard with the dogs to greet them, standing on the spot where Harry had first seen her when he arrived afraid and excited with Rob, that first Sunday afternoon. Where once Mamoon's temper and Liana's will had kept everything alive, the house and gardens were beginning to look as if the original wilderness would return. Mamoon wouldn't use his writing room again; Scott was growing weed in the greenhouse, and renting the former 'archive' barn as a repairs workshop. The yard was scattered with semi-dismantled cars and metal parts.

Scott himself stood there dirt-smeared and bare-chested, idly knocking a monkey wrench against an oil can, with two of his gang beside him.

Julia greeted her brother, and then went to look for Ruth, to console her. A couple of weeks back, one night, a male friend of Ruth's – perhaps a paramour – had attacked another of her friends in the house, stabbing him with a broken bottle, almost murdering him. There had been blood and despair; there would be a court case and prison. Before his second stroke, Ruth had gone to Mamoon, the patriarch, and begged for help, consolation and wisdom, but he only gave her a look of pity that said, 'How can anyone live like you?'

Liana had had an operation to remove a growth; her eyes, behind thick glasses, were tired, and she wore no make-up or jewellery, just jeans and a too-large sweater. She'd never been so thin or so sad, she said, or so happy to see her friends and the 'grandchildren' she adored.

After his strokes and heart failure, as well as weeks in hospital, Mamoon had stubbornly insisted on being at home, and, despite her own weakness, Liana was determined to look after him. She had had Scott bring a bed into the library, where Mamoon, propped up and surrounded by roses, could see out into the garden, watching Liana as she worked.

Ruth and her sister Whynne bathed and changed Mamoon; Scott moved him about, and Liana sat and whispered poetry into him, books from his childhood, *Alice in Wonderland*, parts of Dickens, stories from the *Thousand and One Nights*, the sports news and, his favourite, the Song of Songs – 'I am my beloved's, and my beloved is mine; he feeds among the lilies. Thou art beautiful, my love' – because he said he liked to hear her voice, to know someone was there.

Alice was keen to see Mamoon. She missed the stillness, and sense of distance and space, you got at Prospects House; she missed Liana's cooking and the energetic talk. All the same, she had been uneasy about going; she had rung Liana often and knew how unwell Mamoon was, yet she was still shocked and upset to see him. She wanted to keep on good terms with Liana, and perhaps work with her in the future. But Liana was too wretched, preoccupied and weepy to think about that. She was delighted to have them there.

Insisting that Mamoon had become very fond of him, Liana asked Harry to sit with him. And Harry did sit there, wondering about the relation between his book and the man, even holding the old man's hand. Harry missed their combative conversations; nobody had been so tough on him, or made him think so hard. At one point, when Harry wiped saliva from Mamoon's mouth, and dared to take out his phone and photograph him, Mamoon looked directly at him and said, 'How long can you stay, Latif? Did you bring your homework? Is the story finished?'

In this house of the almost-dead, Ruth, her sister and Liana were delighted to see the babies, which meant that Harry and Alice could walk again in the familiar woods and beside the river, with the dogs.

Alice would get a flat, as would he; Julia would find a room nearby. He and Alice had almost stopped speaking about anything except money and the children, and how their care for them would be divided up. Now Harry said to her, 'Did you read Mamoon's new novel?'

She shook her head; he explained that, as far as he knew, it concerned the love of an older man for a younger woman, the partner of a journalist.

'He did it then, he wrote the fiction he'd been talking about,' she said. 'He'd been sitting in that room every day for months, staring at the wall, while you burrowed into his privacy. I said I understood that,' she said. 'I have that desolate nature.'

'You do?'

'But you have helped me with it, Harry, listening to me. I respect you for that, as well as for you being relatively stable and all.'

He thanked her.

'I didn't believe Mamoon, in fact. His bin was full of screwed-up paper. I opened one out, thinking it might make a souvenir for the children. It was covered in doodles. He really did believe he was finished.' She went on, 'And you were asking him questions about things he couldn't, or didn't want to remember – certainly not in *that* way – questions which made him feel his life was being retold as farce by an idiot. There was something else.'

'There was?'

'He'd reread *Anna Karenina*. He worshipped Tolstoy for his understanding of marriage, of women, and of children. He'd done his best, but he knew he'd never do anything as true, as sympathetic, as universal.'

'Why didn't he talk to Liana about these things?'

'He was afraid. She was demanding, asking for more love, sex, money. He couldn't work and he couldn't satisfy her. What was it with women and him that always went wrong?' She said, 'I suggested it must be more than peculiar, disorienting, in fact, having someone write your life, interview you about it as if you were almost dead, while living in your house. At that moment he had the idea of writing about what you were doing and how it made him see himself differently.'

Harry said, 'He finally flogged the archive and some of his land. He rented the London flat to calm Liana. He was able to see you regularly at a friend's place.'

'Does it say all that?'

'Liana didn't know.'

'I couldn't hurt her. She would have misunderstood.'

'Nor did I know. You deceived me. God knows, I've

done the same to you in other ways.'

She said suddenly, 'I've had enough of you.'

'The same. Bored to death.'

'Why won't you just fuck off?'

'Don't hit me like that,' he said, taking her arm. 'Alice, I know Mamoon considered me mediocre—'

She giggled. 'Yes, and impatient and seething with fury. And perhaps with a personality disorder!' She went on, 'Does it say in the book that he insisted I give you up for him? He liked to be massaged – otherwise I didn't have to touch him. I could have lovers. All I had to do was talk to him.'

'Why?'

'I guess he was in love.'

'How nice was that for you?'

'I was flattered, I liked the attention. You didn't give me much.'

'Nor you me.'

'He was too forceful and demanding, but it was a good experience with him. To be close to a man like that, to have the chance to learn to think, it's unforgettable.'

He said, 'What was your reply to his request?'

'I reminded him of his duty towards Liana. She is a great friend to me.' She shrugged. 'I won't read the book. I know it's a story. I became his hallucination, all made up and left behind with nothing. Sometimes you can know too much. I feel as if I've been shredded. I can't take any more life right now, if these terrible coils and circles are life. Are they, Harry? Do you know? Won't you answer me for once?'

He had heard enough. He began to walk back, and she followed him. He said, 'I wish he could hear about the new and well-paid job I have lined up.'

'What is it?'

'It is a gift from Rob, because he pities me after the last job, and wants to give me an easy time. While working on the book about Mum, I will be ghost-writing the autobiography of an international footballer. I will be a centre forward's horse whisperer. I can safely say we have class, at last, as a family.'

But they were not really a family, and, as she laughed, he recalled his father's words to him about his mother, which were, roughly: *She was your mum, Harry, but to me she was just another girl.* Harry wondered if, in twenty years' time, he'd say such a thing to his sons.

Perhaps Alice was thinking something similar. 'I'm sorry it didn't work out between us. But we're very pleased and grateful, Harry, that you can support us all.'

'Any time.' He said, 'Please hold me, hold me one last time.'

'Never.'

It was Lotte's idea that they return to the house and Harry add the account to the end of the book: a few paragraphs about the dying writer. Now, before supper, Harry stood at the open door of Scott's barn, the place where he'd sat for hours with a magnifying glass. Peggy's diaries were gone, taken to the American archive, as if Peggy herself had finally been taken away. Harry had brought them all back to life, reclaiming her in the book, stressing her contribution to Mamoon's work, and how he needed her; Ruth also appeared, sending Mamoon forth, and there was enough about Marion, and how she'd led him towards himself at last.

In the kitchen, that night, they all had supper together, and when the children were asleep, chrysalises wrapped tightly in their white blankets, everyone apart from Liana and Harry went to bed early. He watched her poking at the fire in the library, and, at last, had the courage to ask for her view of the biography, and whether anything in it pleased her.

'I wondered when you'd ask,' she said, and left the room to return with a piece of paper. 'I haven't had much time, I haven't even read Mamoon's last book. Did you read it?'

'I'm going to.'

'Yes. Now, some of these mistakes angered me very much,' she said, twirling her pencil and giving him a glorious glare. He was glad to see she had temporarily returned to her old go-getting self. 'My eyes are not good. My mind won't stay. But marvellous, in the main.

I don't care so much about this now – it's you I adore, Harry. You are one of the people I like most. You'll always have time for me, won't you? These are my thoughts.' She put on her glasses. His stomach plunged; he was ready to scribble in his notebook. 'Didn't you bother to research thoroughly?'

Her father had been a pharmacist, with a chain of shops in the region. It was true that their name appeared on shampoo. He had founded a country club, with real art on the walls, and built a library. Where did he get the idea she only spoke three languages, rather than four? She had always ridden horses, and for long distances too. And so on. It wouldn't take him long to make those corrections.

He went out into the yard, where he had spent many evenings worrying, agitated, pacing up and down.

'I got the gush from Liana,' he said to Rob on the phone. 'She called it "splendid, marvellous". Write that down. Send apologies and money immediately.'

Looking back towards the kitchen, Harry saw that Liana was weeping in the doorway. He dismissed Rob, led her outside into the night air, and asked her what was wrong.

'At the end, in London, before he became sick, when he fulfilled my wish at last, bless you, because I think you insisted – you were kind, dear boy, kind! – we became close again,' she said. 'He wanted to dine with me.'

They strolled in sunny parks; he wanted to buy clothes, and take her advice; something made him talk about his childhood. One afternoon, after coming home, he stroked her hair; he closed his eyes, let her touch him and say her dream about falling over the cliff. He gave his view, his voice was gentle like a blissful kiss. She could have devoured him, her beloved husband, with love. One night, he even took her breast into his mouth.

'And so, soon, after I have reread his complete works, I will gulp down everything written about him, including you. So thank you for keeping his name in the world. We are grateful, and I love you.

'But now – now I want him back,' she said. 'Where has it gone? I want him back, as he was then! Bring him back to me! Life is too cold without him!'